Marriage Vacation

A NOVEL

Pauline Turner Brooks

MILLENNIAL PRINT

SIMON & SCHUSTER

NEW YORK LONDON TORONTO SYDNEY NEW DELHI

Simon & Schuster
1230 Avenue of the Americas
New York, NY 10020

First Simon & Schuster hardcover edition June 2018

SIMON & SCHUSTER and colophon are registered trademarks of Simon & Schuster, Inc.

For information about special discounts for bulk purchases, please contact Simon & Schuster Special Sales at 1-866-506-1949 or business@simonandschuster.com.

The Simon & Schuster Speakers Bureau can bring authors to your live event. For more information or to book an event, contact the Simon & Schuster Speakers Bureau at 1-866-248-3049 or visit our website at www.simonspeakers.com.

Interior design by Carly Loman

Manufactured in the United States of America

10 9 8 7 6 5 4 3 2 1

Library of Congress Cataloging-in-Publication Data is available.

ISBN 978-1-9821-0017-9
ISBN 978-1-9821-0021-6 (ebook)

For everyone who has dreamed of running away,
and longed for home

Prologue

I blew up my life a year ago and now I wanted it back.

I knew I didn't deserve it. But there I was, standing at my own front door, hoping for a second chance.

We painted the door red when we moved into this house ten years ago. Karl and I loved the idea of a door the color of a fire engine, or a brothel, a door completely incongruous with the rest of the navy and slate-gray entryways on East Eighty-Second Street.

A red door was meant to be cheerful and welcoming . . . maybe a little scandalous.

But standing there, after being gone so long, it intimidated me. It conveyed anger and urgency, like a siren, a warning.

I told myself it was just a door.

I tentatively reached to touch the peeling paint near the brass door knocker while my other hand gripped my house keys in my pocket. The metal warmed as I rubbed my thumb and forefinger back and forth, over and over. How easy it would be to pull the key from my pocket and open the door without knocking, wander into the foyer and up the stairs where Karl would just be waking up, where the girls would be stirring in their beds, kicking their quilts with their tiny feet and peering out at one another, daring the other to be the first to get up, to run and wake up Daddy. This was the Saturday-morning ritual I'd missed for so many Saturdays.

I didn't have a suitcase, just a heavy canvas duffel slung over one shoulder, the strap slipping toward the crook of my elbow. When I left here I brought along one of our expensive pieces of luggage, the kind with wheels that spin in all different directions, a part of a set, a wedding present. It lost its wheel in the middle of the jungle and I traded it for this duffel, which was stuffed to the point of barely closing with presents for the girls.

I wished I had taken more time to fix myself up in the taxi from the airport, but at least my clothes—jeans, a white T-shirt, and an old cardigan—were clean, if hopelessly rumpled.

I dropped my hand from the door knocker and ran it through my hair. It was duskier than when I left, the roots darker than I'd ever seen them, though the ends remained a sweet honey blond.

What the hell am I doing? The thought seized me. What kind of woman thinks she can leave her husband and her daughters and then just waltz back into their lives? What would Karl say when he saw me? I knew in my bones that I deserved every terrible thing he could say to me. If he told me to leave and get the hell out, I would deserve that too.

But maybe, just maybe, I thought, *he'll understand*.

I pulled a large manila envelope out of my bag. What he chose to do with the stack of paper in the envelope would decide our future together.

I reached out again to knock, and this time my hand made contact. The sound echoed through the tall entryway and traveled up the stairs. I knocked like a stranger, or the Seamless deliveryman, slow and tentative, as if apologizing for the intrusion, for my presence. I'd never knocked on my own door before.

No one came.

A part of me was a little relieved. A part of me thought this was a ridiculous idea. I took a small step away from the door and then a larger step that put me on the stairs of the stoop.

I thought about going to the coffee shop down the street, ordering an espresso, texting Karl, and asking him to meet me on his terms. I should have done that in the first place, but I wanted the element of surprise when I arrived unannounced. I thought if he was surprised when he saw me then maybe his expression would reveal how he really felt about me coming home. If he were to meet me in a coffee shop he'd have time to collect himself, time to put on a mask.

The duffel was getting heavier. I had bought too many presents, silly trinkets my children would definitely forget about in less than a week. I tried not to think of them as bribes to regain their affection. As the bag slipped from my shoulder, I stumbled a little on the last stair and heard the door swing open.

"You're back."

I was still staring at the ground as I turned around, which was why the first thing I saw were Karl's plaid pajama bottoms.

My bag slid off my shoulder and fell with a thunk onto the ground. If we were in a movie, Karl would smile. I'd throw my head back and laugh as tears ran down my face while I dashed up the three cement stairs and collapsed into his arms. He'd press his body into mine and I'd tilt my face toward his for a long and passionate kiss, the pain, tension, and resentment of the past year, the past ten years, really, melting off us onto this stoop. His hands would slide down my hips and cup my ass. If this were a movie we wouldn't even make it up to the bedroom.

Then again, if this were a movie I would probably be a man, the husband returning from a long trip away. Wives and mothers, in fiction and in real life, don't leave their families.

But it wasn't a movie. It was my life and I was fucking terrified. I bit the inside of my cheek to keep from crying and straightened awkwardly as I looked up to see Karl's face, his eyes heavy with apprehension. He looked back at me. "You're here?" he asked.

I handed him the envelope.

Eleven months earlier . . .

Chapter One

I've always loved a good wedding—the perfectly average food, the worse dancing, the over-the-top flowers, the open bar, the sense of possibility that comes when two people are surrounded by everyone they love and still naïve enough to believe the best is yet to come.

And there are actually few things I love more than attending weddings with my husband. After ten years of marriage and two children, attending someone else's wedding brings out the very best in Karl and me. We both put in the effort. I shave my legs above the knee and Karl wears that cologne I like, the one that smells like burnt oranges. Unlike the stuffy social obligations we attend together for his job, at weddings we can both drink as much as we want and laugh too loud. My husband is a remarkable dancer. You wouldn't know it to look at him walking down the street in Manhattan with his broad shoulders and slightly lumbering gait. But at weddings he's suddenly Fred Astaire, twirling and dipping me, amid a sea of other middle-aged men doing their dad moves—karate kicks, the sprinkler, and a sad running man. I delight in watching other women watch Karl and then wrapping my arms around his neck and drawing his face down to mine to remind them that he's with me. This graceful, handsome, perfect man chose me. In those moments I felt as lucky as I did the day he proposed to me.

But right now there was a gaping Karl-size hole next to me. I was at this wedding alone, and my husband was three thousand miles away. I tried to shake off my disappointment at this fact, determined to make the best of it.

My stomach churned with a mix of wistfulness, nostalgia, and nerves as I looked around the immaculate grounds of the rented Victorian mansion overlooking the Pacific Ocean, where two of my oldest friends in the world—Beth and Lauren—would imminently tie the knot.

A young waiter wearing jaunty suspenders and a pubescent mustache smiled at me as I snatched a glass of pink champagne off his tray. I was hoping the bubbly would help fortify me. As clichéd as it was, it felt simultaneously like yesterday and another lifetime that we were getting our MFAs at Columbia, ready to take on the world with our sparkling prose. And now, seeing all my old grad school friends had for some reason put me on edge. I felt like I was living that dream where you show up naked for an exam that you never studied for.

It didn't help that neither Beth nor Lauren informed me that the dress code for their wedding in Big Sur was an aesthetic that could only be described as bohemian chic and would be downright unacceptable anywhere but Northern California. Everyone, the men included, wore loose linen clothes in rich earth tones or Moroccan print kimonos. I'd translated "cocktail attire" on the invitation to mean a royal blue wrap dress and gold statement necklace—the kind of thing I would wear to an actual cocktail party back home in New York.

Getting dressed alone in my room I thought I'd looked nice, pretty even, but here now, in this sea of boho haute couture, I looked like a real estate agent, the kind who flashed you a toothy smile from the back pages of *New York* magazine and tried to sell you a pied-à-terre with a view of New Jersey.

I'd flown into San Jose this morning and driven the few hours south alone in a rental car. I'd arrived at the preceremony cocktail hour only fifteen minutes ago, but already every interaction with all of my old friends from grad school, the ones I thought I'd be so excited to see, had become a minefield of questions that made me feel anxious and insecure.

"What have you been up to?"

"How's the writing?"

"You're so fucking brilliant, Kate. You were always the best of us."

I smiled until it hurt and said a lot while saying very little, a skill I had honed over years of hosting dinner parties for a never-ending parade of Karl's colleagues and authors.

Telling them the truth about what I was up to would bore them to tears.

I just found myself repeating the same thing to everyone: "Oh, you know, just raising my girls. They're four and six now. Mom stuff."

The looks I received in return were at best polite disappointment and at worst barely disguised disdain that after going into debt to get a graduate degree in writing from an Ivy League university I would choose to be a stay-at-home mom. If Karl had been here it would have been easier. He was a champion at small talk, and with him by my side my life choices felt more easily justified. Also, given that he was one of the most powerful publishers in New York, putting him in a roomful of writers would be like paparazzi on a Kardashian.

As for my own writing, it had been at least five years since I'd actually put pen to paper. Writing was probably the only luxury I could no longer afford.

I hastily finished my first glass of champagne and then grabbed another, sticking to the edges of the party and avoiding eye contact with anyone I knew. I made light chitchat with a relative of one of the brides, Aunt Peggy, a husky older woman from Houston with a bleached blond perm, too-white teeth, and a jewel-toned tunic—the only other person who also looked like a real estate agent at the party.

When I spotted Nina it was like seeing a mirage in a desert. It was hard to believe I hadn't seen my old grad school roommate in more than ten years. She carried two glasses of tan liquor, almost the same color as her perfectly bronzed shoulders peeking through her off-white bandage dress that left nothing to the imagination.

"Solo at a lesbian wedding?" Nina grinned as she sauntered over to me and finished one of the tumblers in a single gulp. "Want to make out later?"

I excused myself to Aunt Peggy and hugged Nina tightly, inhaling her rich, spicy smell of clove cigarettes, jasmine, and the charcoal natural deodorant she began using years ago before everyone started using natural deodorants and you could find them at Whole Foods. I marveled at my old friend's bright red lipstick, which stood out boldly against her skin and sleek dark lob. It wasn't that I didn't wear makeup. I wore plenty of masks, lotions, and extracts of snail slime that Vogue promised to smooth, de-wrinkle, and highlight, but lipstick hadn't been a part of my repertoire since I'd had kids and developed the uncontrollable habit of kissing them on their heads and faces and hands and feet every time they were within my reach.

I stole a gulp of Nina's remaining drink.

"Have you met Aunt Peggy's date?" She dropped her voice to a sultry conspiratorial whisper.

"She's not here with Uncle Martin?"

"Divorced. He ran off with his gardener, Rico. Apparently it's Uncle Martha now. He's been stealing Aunt Peggy's control-top grandma panties and padded bras for the better part of two decades."

"Poor Aunt Peggy!"

Nina laughed a low throaty chuckle. "Well, Aunt Peggy's getting her own. See that tall drink of cocoa by the bar."

It was hard to miss the nearly seven-foot-tall black man and not just because he was towering above a sea of pasty white people, but also because he was jaw-droppingly gorgeous.

I burst into a delighted cackle. "I wouldn't have thought Aunt Peggy had it in her."

"Oh, she's had it in her."

I swatted her. "Nina!"

"That's why she walks with a limp."

"I just figured she had a bad hip."

"She probably does. I'll bet he's moved everything out of joint. His name's Alex. She claims he was her Zumba instructor. Oh, and she

likes to be spanked." Nina offered these two improbable facts with the conviction of a Fox News anchor.

I tried to picture demure Aunt Peggy, who had just given me her recipe for tart lemon squares, bent doggy-style over a bed being smacked with Alex's massive hand.

I threw back the rest of the scotch in Nina's glass to get the visual out of my head. "I need another drink."

As we stood in the interminable line at the bar Nina switched gears to her favorite subject—Nina. She caught me up on her life with a succinct highlight reel of the past decade she appeared to have perfected with repetition—recounting with false modesty how she'd barely squeaked onto the Young Lions 40 Voices Under 40 list, how the *New Yorker* called her "our generation's Anaïs Nin with a dash of Hunter S. Thompson," how her latest book nearly spent more weeks on the bestseller list than Gillian Flynn's, which was a triumph since, according to Nina, "Everyone buys that kind of slasher trash in airports." She concluded with how exhausted she was. She landed in California the night before, arriving straight from Norway, where she'd spent the previous three weeks aboard an icebreaker ship bound for the magnetic North Pole. "God, Kate, it was cold enough to freeze your clit off . . . but luckily I found ways to keep warm."

That was the shtick of Nina's writing—hard-hitting adventures and sexual escapades in 122 different countries. Not too long ago, I'd spent a week furiously reading all of Nina's books from her debut— *She Comes First*—to the most recent, *She Comes Everywhere*—and enviously devouring the glowing profiles written about her.

Now, I marveled at how quickly we settled back into our old roles, even after all this time—Nina the self-anointed star, me the attentive audience and sidekick. Although in this particular moment, I was grateful for her self-involvement and her chatter because it meant I didn't have to talk about myself.

We hurried to grab our dinner table assignments before making

our way to our seats. I tried to crumple the piece of paper that read
KARL CARMICHAEL—TABLE 3 before Nina could see it, but Nina noticed everything.

"Why did Karl ditch you?" she asked with a self-satisfied smile. I
knew from reading Nina's books that she considered marriage a bear
trap around the ankle of the modern woman. She wrote about married couples with a smug condemnation usually reserved for ruthless
dictators and Taylor Swift.

"He had to work. He had a hysterical author. You know how it is."
I could only imagine that Nina had caused an editor or two plenty of
drama along the way.

"Yeah, he's got a lot going on. I saw a profile of him recently in
Poets and Writers. They had a picture of him from the National Book
Awards. He's as hot as ever. That must be so annoying having a hus-
band who just keeps getting better-looking with age."

Leave it to Nina to offer the pitch-perfect backhanded compliment.

The truth is, I didn't find it annoying. I found it remarkable and a
bit of a cliché, and slightly unfair, but not annoying.

What *was* annoying was the thought of sitting down at our table
for eight and having a conspicuously empty seat next to me. Until
three days ago Karl had planned to come, so I didn't even have time to
alert the brides. It would have been our first real time away since our
girls came along, and I had been so looking forward to it. We needed
to shake things up. Our sex life had become routine but serviceable,
like the many Italian bistros of the Upper East Side.

Karl and I once promised ourselves that we would never be the
couple who had to schedule sex on their Google calendars and I never
thought I would be a wife who would have trouble remembering the
last time she had sex with her husband. But here we were. Actually, I
do remember the last time we had sex, and that's the problem. It was
over two months ago. We had to end our dry spell.

But then something came up at work—one of his big-deal authors had a meltdown, shaved her head Britney Spears–style circa 2007, took a handful of prescription diet pills, and threatened to erase her manuscript from her hard drive if Karl didn't take a meeting with her in her bathroom on Friday morning. I'd held out hope that the situation would be resolved by Friday afternoon, but the tabloid-worthy crisis continued until the moment I finally boarded the plane alone this morning.

"She has an editor and a publicist, an agent, and three ex-husbands who can talk her off the ledge," I'd argued, even though I knew it was useless. Karl promised he would make it up to me, but he was distracted and frustrated. There was no way to explain to him how much I needed this trip now. How much we needed this trip now. I couldn't find the right words to say that maybe a wedding would help us reignite our spark, that it might give us the time and space to talk about the emptiness I'd begun to feel now that both girls were in school.

"This is the fanciest lesbian wedding I've ever been to," Nina whispered as we took seats in one of the last rows for the ceremony.

"Come on. Lauren has better taste than you," I teased her. "And better sense than to wear white to someone else's wedding."

"No she doesn't." Nina laughed. "Remember how she wore hiking sandals with socks every day for a year. I didn't think anyone would ever want to muff-dive her. Even someone as butch as Beth. How was that not a deal breaker! It must have been true love if Beth could see past those. I can't believe they're only just getting married now. It's been at least ten years since they first got together."

Nina was terrible at keeping track of time. It had actually been fourteen years since Beth and Lauren met and twelve since the four of us—Beth, Lauren, Nina, and I—finished our MFAs at Columbia together. I saw Beth and Lauren much more than I saw Nina. They'd both been in my wedding, even though Lauren had been massively pregnant with Colin, their first. Beth and Lauren and Karl and I hung out a lot in those early days when we all still lived in the West Village. But then Beth got tenure at Berkeley and they moved across the country.

Meanwhile, I hadn't seen Nina since the day we both moved out of our roach-infested one-bedroom on 116th Street above a Korean laundry that was also a brothel, judging from clientele wearing tailored suits and baseball caps pulled low over their brows. I hadn't expected to see Nina here at all. She'd turned down the invite to my wedding ten years ago, claiming exhaustion after a yearlong tour for her first book. We were all surprised that she would miss the chance to lord it over all of us that she had been the first of our classmates to be published. But no matter how much time had passed, it was easy to fall right back into step with Nina. Her sarcasm and quick wit made anyone feel like they could be her best friend. I realized I missed her. Or maybe it was the feeling of being around her I missed—she always made me feel lighter, freer, like a much cooler version of myself. It was just as seductive now as it had been when I was twenty-six.

"You know how it is when two ladies get together," I replied. "First you move in together the week after you meet at grad school orientation, then you adopt a cat and then another cat, and soon one of you finds some sperm and gets pregnant, and then the other one gets pregnant, you pick up and leave New York to move to the expensive part of Oakland, and ten years later you finally tie the knot in a gorgeous wedding in Big Sur with a fabulous wedding planner named Hugo."

"This place was definitely Hugo's idea." Nina nodded toward the wedding planner, a petite well-Botoxed man wearing a hemp suit and a bolo tie furiously giving orders into a headset. "If this wedding had happened ten years ago we'd be drinking beers on a roof after a goddess ceremony."

"People change. We've all changed." I glanced then at Nina and thought about how she hadn't changed a bit. And then I looked out at the ocean to avoid thinking about how much I'd changed.

The view of the Pacific was postcard perfect. Sheer white cliffs plunging into turquoise waves. The rest of the shoreline disappeared into a grove of coastal redwoods. The air smelled of salt, citrus, and eucalyptus.

"This place must have cost a fortune," Nina said, raising her eyebrows and pushing a lock of inky hair out of her face. Her hands were smooth, but her nails ragged. Her cheeks had more freckles and a few more wrinkles than the last time I'd seen her, but somehow Nina could still pass for being in her late twenties, while I knew I looked every bit the forty-year-old mother of two. I reflexively and self-consciously reached up to touch the skin near the corners of my lips and cursed myself for not getting fillers before this wedding.

"Beth might be living on a professor's salary, but Lauren makes good money off her books. Who knew a children's book series about a homeless dwarf with a lisp could be turned into a blockbuster movie with Tom Hanks?" I said. Then I shushed Nina before she could speak again once the flutist began the first twinkling notes of Pachelbel's Canon.

"So traditional," Nina said in a stage whisper.

"Sometimes tradition is nice."

"Fuck tradition."

I raised my phone and snapped a picture of Lauren and Beth's three kids as they tossed tiny crushed nuts from handwoven baskets. An asterisk in the program explained that the brides preferred to feed crushed nuts to the native wildlife than to rip the petals off innocent roses. You can take the girl out of the goddess ceremony, but you can't take the goddess ceremony out of the girl. Their daughter Anna nervously tugged on the edges of her paisley peasant dress. I waved at her and she waved back, reminding me of how my youngest, Matilda, had recently started indiscriminately waving at anyone on the street. Karl and I agreed it was both adorable and an invitation to pedophiles, so we gently discouraged the behavior in crowded public spaces.

I felt an ache, missing them. This trip was the longest I'd been away from my girls since they were born, even though I'd only been gone less than twelve hours and I was due back out on the red-eye tomorrow night.

"Guess what?" Nina whispered in my ear as the brides walked down the aisle, elbows entwined, genuine happiness lighting up both of their faces. "I have a surprise for you later."

After the entrées I snuck away to FaceTime the girls before they got into bed. They were already snuggled into matching pajamas. At four and six they still got a kick out of dressing alike, and I desperately wanted it to last forever. Each time I thought about them getting even a minute older, I considered having another baby and then remembered how hard it was to get pregnant the first two times. I knew plenty of women in our neighborhood who got pregnant after forty. There were doctors in my zip code who specialized exclusively in geriatric IVF, but I wasn't sure my sanity or marriage could withstand another child.

The girls loved FaceTiming. Isabel insisted on playing me a piece she'd learned during her piano lesson and Matilda wanted to show me the somersaults they did in gymnastics, and they both wanted to see the Pacific Ocean and a picture of the brides. Brides to them were similar to princesses and the fact that this wedding had two of them made it more special.

"Put Daddy on the phone?" I finally asked gently.

"He's busy." Izzy rolled her eyes, an affect she clearly learned in the first grade or from an episode of *Real Housewives*.

"So busy." Tilly mimicked her older sister. "He's been in his library like all of the night. Marley made us dinner and is reading us our bedtime stories."

"I will tell him you called, Ms. Carmichael." I heard Marley's disembodied voice, heavy with her thick Irish brogue, come from somewhere in the room.

Thank god for Marley, our au pair, an adorable Irish girl who the other moms on the Upper East Side envied for both her charm with my children and her wide waistline, an asset, they all claimed, in a live-in who you didn't want screwing your husband. I'd assumed somehow that having an au pair, even one who was part-time since she began taking classes at NYU, would give me more time for myself, but that extra time was immediately siphoned into managing other kid things, family things, Karl things, and even with Marley around I still wanted to be with my daughters as much as humanly possible even when they exhausted me or bored me to tears, which was more often than I cared—or dared—to admit.

"Thank you, Marley." I kept my voice light and my tone cheerful.

"Mommy, we have to go," Isabel said. "It's time to read about the dragons and tacos with Marley." Her dismissal stung. At six and four they were already too old to miss me.

"OK, sweetie. I love you very, very much. Do you know how much?"

"Very, very much, even more than you love yourself," Matilda said with confidence, repeating a mangled version of a line from *The Giving Tree* that I'd whispered to her almost every night since she was born.

"Yes. Very, very much." I leaned in to kiss my screen.

The dinner and reception were in full swing by the time I made my way to the large tent in the backyard, with the two hundred guests, including kids and elderly relatives, spilling over the wraparound porch and lawn and dancing wildly to a bluegrass version of "SexyBack."

As the band switched from JT to Van Morrison I watched a handsome couple, maybe a few years older than Karl and me, glide across the dance floor. His hand gripped the small of her back just above her ass. She threw her head back and laughed before he twirled her out of his embrace and then back to him again. His eyes were fixed firmly on her breasts. The crowd focused their attention on the couple. Someone even clapped.

That should have been us.

I thought about the last time Karl and I had danced to this song. "Crazy Love," one of my all-time favorites. We'd attended his Yale classmate's wedding in Montauk just two months after Tilly was born. I was still breast-feeding, and the baby was asleep in the hotel about two dozen yards away. I had worn a maternity dress, since it was the only thing that fit my postpartum stomach, and at least two wedding guests had asked me when I was due. My feet were so swollen I had to put them on top of Karl's to dance at all. My engorged breasts had just begun to leak and sour milk dripped down my belly. If I closed my eyes now I could still feel Karl's hot breath on my cheek as he whispered in my ear, "You're the most beautiful woman here."

Nina snapped me away from the happy memory. "Beach, now," she hissed in my ear, a bottle of prosecco in one hand, and a worn leather tote slung over her bare shoulder.

I looked skeptically over the cliff, which plummeted directly down into the sea. "Do you have a rope? How do we get down there? Are we going rock climbing, because I'm not wearing my rock climbing formal wear?"

"There're stairs. I went there this morning. Come on. It's low tide."

"How do you know that?"

"It's one of those things that I know."

It was as easy to inherently trust Nina's knowledge of tide charts as it was to trust her familiarity with astrology, Greek mythology, Sufi mysticism, and every lyric to every Rolling Stones song ever written.

The worn wooden stairs leading to the beach were a small-magnitude earthquake away from being swept clear to Asia and I would have turned back if Nina hadn't raced ahead. As usual I was seized by the urge to mother her, to rescue her from the worst versions of herself. When we lived together for those two years, I was the one to buy the groceries, to pay the utilities on time, to cook dinners of noodles doused in Tabasco sauce and butter eaten while the two of us pecked away at our laptops until dawn. I'd held her hand in the waiting room before an abortion. I'd run her a cool bath when she came down with the flu.

"Hurry up!"

"Will we be washed away?" I was slightly out of breath.

"Maybe. Wouldn't that be a fun adventure?"

Nina's life seemed like nothing but a fun adventure. As far as I could tell her bestselling books had given her plenty of money to fuel the circumnavigation of the world and exploratory sexual activities.

"Let me catch my breath." My feet sunk into the wet sand with a pleasant slurp.

"I thought all you yummy mummies on the Upper East Side did Pilates all the time," Nina teased. "How can you be out of breath already?"

"It's actually barre classes now. Pilates is passé and I'm out of shape anyway," I clarified.

"Do the honors." Nina handed me the bottle of prosecco. I aimed it toward the sea and let the cork fly into the air. Nina pulled me down next to her on the sand and grabbed the bottle, taking a generous gulp.

"So, ready for your surprise?" I could tell she was grinning even as my eyes adjusted to the dark. She pressed her bony shoulder into mine as she dug into her bag. The water was closer to the cliff face than I expected even at low tide, and I wondered how quickly we could reach the stairs before a rogue wave engulfed us.

She handed me a tiny brownie wrapped in a napkin.

"That's my surprise? Dessert, from the wedding? You shouldn't have. I wanted to check out the chocolate fountain on my own."

"No . . . that's just a snack to tide you over while I get you the real surprise."

I popped the entire petite pastry into my mouth in a single bite, savoring the rich, creamy chocolate. I promised myself for the fourth time that night that I'd start the Whole30 next week and book one of those Taryn Toomey classes, the one where you writhe around on the floor and pretend to give birth to tone your core.

Nina banged something hard against my thigh. I squinted down at it. A notebook—thick black Moleskine.

"It's yours!"

I scratched at the back of my neck on a spot that hadn't itched a moment earlier.

"Why do you have this?"

"You must have left it at our old apartment and I packed it with all my other shit. I found it in my storage unit last month and figured I could give it to you here."

There was a time in my life, before Karl and the girls, when these notebooks were my everything. In a week I'd fill one with an entire story, writing everything longhand, always longhand, before committing it to the computer screen.

"Did you read it?"

"Of course not."

"Liar."

"I read every word."

"What's in it?"

"A short story. It doesn't have an ending, but then none of your stories ever did. We all thought that was part of your virtuosity, your obsession with pushing the boundaries of literary theory. You were so fucking pretentious." She nudged me again playfully.

The truth was I never knew how to end anything. Beginnings came naturally to me, the middle always wrote itself, and the end eluded me. "What's the story about?"

"It's the one with the truck driver with the dead wife. Every town he stops in he thinks he sees her and then he meets a stranger who tells him something he never knew about her. To be honest it's very *Black Mirror*."

I remembered it. It was a story that broke my heart when I began it twelve years ago. For most of the narrative, the reader believed the trucker's wife was still alive, only learning toward the end that she was killed in a car accident on the same highway just six months earlier. "I missed my calling. In another life I could have written for streaming television."

Nina snorted. "You talk like your life is over. You're barely forty. And the story is great, Katie, even without an ending."

She could have been right, I just didn't know. I had no sense of my talent anymore. Was I any good? The truth was I wrote because I loved it, not because I'd ever felt good at it. I'd loved writing those short stories, but I'd always wanted to write a novel. Admitting that now sounded as preposterous as saying I want to become a YouTube star or a celebrity chef. They seemed out of reach and completely absurd. Everyone talks about the incredible things you get out of being a mom—unconditional love, seeing the wonder in a child's eyes, the gratification of creating a new life—but no one talks about the things you have to give up, the sacrifices you make in the process. I'd sacrificed being a writer. That was all there was to it.

I fingered the cover of the notebook. "Why'd you bring this here?"

"I thought maybe you'd want to finish it."

Actually, I wanted to toss the book into the sea. I didn't want to open it, didn't want the words to become a liability, a reminder of yet another thing I hadn't accomplished. The heat of anger rose from my stomach to my chest and landed in my throat, where I forced myself to swallow it.

Shame warmed my cheeks. "I don't have time to finish it, Nina."

"Oh, give me a break—you have a husband and a nanny and no job. Surely, you have time to write. You're making excuses."

Her words, as blunt as ever, stung on so many levels.

"Actually, Nina, you know nothing about my life. You've barely been in touch over the last decade." *What a bitch.*

"I know you live in a ten-million-dollar town house on the Upper East Side. I know you're married to the head of Paradigm, one of the top publishing houses in the country. You have two beautiful daughters and a perfect little life. I bet you have some gorgeous study with floor-to-ceiling books and a grand desk. In fact, I know you have a gorgeous study with a grand desk because I saw it on Zillow and in *Architectural Digest*."

There was something sickly satisfying about knowing that Nina, who claimed she shunned social media and most technology, spent the time to google me, to look up where I lived.

I repeated myself, my cheeks still burning. "You don't know anything about my life." Karl had the grand study in our house. We shared the master bedroom. The girls shared a room and had a playroom. There was a guest bedroom and a room for Marley, but somehow with all of those rooms I didn't have a room of my own. Virginia Woolf would be horrified. But whose fault was that? Karl's? Mine? You can't blame the children. They'll never understand what their parents gave up for them until they have kids of their own. Sitting here on the beach, it was Nina's freedom that felt perfect. Had I made a few different decisions along the way, her life could even have been my life. I could have finished my novel. I could have been the one to win the awards and get the acclaim and travel the world writing things people actually wanted to read. Instead I was just a wife and a mother.

Nina passed me the bottle, lighter now, half-empty, and I took a swig and stared ahead. The sea began to sparkle. Each wave sent a shimmy of light rushing toward us.

"Shit. I didn't mean to upset you." Nina wrapped an arm around my shoulder. It felt good, familiar. It had been so long since I had spent any time with anyone I considered a real friend.

"I'm fine. Maybe I'm drunk. You're right. I do have the perfect life. Blah, blah, blah."

Nina softened and took my hand, lifting it in front of us and whistling dramatically as she admired my diamond ring shimmering in the moonlight. I yanked my hand away self-consciously.

"Hey, I have an idea. You can take a vacation, right? Without your kids. I know this place, this goddamn perfect place in Thailand on the border of Burma . . . even though I know, I know we're not supposed to call it Burma anymore. It's in the jungle in the Dawna mountains, a zen center, all tree houses on stilts and silence. I wrote my last book there in two months. I have to go to L.A. for a quick hop. They want to cast Jennifer Lawrence as me, and she is trying to convince me she can pull off multiple orgasms. I don't buy it. Anyway, after that I can meet you there. We'll go to the jungle . . . decompress, get five massages a day, and then stop in Bangkok on the way home. We can dance all night, get tattoos, and flirt with boys . . . and maybe some girls."

The sound that came out of my mouth wasn't a laugh, but more of a croak, a choking sound.

"I can't exactly just leave everything, Nina."

"Just for a week, maybe two. You'll be back before they know it."

I thought about it then.

I couldn't believe it was something I would even think about, but the booze must have been going to my head. I scooted closer to Nina and began to gently sway to the wedding music echoing off the cliff. I loved this song. I couldn't remember the name of it, but I knew I loved it. I wanted to stand and dance to it right then. I wanted to take off my dress and run into the water and dance.

Nina pulled the bottle away from me and finished it in one swift pull. The water was now mere inches from our toes, and before long it would rise to meet the cliff face.

I stood and grabbed Nina by the elbow.

"Let's dance."

"Yeah, mama. That means you're coming."

I didn't say no.

"Race you," I said as I dashed up the stairs. I should have been out of breath, but I had more energy than I'd had in years. I felt like I could conquer the world. Everything was alive with possibility. I could go to Thailand, why not? I could write a novel? I mean, why had I stopped writing, anyway? Nina was right, I was making excuses. The truth was

I could do it. I could do anything. I felt a surge of electricity—I was goddamn invincible. I turned to look up at the moon and I swear I saw a big eye wink at me.

"Tag. You're it." Nina smacked my ass and tugged on my hair as she passed me, stilettos in one hand, bare feet jogging to the dance floor.

I got there just in time to see Nina pull Alex away from a flummoxed Aunt Peggy and begin a sultry tango to Lady Gaga's "Bad Romance." I joined the two of them, wrapping Alex in a Kate-and-Nina sandwich, a move we'd perfected, teasing men in the sweaty meatpacking clubs we used to frequent when we got sick of literary theory.

If only Karl could see me now. I slid my hands up Alex's taut back, feeling every muscle strain and flex. I reached my hand back to pull my hair out of its tight chignon and shook my head like a wet dog.

Nina slinked around Alex's stomach and began dancing with me.

"How great is this? I fucking love dancing on molly."

I could hardly hear her above the booming bass of my own pulse in my head. I rubbed my hands up and down my thighs and swung my head from side to side. "Dancing to poly? Is that some kind of new electronic music?"

Nina threw her head back and opened her mouth so wide I could see the soft pink skin in the back of her throat. Alex was grinding low behind her. His eyes were a golden brown, like a perfectly cooked chocolate chip cookie. I wanted to lick one.

"Dancing on molly, Kate. I laced those brownies with MDMA. How good do you feel?" She leaned in so close to me, I thought she was going to kiss me on the mouth, her upper lip slick with sweat and saliva.

It still took a few seconds to sink in. *Molly. MDMA . . .*

I stopped dancing. "Ecstasy. You put Ecstasy in those brownies?"

Nina never stopped moving. "Technically it's a more pure form of Ecstasy. We're gonna roll all night, girl!"

I should have been furious. I should have screamed right in

her face. Instead I laughed. It came out sounding raw and feral. I'd done my fair share of fun drugs in my twenties, but I'd slowed and then stopped when I met Karl, who was as straitlaced as a Supreme Court nominee from New England. I'd have been lying if I said I didn't miss this feeling, like the bottom of the world could fall from beneath your feet and you wouldn't care, you'd be glad to allow yourself to float in some glorious orgasmic free fall. There was something even better about how furtive it all was, how Nina and I had shared a secret from everyone else at this wedding, except maybe Alex. As I watched his eyes roll into his head as he slid his hands up and down Nina's hips, I began to suspect he had partaken in Nina's stash.

The band began to play the requisite wedding version of "Shout," and even more guests crowded onto the dance floor.

A *little bit louder now* . . .

I found myself in hysterics in a tangle of limbs with Nina lying on the floor before we exploded back onto our feet.

Shout!

Alex dragged Aunt Peggy back onto the floor and gave her a little love. Nina held hands with three little girls and skipped a ring-around-the-rosy dance. I began to twirl all alone, letting the cool ocean breeze tickle my skin.

Before I knew what was happening I was running back toward the ocean. My shoes were long gone. We half ran, half fell down those rickety stairs. Nina, Alex, and me and a handful of other guests I didn't know who Nina had befriended the night before at the rehearsal dinner when she offered everyone some of her medicinal pot. Clothes were flung onto the stair railing and into the sand.

We waded into the freezing surf. If we'd been in our right minds it would have killed us, the northern Pacific isn't exactly bathwater, but we didn't care. In the moonlight Alex's naked body glowed like a god. I loved my own skin. Gone was the self-conscious anxiety I often felt among the perfect size-twos at the beach in the Hamptons, all of them tucked, tightened, and buffed to perfection. Right now, I felt beautiful.

I wanted Karl then. I wanted him here in this ocean. We'd once skinny-dipped in the Aegean off a secret beach in Mykonos. I'd wrapped my legs around his hips and eased him inside me right there in the water, bucking and grinding against him in time with the waves, letting him nearly slip out of me before bringing him back to me with a violent thrust. We crawled out of the water, our limbs still trembling, and collapsed on the sand, sticky and satiated.

I wanted my husband more than ever, needed him more than ever. Only one lingering thought punctured my ecstatic reverie: *Did my husband still want me?*

Chapter Two

The sunlight streaming through the large window next to my bed assaulted all of my senses before I opened my eyes. I lay splayed naked on top of the covers. My body was dry and warm from the fire raging in the fireplace in my room. I had a spotty memory of coming back up here with Nina and Alex and building a fire and drinking two stolen bottles of wedding wine while Nina braided my hair and Alex smoked a joint in the corner. While Nina would have been down for an orgy, the night devolved into a vaguely awkward massage chain.

My hair was still damp and smelled of salt and sea, a faint reminder that I'd taken my clothes off and run into the freezing ocean.

My head pounded, my mouth tasted like a shoe. Not a nice shoe either, a dirty old Croc some old lady would have worn in the garden.

The thought of an old lady in Crocs reminded me of Aunt Peggy, and I felt a twinge of guilt for my complicity in tearing Alex away from her for the evening.

I heard a bold knock at the door and thought for a split second that it might be Karl coming to surprise me. I ran my hand down between my legs, still slightly tingling from the memories I'd conjured the night before.

"Can I come in?" Lauren's voice, with its fading Southern twang, traveled through the door.

What time was it?

"Hold on a second. Let me get decent."

When I sat up, my entire body felt as though I'd rolled in broken glass. I looked around the room, half expecting to see Nina cuddled up in a pile of cushions in the corner.

I grabbed a cozy white bathrobe from a brass hook behind the bathroom door. "Come on in. I don't think it's locked."

I rubbed the sleep from my eyes and found my phone within the folds of the crisp sheets. It was already close to noon. I couldn't remember the last time I had slept this late. I didn't have any missed calls—Karl had apparently been too busy to call me back.

"You missed brunch." Lauren surveyed the empty wine bottles and glasses littering the tops of the furniture and a tumbler filled with cigarette butts and a half inch of red wine on the balcony.

"You had more fun at my wedding than I did," she snorted. "Did you guys do drugs? Did you do drugs at my wedding and not give me drugs, because if so that's the shittiest thing a friend could do."

I lay back down on the bed and flung my arm over my eyes and groaned.

"Ohhhhhhh, honey," Lauren said with real sympathy. "There's nothing worse than a hangover in your forties is there? I have three glasses of wine these days and I wake up feeling like a donkey kicked me in the face."

"I want to die," I murmured into the crook of my elbow.

"At least your kids aren't here. Actually what's worse than a middle-aged hangover is trying to parent through one. All you want to do is hit pause on those little terrorists for six blessed hours while you recover . . . but you can't because you're being held hostage."

"You can't call your children terrorists," I said. "Someone will take them away."

"They'd give them back in a heartbeat." She laughed.

"I can't get on a plane today," I whispered. "I think I'm going to puke."

"So don't leave. Snuggle into that bed as long as you can . . . as long as you want actually. We had to rent this place for the whole damn week just to get it for the weekend."

"Wow. Are you staying?"

"No. We need to get the kids back to school tomorrow, and I didn't get any of your good drugs so I'm doing OK this morning. But, I hardly got to talk to you last night," Lauren said with a sigh.

"It was your wedding. You never talk to anyone at your own wedding."

"I know. But we're so old. I thought it would be different if we had the wedding after we already had bunions and neck waddles. I thought we'd get to enjoy it more. I wanted to catch up. It's been too long."

"Come to New York—visit us soon, we'd love that."

"Or you could come to us." We both laughed at the verbal tango of friends with kids.

"We'll figure it out."

Lauren spied the notebook before I did, the one Nina had handed me on the beach. I couldn't remember how it had gotten up here.

"What's that?"

For a second I considered making up a story, but then I told the truth. "Nina brought it. It's an old one from school. It had a story in it I never finished."

We sat in silence for a few moments.

"Do you miss writing?" Lauren asked.

"You know how it is." I tried to brush off the question. "There's not a lot of time."

"That's not what I asked."

Suddenly, before I could stop myself, the words poured out, coming from that dark place of self-pity the brain only goes into when it's coming down from something that was so delicious only eight hours earlier. "I feel like I'm running in place while my girls grow up and start to become these magnificent human beings. I want them to be proud of me, to see me do something real with my life, and I'm not even proud of myself. I just feel like I don't even recognize my life—or myself sometimes."

Lauren lay down and stretched her long willowy frame next to me. "Does Karl know you feel like this?"

"Of course not. He's busy. All the time. Busier than ever. Since his dad passed, you know he took over everything. And publishing is a hard business. E-books, Amazon, nonexistent attention spans, self-publishing. He's reinventing Paradigm every week. It's hard for him."

"I get that. Maybe you could see someone together. That's what Beth and I did. Did you meet her last night? Our therapist? The one with the bright red hair and the strange mole on her chin that looks like Ronald Reagan. We invited our therapist to our wedding because without her we wouldn't have walked down that aisle."

Karl and I talked about seeing someone after Isabel was born, when the lack of sleep drove each of us to the brink of our sanity and, for the first time in our relationship, we began to argue, really argue. Everyone we knew had a therapist, sometimes even three of them — his, hers, and theirs. But we never went to anyone.

Forget couples counseling, *I* should have gone to someone by myself after Isabel was born. I'd never felt as alone as I did those first few months with a newborn. It was a time when I should have been surrounded by family and friends, when I needed a tribe of women to help me figure out how the hell to be a mother, but I had no one. Lauren and Beth had already packed up their small family and moved to the West Coast. My mother had been dead for almost five years by then and my older sister was busy with her own teenaged children back in Milwaukee. Karl went right back to work two days after we came home from the hospital. There's no paternity leave when you're the boss. My body ached so badly I felt like I'd been hit by a truck. The baby wouldn't stop screaming and then she wouldn't eat. When she finally latched it felt as though my nipples were being sliced open with glass every time my milk came in.

Not too long after that Karl and I started trying for another, and then I was pregnant, and then I wasn't pregnant anymore, and we should have seen a therapist then, but soon I got pregnant again with

Tilly and we began the cycle all over again and I never took the time to mourn or heal. The babies turned into toddlers and I began the lengthy process of enrolling them in the right preschool so they'd go to the right elementary school so they'd eventually attend Harvard and get to go to Davos and rule the world. We renovated our town house, then the place in Connecticut, then the place in East Hampton. I knew full well how it sounded to say that overseeing the renovations on three properties became a full-time job, one I didn't even particularly enjoy, but it was the truth. I became an ace trouble-shooter and project manager, sometimes even a general contractor, all work I could never put on a résumé, not that anyone would ever hire an MFA with no work experience save waitressing, bartending, and teaching English as a foreign language.

And now, somehow Karl and I had gotten to a point where we mostly spoke about and through the girls. I couldn't pinpoint the last time we were alone for more than an hour when both of us were awake. It had become our new normal, and I'd become almost numb to the fact that it wasn't normal at all. I'd been hoping we'd talk while we were here—really talk.

"Maybe we'll see someone when I get home."

I rubbed the tip of my index finger along the cover of the note-book and flicked it open.

"I haven't written a word in a five years."

Lauren put her hand on top of mine and squeezed. She under-stood everything I was trying to tell her. We were writers. Writing was what fed our souls. To admit that you had stopped was like saying you no longer breathed.

"I meant it when I said you could stay as long as you'd like. Stay all week. Keep this room or move into one of the bigger suites down-stairs. You still have that chubby au pair, right? The girls will be fine. Karl can fend for himself. Trust me, I know what it looks like to need a break. And you need a break . . . even if you did do all of the drugs last night . . . actually especially if you did all of the drugs last night."

"I can't."

"Why not?"

Why not?

The truth was that I had everything at my disposal to be able to stay. I knew plenty of women who built "me spa-cations," where everyone eats activated charcoal and grass and lets bees sting their ass on purpose, into their gospel of self-care routines, jetting off to Canyon Ranch or the Greenbrier for a long weekend. I'd never felt like I deserved that kind of break—even planning for this trip, where I would be away from home for less than forty-eight hours, left me feeling guilty and on edge. Maybe it was because I had committed myself to being a stay-at-home mom and secretly didn't believe I was doing real and worthy work beyond that. If I were a corporate lawyer or even an actual full-time writer, I would allow myself downtime once in a while. But everyone deserved a break and some downtime, and the offer was incredibly tempting. Surely Karl and the girls could survive another day without me. Imagining the peace and quiet, the luxury of time completely to myself in this paradise, made my heart quicken with a giddy anticipation—like knowing your favorite dessert was coming after dinner.

"Actually, maybe I could stay an extra few nights." I began to run the logistics in my head. The airline would charge me a $250 change fee, the rental car would be another couple hundred, but that's what money was for, right? Buying convenience. After a childhood and early adulthood of pinching every penny, I still flinched when it came to spending on myself. "Is Nina still here?"

"She left early this morning. Said she needed to drive down to L.A. for some meetings with Jennifer Lawrence? Something about multiple orgasms? Said to tell you she'd text you."

My first thought was surprise that Nina was in any shape to do anything, but for all I knew she did molly every night and could bounce back like she'd popped a couple Advil and a melatonin. Then there was a fuzzy memory of the last thing Nina had said to me before she left my room. She'd kissed me square on the lips, pulled back, and stared into my eyes like she could see my soul. "We're going to fucking Thailand!!! This is going to be so much fun!"

The memories rushed back then in broken fragments—Expedia, American Airlines, Nina screaming "YOLO" off the balcony. Me wondering what YOLO meant. Her explaining it to me. *Oh God, what did I do?*

Lauren went downstairs to say her good-byes, pack her bags, and get her kids and her wife into their minivan. Suddenly I was alone with my hangover.

I took a deep breath and checked my e-mail. My hands flew to my face Macaulay Culkin–style. There it was, the first message in my in-box: a confirmation for a one-way ticket to Bangkok leaving on Tuesday at 9:00 p.m.

What the hell was I thinking?

I wasn't. That was the point. I hadn't been thinking. The drug had loosened something in me and allowed me to lose my mind. It had been so glorious, it was almost worth the worst hangover I'd ever experienced. But it was also stupid. I'd need to cancel the ticket and probably wouldn't be able to get my money back. I couldn't go to Thailand.

At the same time, there was no way I was getting on that plane back to New York today. The idea of a break, now that it was lodged in my mind, was too tempting. I could take Lauren up on her offer and stay here in California a couple of days. I'd sleep. I'd recover. Who knows, maybe I would write.

When I called Karl to tell him the plan, his phone went straight to voice mail, which meant he was taking a run. His forty-five minutes of daily exercise was the only time he ever turned his phone off. It was just past three in New York on a Sunday afternoon and he would reliably be halfway around the reservoir. I went downstairs and foraged for food, but the kitchen was pretty bare.

I wandered down the lawn and out to the edge of the cliff to try Karl again.

"How was the wedding?" He sounded distracted and out of breath when he finally picked up. I could picture him checking his Fitbit as he cooled down. "When are you driving to the airport?"

I paused, unsure how to put this. "I thought maybe I'd stay an extra day or two. I might try to . . . to relax a little. Fly back on the red-eye Tuesday instead of tonight." In those few sentences, I wanted Karl to hear everything I wasn't telling him. I wanted him to hear how much I needed a break, how exhausted I'd become, how I needed some time to figure out what the hell I wanted to do with my life now that both of the girls were in school during the day. But I didn't say any of those things.

"We have that fund-raiser for Room to Read tomorrow night. We bought a table," Karl said briskly.

I didn't want to hear that he wanted me to come home for some benefit. If he were going to tell me to come home why couldn't it be because he'd miss me.

"You'll be fine without me. That event runs like clockwork. Donna wrote you an incredible speech for it. I looked it over before I left. You don't need me."

"I know it'll be fine. I'm just telling you that you'll miss it." His tone softened. "Don't worry about it. You deserve a break. We'll see you later this week."

"Will the girls be OK?" I hated that I would miss bedtime with them for another three nights. Bedtime was always our time. Even when Karl and I had obligations at night I tried to work them around the girls getting into their pajamas, choosing a book to read, and then piling on top of me in one of their beds, their minty breath on my arms, neck, and hands.

"Marley's here. They'll be fine."

"I miss you guys."

"The girls miss you too." *But do you miss me?* I thought.

"I wish you'd come this weekend." I regretted saying the words the moment they came out of my mouth. I didn't want to pick a fight, not then.

"You know I couldn't. I had to deal with this. In fact, I'm still dealing with it. I'm going to meet Annabel in an hour to try to talk her off yet another ledge. We need her finished manuscript. We needed it weeks ago if we wanted to publish it on the spring list."

"I understand," I said, even though I didn't.

After sleeping for fifteen hours straight, I woke up on Monday morning with no one to answer to but me. *This is how Nina feels every day of her life.* I stretched my arms over my head, opened my eyes, and then closed them again for as long as I wanted. I didn't need to make breakfasts or pack lunches or find my husband a matching sock. For just one day I wasn't anyone's wife, anyone's mother.

After I got off the phone with Karl yesterday afternoon, I had wrapped a scratchy Pendleton blanket around my shoulders and pulled a chair onto the balcony. The notebook dared me to open it. The pages had yellowed some with age. Some sentences perfectly matched the parameters of the Moleskine's parallel lines while others passed diagonally across an entire page. The letters were neat and close together, the script strong and confident. I began to read the story of the truck driver.

Every time that song, their song, came on the radio he looked over at the passenger seat and was surprised all over again to realize she was no longer sitting there next to him . . .

Even with my gruesome hangover, something had shaken loose inside of me, and I began writing, as if in a fever dream, all day—

taking only a quick break to scrounge in the kitchen for wedding leftovers—and then writing a few more hours until I'd collapsed into an exhausted sleep at 9:00 p.m.

I reached for the notebook again before getting out of bed and quickly skimmed what I had written. It was solid, if uneven in places. I didn't mind trashing some of it. There was something so gratifying in destroying something I'd created, knowing I'd have the time and space to create something new later that day.

I threw on jeans and a T-shirt, grabbed a banana, and strolled the palatial grounds for a bit, soaking in the solitude. Then I took the rickety steps two by two back down to the sea, letting my mind empty as the waves rolled over my feet, no longer afraid that they would rush in and engulf me. In the distance dolphins shimmied on the horizon, their sleek backs rising and falling in symmetry with the swells. For the first time in a long time I felt like I was on the cusp of something new.

My phone buzzed in my pocket. It was a text from Lauren.

I love that you're still there. Self-care FTW. You need to drive out to Henry Miller Library and hit up Esalen at 2 am (if you can stomach the naked old men . . . so much flabby dick). Treat yo self mama. You deserve it.

Visiting the clothing-optional hot springs of Esalen in the dead of night was definitely more than I could handle with the lingering remnants of my hangover, but a library dedicated to one of my favorite writers was simple and the perfect short drive from the house. Suddenly eager to get off the property, I turned around and climbed the steps two by two back to the house to grab my bag and head out.

Somehow I'd always thought of Big Sur as a town, an idyllic little village south of San Francisco. I had no idea there was no town at all, rather an eighty-mile stretch of coastal road dotted every so often by hiking trails, hobbit-style houses, campsites, and small businesses, half of which appeared to be shuttered, perhaps forever, or maybe just for the afternoon.

Midafternoon traffic on Highway One was light enough that I could drive my rental car at a leisurely pace but never sit in traffic. It was a perfect fall day, crisp and cool and punctuated by bright sun, an ideal day for a road trip. I couldn't remember the last time I'd taken a road trip. Once upon a time getting behind the wheel and driving for hours with no set destination, driving just to drive, radio blasting, wind in my hair, had been one of my favorite things to do.

Now, as I cruised down one of the most scenic roads in the country, I tried to savor it. I pulled off on the side of the road to take in the stunning vistas of coast and took selfies for the girls. I'd forgotten what it felt like to drive in a car without my children, to be able to listen to whatever I wanted on the radio, to be able to roll down all of the windows without worrying about blowing wind or dirt in their faces, to be able to empty my mind of everything but the yellow lines in front of me on the asphalt.

I drove past the unassuming entrance to the library twice. It was easy to miss the simple sign painted in yellow on a few planks of wood that promised three things—BOOKS MUSIC ART. I'd been expecting a grand structure, not dissimilar from the home I was staying in. I was unprepared for a slightly spooky cabin in the woods.

But the inside of the library quietly fulfilled Lauren's promise that it was something special. Though I always associated Henry Miller with New York and Paris, the evidence of his life here, from 1944 to 1962, was all over the rough-hewn wooden walls. I particularly enjoyed a letter from Miller to a friend as he was on the cusp of writing *Tropic of Cancer.*

> *I start tomorrow on the Paris book: First person, uncensored, formless—fuck everything!*

"Fuck everything," I whispered to myself. "Fuck everything." I repeated it like a mantra.

According to a small flyer posted on a table in the back of the main room, the library never belonged to Miller. It was the home of his friend the painter Emil White. Miller also never knew of the existence of the library and memorial. They were created by White and an eclectic group of Miller enthusiasts the year after he died. It wasn't a library as much as a shrine to the writer, with his books and paraphernalia for sale. I felt a twinge of jealousy for a man who inspired such loyalty and fanaticism after his death. This quickly slid into a morbid train of thought about how if I died, my legacy and memorial would consist entirely of a few notes I'd penned to my children's teachers and a copy of my husband's calendar.

An enterprising entrepreneur with a literary spirit had emblazoned hand-crafted ceramic mugs with some of Miller's more famous quotes. I rattled the mugs around on the table, hoping to find one with the quote I'd written on the first page of every notebook I bought during my twenties: "One's destination is never a place but rather a new way of looking at things." I couldn't find it and felt too embarrassed to ask. Instead I picked up a mug for Karl that read *we live on the edge of the miraculous*. Henry Miller was a seminal part of the discussion Karl and I had over oysters on our first date. That night, Karl had told me that he wanted to follow Miller's example of championing writers who had been disregarded and cast aside. He wanted to publish the kinds of literature that would challenge and trouble the elite of our day. Karl was so optimistic back then, and it turned me on more than I'd ever been turned on in my entire life. We talked for hours about literature and life and art and sex and by the time we left the restaurant we nearly finished one another's sentences.

I bought the mug and a new notebook and wandered to the back of the cabin where there was a table with coffee and muffins and a tin box with a sign instructing visitors to pay what they wished, with the knowledge that the organic muffins were handmade with love by a local writer using local ingredients. I slipped a twenty into the box, picked up the plumpest muffin, and poured a cup of coffee to enjoy on the cabin's porch. Once I sat down, I pulled the notebook from its paper sack and lost myself writing for the better part of an hour before I heard someone clear his throat above me. I shaded my eyes with my hand and looked up to see a store clerk with a precarious man bun bobbling like an uncircumcised penis on top of his head. He held the pot of coffee in his hand and lifted it a few inches to offer me a refill.

"Free refills for writers." He smiled so earnestly that I felt a flush of embarrassment.

"Thanks," I said shyly. "This coffee's really good."

"Folgers." He grinned back. "I should tell you it's some of that fancy shit they roast up in San Fran, but since the mudslides took out parts of the road down here it's easier for us to just get the corporate standbys."

"It is the best part of waking up," I agreed.

"Do you want another muffin?" he asked. He was too young to get the joke. He'd probably never watched television with commercials. "On the house. We like to feed writers when they're working here. We actually have a lot of events for local and visiting writers. We're a small community, but we bring in a sizable crowd."

I blinked a couple of times. "Oh. I'm not a writer."

He cocked his head and cast his kind brown eyes at my notebook. "You're writing, aren't you? Sure looks like it to me."

"This is just . . . I'm just trying something new."

"Aren't we all?" He turned on his heel and headed for the door, his hair jiggling in time with his hips. "I'm going to get you a muffin."

I felt an intense urge to leave before he returned. Our brief conversation made me feel like a sham. What was I playing at? I was a wife and a mom, just a wife and mom from the Upper East Side, a place that felt like another country compared to this bohemian enclave.

I was already at the end of the gravel driveway when I saw the clerk balancing a plate with a muffin in my rearview mirror.

I was living in Paris when I first met Karl, who was living in New York. Back then, the two of us would have marathon phone calls that lasted until dawn. Listening to his voice in my ear as the sun came up in my little studio apartment in the Marais were some of the best moments in my entire life. Even better were the nights where we would fall asleep with the other person breathing on the line, as if we were next to each other. And even better than that were the nights where the calls devolved into steamy conversations about various things we planned to do to one another just as soon as we were together again.

I missed that early version of Kate and Karl so much. I thought about them as I called him later that night. Perhaps we couldn't talk until the sun came up, but maybe we could talk tonight, really talk. Maybe I'd say something about Paris, or that night in the water in Greece. Maybe he'd get out of bed, cross our bedroom, and lock our door and reach beneath the covers . . .

"Kate?" Karl answered on the second ring, his voice groggy. I'd forgotten about the time difference.

"Were you asleep?"

"It's after midnight. Yeah, I am."

I'd heated myself up a small dinner of pasta and a beet salad I purchased at the market down the road and poured myself the remainder of the wedding wine.

"Have you ever been to the Henry Miller Library?"

"Is everything OK?"

"I'm great," I said with too much enthusiasm. "Have you ever been to the Henry Miller Library?" I repeated. I needed to tell him everything about my day. I couldn't wait to tell him how, from the moment I walked into that library, I knew it was the kind of place he would have loved once upon a time. I needed to tell him how it smelled like old books, a scent we once agreed was our favorite smell in the entire world. I wanted to tell him about the story I'd finished the day before and then the one I started today.

"Kate, I don't know what you're talking about. A library?"

"Did you know Henry Miller lived in Big Sur?"

I could hear my husband sit up in bed and flick on the bedside lamp. His voice was a little more clear.

"I did. That's where he wrote *Big Sur and the Oranges of Hieronymus Bosch.*"

"I bought a copy of that today." My voice rose with excitement.

"You bought a book at a library? Aren't you supposed to borrow books from a library?"

I began to ramble about the library that wasn't really a library and the memorial and how he would have loved it.

I started telling him about the wedding and how I thought about him when I was on the dance floor, how I imagined him wrapping his arms around me and touching me.

Then I heard Karl yawn. Loudly.

There would be none of that kind of talk tonight.

"Are you drunk? It's late. Do you need Sara to arrange a car for you from the airport Wednesday morning? We have Alexander Brozny coming for cocktails at seven with his agent on Thursday night."

Alexander Brozny was a transgender Ukrainian novelist who had written a beautiful memoir connecting his harassment and intimidation from the antigay government with his half-Jewish grandmother's persecution and imprisonment during the Second World War. He intertwined their two stories seamlessly, and the result was a gorgeous meditation on love and identity, cruelty and kindness. I'd adored his book and devoured the galleys in just two nights. I'd been excited to host him in our home, but now the cocktail party had lost its sheen. It would be just another night where I became a fly on the wall observing someone else fulfilling their dream.

"Kate, are you there? Do you need a car?"

How did I get to a place where the thought of going home filled with me a cold sense of dread?

"I can get an Uber," I said flatly. I couldn't believe how quickly my mood changed, my earlier buoyancy now dissolved. I felt like my epic hangover had returned, and a dull ache took up residence at the base of my skull.

"OK. Sara will e-mail you the guest list tomorrow morning. She has a question about the menu. Oh, and the bartender canceled. Can you call those bartenders we used for that party with Dan Brown last month?"

His shift to logistics crushed me. "Sure."

I heard him yawn again and I wanted to yell at him: *Am I boring? Do I bore you?* But I said nothing.

"Thanks," he said, filling the silence. "I need to get back to sleep. Love you."

Moments earlier I'd been starving for conversation and now I was desperate to stop speaking to my husband. The only way to respond was with a phrase that had begun to lose its meaning.

"I love you too."

I'd later think of that phone call as a turning point, a pivotal moment shaping everything that would come after.

When I hung up the phone I stood dumbly in the middle of the room, staring out the window at the inky-black expanse of sky and ocean. I knew that as soon as I boarded the plane back to New York my life would return to normal. I'd arrange cleaners and bartenders and make sparkling conversation about someone else's great accomplishments. These expectations weren't unreasonable. This was the person I'd become in the past ten years. I couldn't even tell if Karl actually liked me any longer, or if I was just another person who helped make his life and his business run smoothly. The more I thought about it the angrier I became. The clerk at the library mistook me for a writer. My old friends from school mistook me for a writer. My husband had forgotten I was a writer. He knew who I was when he married me, and yet he let that part of me slip away. In the early days of our relationship we'd promised to help the other one realize our dreams. It was part of what bound us together in the first place. I'd kept my end of the bargain. Why did he break his promise?

I lay down and stared at the cracks in the ceiling and then stood and paced the room. I was angry and sad and frustrated. I directed my rage first at Karl and then at myself.

Sometime before dawn I abandoned the idea of sleep altogether and cracked open my laptop, determined to do my duty and find the e-mail of the man who arranged the bartenders to make sure he had two available for the Brozny party.

At the top of my in-box was an e-mail from Lois Delancey. "Where Are You?" was the subject.

I didn't see you at drop-off or pickup today. Have you left Karl?
LOL

I wondered, not for the first time, whether I was the only adult left in New York City who didn't use abbreviations or emojis in e-mails. The tone was playful, but the snappy subtext was clear if you spoke "Upper East Side mom." There was no doubt that Lois, the enfant terrible of the mommies at the Atherton School, had already floated any number of speculative theories about why I hadn't dropped my children off at school. Lois, a graduate of Harvard Business School who never missed an opportunity to remind you that she went to Harvard Business School even when you didn't ask, had the perpetually bothered expression and pinched tone of voice of a woman given a surprise enema. I could hear her high-pitched accusation in my head. Drop-off was a necessary evil in our world. No matter how much help any of us had, and my part-time au pair was considered a skeleton staff compared to most of the moms from Atherton, parents (mostly moms) almost always made it to drop-off or pickup. It was part of the facade we all cultivated that we were absolutely fucking doing it all.

We were good mothers, we were in the best shape of our lives, we looked better than we did in our twenties, and we did meaningful work, mostly charity, outside of our home. We were superwomen, and our daily presence at the school added the exclamation mark on that falsehood. It didn't matter if you had two nannies and a night nurse the rest of the time. If you were at drop-off, you were a good mom.

Lois, a former exec at Google turned mom-trepreneur who was making a fortune selling panties that you could essentially pee in, was probably trying to dig up dirt on me to diffuse the gossip about her own latest drama. She'd recently stolen a personal chef from Ainsley Harrison. What made it especially bizarre was that it was a personal baby-food chef, a top-notch graduate of Le Cordon Bleu hired specifically (with a six-figure salary) to puree organic vegetables for a six-month-old. It was Ainsley who originally discovered the culinary prodigy. She'd bragged about him every morning for months, before Lois secretly e-mailed him and offered him double what Ainsley was paying him. It got juicier. Some mommies speculated that Lois had snagged the chef to cook for her and not for her baby. The latest was that she put herself on a baby-food-only diet in order to shed her baby pooch. These women were more ruthless than Breitbart in their genesis of fake news. The Facebook groups, the e-mail chains, the mommy listservs, the whisper down the lane at pickup and drop-off. I wished I could say I'd become numb to it, but I hated the toxic culture of Upper East Side mothering as much now as I did when I first entered it. That said, it felt like there was no escape—for better or worse, this had become my social circle.

I considered not replying to Lois, but leaving a vacuum would only give her space to fill.

Had to fly to the West Coast. Helping out some old friends with a situation here. Resolving now. Home Friday. Coffee next week?

The word *situation* was both vague and important-sounding, as if I'd come out here to help someone with their sick mother. It would keep the chatter to a minimum. I imagined Marley had done both drop-off and pickup, or maybe just one of the two. Karl liked to get the girls to school when he could. That was the thing about Karl. He was a great father. If he weren't I couldn't have imagined leaving my children for even a day.

I closed Lois's e-mail, picturing the look of horror on her face if she could see me now—the room was still a bit of a mess from our after-party, an empty cigarette pack in the corner, the lingering smell of weed, my clothes in various puddles around the room, as if it belonged to a recalcitrant teenager. I tried to imagine Lois ever doing molly and decided it would do her some good.

I gazed over at my empty suitcase. There at the bottom was a rust-orange vial filled with a prescription for Zoloft from our family general practitioner, Dr. Sullivan. I had another one for Xanax. Both were prescribed at my annual physical last year when Dr. Sullivan asked how I was feeling. I had a rare moment of honesty that I later regretted. I confessed to him that sometimes when I woke in the middle of the night I felt as though I were drowning. That I would then lie awake for hours, dark thoughts spinning, like imagining I was in a coma like a daytime-soap star, beautiful and serene, while the world went on without me. Dr. Sullivan prescribed the anti-anxiety medication and recommended a therapist and gluten-free diet. Since then I kept the drugs with me all the time. Karl had no idea about the prescriptions. But it didn't matter. I'd never taken a single pill.

For me, taking the drugs meant admitting I was depressed, admitting I was unhappy with my life, and that brought on a roaring wave of anger at myself. Like Nina had said on the beach, didn't I have the perfect fucking life? I didn't deserve to be depressed. I had a good, if occasionally absent, husband. I had healthy, beautiful daughters, and we had enough money to never think about money for the rest of our lives. If I took the pills it would be like admitting those things weren't enough for me, and that seemed like courting disaster, even if most every woman and child over the age of eight in our zip code had a script for some kind of SSRI if they hadn't already moved on to medical marijuana. After all, we were the fucking one percent. What right did we have to complain.

I had actually tried to talk to Lois about it once, during one of our rare conversations about anything more than school gossip or our children.

She laughed at me in a way that wasn't mean but also wasn't nice. "Oh, Kate. Why don't you just eat your feelings and then throw them up like everyone else we know." Her laugh turned into a cackle. "Kidding! I'm just kidding. I'm not talking about me, of course. But I did hear Ainsley the other day talking about a baker in Koreatown who makes sheet cakes laced with laxatives and ipecac."

I laughed then. I wish I hadn't, but Lois's approval used to mean so much to me.

She swiftly changed the subject back to her waterproof underwear. "Kate, you must check out our new sports line, Jinx Joggers—Lululemon just took a huge order."

We never spoke about feelings again.

My passport was also lying in the bottom of the bag. I'd brought it along instead of my driver's license when I realized, two days before this trip, that the license was expired and I wouldn't have time to go to the DMV.

"You really should be able to pay an extra fee and cut in front of the gen pop at the DMV," one of the mommies at school drop-off remarked when I told her about the nuisance. *Gen pop* was something some of the moms were trying out to refer to the "general population." This sounded perfectly natural coming out of the mouth of a woman who paid $10,000 for her kid to cut to the front of the line of Space Mountain during their recent trip to Disney World, a place, she remarked upon her return, that had way too much gen pop.

I tossed a shirt on top of the pill bottle and my passport and returned to my computer screen. The bartender. I had to e-mail the bartender.

It took forever for the e-mail to load again and I bit my fingernails in the meantime, a nasty habit I'd abandoned when I began getting de rigueur weekly manicures. I thought of Nina's ragged, dirty fingernails then, and as I thought of her, she came to life on my computer screen. At least her e-mail did. Her name appeared in my in-box like a spirit conjured at a séance where no one believes in ghosts. The subject line of the e-mail was in all caps and punctuated with cheerful, if insistent, exclamation marks. "THAILAND!!!!!!"

I opened the e-mail.

I'll meet you at the zen center!!!! I can't fucking wait. This is going to be perfect. I love you.

There was a link to her itinerary—she would arrive at the center almost a half day before me. That is, if I went through with this.

I fiddled with the slim gold chain at my neck, the one with delicate charms bearing my daughters' initials. I brought the chain in and out of my mouth, tasting the bitter metal. I thought of Henry Miller, "One's destination is never a place but rather a new way of looking at things." I thought of something else he said: "Fuck everything."

I still had two plane tickets booked on the same day—one back to New York and one to Bangkok.

Chapter Three

If Karl answered the phone I would get on the plane to New York and Nina would just have to understand.

If he didn't answer, if my husband ignored me, or didn't try to talk me out of this, I'd get on the plane to Thailand. There was a part of me that felt ridiculous having created such a melodramatic scenario. Who did I think I was? A character in a Lifetime movie?

But I couldn't deny another feeling: exhilaration. It was like faking a stomachache as a kid—the feeling of being able to play hooky. But these weren't the kinds of games a grown woman with two children was allowed to play with her life.

After I settled into one of the soft booths in a charmless airport wine bar, I pulled out my phone and stared at it for a moment, smiling at the screen saver photograph of Isabel and Tilly staring up at fireworks from this past Fourth of July. I took a deep breath and made the call.

As the phone rang, I played out the ideal conversation in my head. Karl would answer and he'd tell me he couldn't wait to see me when I got home. He would tell me he missed me and he'd wait up for me.

It would be the validation I needed. Thailand would become a foolish memory.

I'd leave the international terminal and get on the plane that was scheduled to fly back to New York and write off this little detour as a mild midlife crisis. When I got home Karl and I would snuggle into bed. I'd slip into that black lace chemise we'd picked up together in Paris and we'd laugh about Nina and Alex. I'd admit I bought a ticket to Thailand and he'd be so relieved that I didn't jet off to the other side of the world that we would screw like bunnies for half the night.

I'd put on a new dress for the Brozny party, the violet Dries Van Noten that had been on back order for a month. The caterers would take over my kitchen, preparing a variety of delicacies on very tiny toast, and the bartenders would arrive and craft a signature cocktail for the evening. I'd name it something witty and hilarious and everyone would compliment me on it and say things like, "Kate, you really should have been a writer," and for the first time in a long time I would say, "Actually I'm working on something."

Sara, Karl's assistant, answered his cell phone.

"Hi, Kate. Is something wrong with your flight?" She sounded flustered. Sara almost always sounded like she hadn't had her first cup of coffee.

"Can I talk to Karl?"

"He told me to pick up. He's on the line with John—he can't talk to you right now."

John Montgomery, head of Pride Capital, was Paradigm's chief investor, and the only thing between Paradigm's survival as an independent publisher and selling out to one of the "Big Five," a move that would have Karl Carmichael Sr. rolling over in his grave. Nothing stressed my husband out more than talking to John, who had built one of the most successful hedge funds in the world, but who could not wrap his mind around the vagaries or nuances of the publishing business, despite fancying himself a bibliophile. Last Halloween he and his husband, Gary, had both dressed as Offred from *The Handmaid's Tale*.

"Can you just tell my husband I need two minutes?"

"He specifically said he didn't have time to talk to you, Kate. I can give him a message."

The last thing I wanted to do was leave a message for my goddamn husband. And even though this was a scenario that had happened dozens and dozens of times before, this time something in me broke. I felt like I was having that dream where you try to scream but you have no voice.

"OK, tell him I won't make it home today."

I clicked the phone off before Sara could ask me anything else and I walked toward the gate.

To hell with it all, I was really going to do this. I'd flown across the country and now I was going to fly halfway around the world to meet a woman I had hardly seen in twelve years in the middle of the goddamn jungle. I expected to feel a crush of anxiety, but I felt fine. In fact, I felt better than fine. I felt a surge of joy and anticipation. I missed my girls. I always missed them, even when they were only a few blocks away, or when they were asleep in their own beds just down the hall. But I didn't worry about them. They were in good hands. They could survive without me for another week or two.

After I made my way to the gate, I quickly settled into a flurry of activity that would make this mad adventure possible. I texted Marley that I wouldn't be home today as expected and gave her some directions and reminders about the girls—that Isabel's piano time had moved this week and that Tilly needed new ballet shoes before Saturday's class.

I'd hired Marley because I trusted her completely. She was more than capable. Everything was going to be OK. I had to keep repeating it like a mantra, or I wouldn't be able to make it through this plane ride.

Next, I e-mailed Nina, telling her I was about to board the plane. Her previous message had the address of her mythical zen center in the foothills of the Dawna mountains. A quick check of Google Earth showed me very little except that it was surrounded by national parks and wildlife reserves and was located just over two hundred miles from Bangkok. I figured I'd rent a car at the airport, drive for a couple of hours, and be there for dinnertime with Nina.

I confirmed with the caterers and the bartenders for the party. Fortunately, these events were a well-oiled machine at this point. Karl would have to host alone. He could do it, but he wouldn't like it. Making sure his events went off without a hitch had become my specialty.

He'll figure it out, I told myself. *It's not rocket science.*

Finally, just as the flight began to board, I dashed to the newsstand

and bought a *New Yorker*. When was the last time I had time to sit and read a *New Yorker* cover to cover?

I settled into my middle seat in the middle of economy—which was the only ticket available with a few days' notice. I couldn't remember the last time I'd flown economy. As soon as I had the thought, I felt a sickening lurch in my stomach that I was the type of person who thought things like, *I can't remember the last time I was in economy*. It was disgusting. A lot of things about my life were disgusting—like the fact that I had become so comfortable always being comfortable. I used to revel in the things that went wrong when I traveled. I loved getting myself out of a difficult situation, didn't even mind when a bag was lost or a reservation canceled because it meant that I could practice a new language or stretch my skills. Now I despised having to share my armrest with a pimply teenager. To be fair, I could see that he was thumbing through Japanese comic porn on his iPad.

I was too polite. I'd surrendered both armrests and now I would have to live with it. I opened the *New Yorker* and skimmed the Talk of the Town before turning to the fiction pages. I almost laughed out loud. Even as I attempted to escape my life, I would never get away from it. The story this week was an excerpt adapted from a new book by Jackson Welch that was being published by Karl. Just a few days before I left for Big Sur, Karl and I had hosted a dinner in our home for twenty people in Jackson's honor.

I realized now, as the plane barreled down the runway, that I could trace so much of my irritation and angst during the past forty-eight hours to that party.

I closed the *New Yorker* and thought back to that night. The guest of honor, Jackson Welch, was an asshole—and worse, he was the type of asshole who cultivated and relished that persona. His bad-boy swagger was like performance art. Twenty years ago he won the Pulitzer Prize and then not two weeks later overdosed on heroin in the bathroom of Odeon. After emerging from a posh desert rehab in Arizona, the kind that charged $20,000 a week for a man-child to make bamboo bird feeders and weave reed baskets while talking about their feelings and why they hated their mothers, Jackson had gone into seclusion in the Smoky Mountains and hadn't written a word for almost two decades. His new novel was expected to be the "big book" of the fall and a boon for Paradigm's third-quarter profits. I hadn't much enjoyed his first book when I read it in college. I remember talking about it with my writing group at the time. "When a male author writes about marriage and feelings he gets the Pulitzer fucking Prize," I had said. "When a woman does the same thing her book is dismissed as chick lit."

When Karl brought home pages of Welch's new book, I vowed to keep an open mind, but from the very first sentence I could tell it was a sophomore flunk. It was a weak narrative about a middle-aged divorcé who falls in love with a prostitute on a train trip from Hartford to New Orleans to attend his mother's funeral. In the midst of it all they solve a murder aboard the train. I bit my tongue to avoid saying that he wrote a poor man's mash-up of *Pretty Woman* and *Murder on the Orient Express* with none of the panache and wit of Agatha Christie or Garry Marshall. The pacing was slow, the characters were caricatures, his prose was pretentious—as if he were trying to *sound* like a good writer, rather than be a good writer—and his disdain for women was palpable. I could tell Karl didn't particularly like the book either, but Paradigm had paid a small fortune for it at auction, so he would never admit out loud that it was anything less than a masterpiece.

We had no choice but to throw a party for Jackson, even though it was the last thing I wanted to do. We invited Jackson; Troy Bachman, his agent; and Kasey, his editor, a rising star at Paradigm in her twenties, the one who wore the practically invisible skirts. I often wondered why she bothered to wear a skirt at all when the slightest shift of her thighs offered the entire room a glimpse of her labia. There was also a reporter from the *New York Review of Books* who was working on a three-part essay on Welch's triumphant return to the literary scene, and Hoda Kotb, who was going to interview Jackson over the weekend (even though she didn't seem pleased by it).

I originally planned to invite some of Karl's other authors, but Troy sent a curt e-mail saying his client couldn't stand spending time around other writers. "Who should I invite?" I e-mailed in response. His reply was curt and straightforward: "Invite anyone who loved his last book . . . and some fuckable single women."

I ignored the entreaty for single women. I wasn't Jackson's pimp. I should have filled the room exclusively with drag queens.

Two last-minute additions were Edward, Karl's corporate accountant and roommate from Yale, and his wife, Penelope. Edward was small and squirrelly and I got the feeling he'd attached himself like a burr to Karl on their first day of freshman year and never let go. He loved reminding people that he and Karl went to Yale, even though they had graduated more than twenty-five years earlier. He also never failed to ask me, "Where'd you go to school again, Kate?"

I always flashed a warm smile and reminded him that I got an MFA at Columbia as I inwardly rolled my eyes and called him a condescending motherfucker in my head. I didn't bother to mention my undergrad degree from the University of Wisconsin. The middle of the country confused people who'd always lived in New York. It was rare that I ever mentioned my life before New York in the company of Karl's friends and coworkers, all of whom had a vague recollection that I was from a "flyover state," but if you asked them which one they were just as likely to say Iowa as Wisconsin.

On the uncommon occasion someone asked me what it was like growing up in Wisconsin, I was honest. "It was totally normal." That was true. Everything about my childhood was normal—two reasonably happy parents, an older sister, piano lessons, cheerleading. For some reason my answer made people laugh and then change the subject because normal was just so boring.

Edward had given both of his children, girls close in age to mine, absurdly literary names: Atwood and Updike. I always thought he did it in a bid to impress Karl.

His wife, Penelope, didn't feign an interest in books, but she adored proximity to anyone with a slight patina of fame. After spending eight years out of the workforce as a stay-at-home mom (with two nannies), Penelope was constantly reinventing herself. She was the kind of woman who believed all of her hobbies should be a career, and she had the rich husband to finance those fantasies. After brief stints as an interior designer, a yoga instructor, and a life coach, she had recently refashioned herself as an Instagram influencer.

As far as I could tell most of her feed was well-filtered duck-face selfies. The most significant consequence of Penelope's foray into the world of social media was that she inserted the word *hashtag* into sentences where it definitely didn't belong.

"Do you ever feel like this room is . . . hashtag . . . too bright, Kate?" Penelope had remarked after handing me her coat when she arrived for Jackson's party. "I just found an amazing light fixture made out of upcycled votives handcrafted by former Guatemalan prostitutes that got more than a thousand likes. You need it."

"I don't know if I do." I shrugged noncommittally.

As an Instagram influencer, Penelope took both lighting and social justice very seriously.

Across the room Karl leaned elegantly against the fireplace, watching Welch's agent make wild gesticulations. A bemused smile played on my husband's lips. Even though he had the propensities of an introvert, Karl was the rare man completely at ease in any situation. I'd seen him wear the same confident expression as he talked his way out of a nasty misunderstanding with some Chilean cowboys in a bar on our honeymoon trek through Patagonia that he wore when he accepted praise from a National Book Award winner in a grand awards ceremony. Lately I'd begun to wonder if his comfort in his own skin was a consequence of his extreme privilege, and, if so, whether that trait would naturally surface in our own daughters, who would never know what it was like to want for anything.

Most of the guests at these kinds of things usually looked right through me. It wasn't just that I was Karl's wife, but more that I wasn't at all interesting to them in my own right. Even Penelope was more interesting than I was. In moments like this, I thought I should have started a blog so at least I could tell people I was a blogger. I think I missed the whole mommy blog moment, though. I'd only recently even started an Instagram account. My twenty-three followers included Marley, our dog walker, and my bikini waxer. She'd peer pressured me into following her account @AllAboutThatBush and then followed me back out of pity.

Jackson was the last to arrive. He stumbled and fumbled in so drunk that Karl asked me to grab him a glass of water and an espresso the second he walked through the door. To his credit, Jackson followed me like an obedient Labrador. When I turned to hand him the tumbler of water in our kitchen he leaned over and placed his palm flat against my breast, a gesture so blatant it was clear that he hoped I might scream and cause a scene. Instead I stared straight into his rheumy eyes. His doughy face was still boyish, but the whites of his eyes were yellow, the skin around them papery and sallow. He wore jeans and a rumpled blazer over a blue button-down that had seen better days. A smear of pink lipstick stained his collar.

"You have nice tits for a middle-aged mom," he slurred. "I'll bet they're new."

Ten years ago I would have told him to fuck off and laughed in his face. Now I had no choice but to politely diffuse the situation so we could carry on with the evening. In a few minutes I'd smile and clap politely as my husband extolled this man's unique genius.

"They're old, actually . . . I like to call them vintage." I peeled his slimy fingers off my body and gently turned him back into the direction of the dining room. It wasn't the first time one of Karl's authors had hit on me or insulted me and I knew it wouldn't be the last, but this time it was particularly grating. *I don't even like your books*, I thought. *I could write circles around you. Why aren't I writing circles around you? You had twenty years and a two-million-dollar advance and wrote utter crap.*

I didn't want to go back into the party. I reached into the pantry for a bottle of whiskey. We hid the cheaper stuff when we had guests. Karl actually preferred Jameson to Macallan, a holdover from his teenaged years spent being a lifeguard with the Irish boys on Martha's Vineyard. I downed an entire tumbler in a surprising gulp.

I wanted to escape then, to run from the town house and sit on a barstool in a nondescript bar and order another whiskey. But, the only way out was the front door, past Jackson and Karl and a dozen people who'd want to know when we would be having the first course. Instead I sank down onto the kitchen floor, not caring if the caterers walked in and found the hostess slumped against the wall with her eyes closed. I just needed a minute. When I opened my eyes, I was staring at the wall-length calendar we kept next to the fridge. It was a complex grid of dates and times, meetings, pickups, drop-offs, and reminders. There was a box for each day, and each contained a name, or several, followed by an activity: Isabel—Japanese, Matilda—knitting class, Isabel—chess, Matilda—guitar, Isabel—meditation, Karl—cocktails Rushdie. My name was nowhere. I created and kept this calendar and yet I didn't exist in it. I kept all the pieces in motion like a silent puppeteer, forever behind the curtain.

I heard steps just outside the door and forced myself to my feet. I pressed my nails into my wrist and admonished myself through gritted teeth. *Pull it together, Kate.* Then I donned a well-practiced smile and returned to finish my hosting duties.

That night in bed, after the guests went home, I needed to talk to Karl about how I was feeling. It wasn't just the humiliating encounter with Jackson but also everything lately. It was the constant anxiety of making everyone else's life run smoothly while ignoring my own needs. I felt hollowed out and empty and I desperately needed to find a way to fulfill my own passions again. I felt dead inside and I wanted to feel alive again, but I didn't know how.

I rolled over and pressed myself into my husband's back.

"Karl," I whispered.

"Mmmm-hmmm."

"I need to tell you something."

"Can it wait until morning?"

"Can we talk now?"

"Kate. Please. I'm so tired. First thing in the morning. I promise."

I should have said no. It couldn't wait. I should have rolled him to face me and told him I felt lost. I was sleepwalking through a life that looked perfect and I needed his help to find myself again.

But, I didn't say those things.

"We can talk in the morning."

"I love you."

"I love you too."

He was already on his way to the office when I woke up. He texted me a few hours later:

I'm sorry we didn't get a chance to talk, baby. But we'll have plenty of time in Big Sur this weekend. I love you.

It took a creative mixture of yoga and fortitude to extract my bag with my notebook, pens, and paper from beneath the seat in front of me without disturbing my seatmates, now sleeping on either side of me. I was too wired to sleep and the soft sounds of the engine and the liminal lighting were like a cocoon, the perfect place to write. I was hoping to write at least a few solid stories and maybe get started on a novel while I was away. But as I put the pen down on the paper, it wasn't a story that came out. It was something else entirely.

Dear Karl,

I am writing you from thirty thousand feet above the Pacific Ocean, on a plane to Thailand. It's surreal to write that: I'm on a plane to Thailand. I'm sure you're wondering how the hell this happened. I'm actually wondering it myself to be honest. It's not like me to go halfway around the world on some impulsive adventure. But actually, Karl, it's exactly like me. At least, the me I used to be. You loved this about me, you loved that I was always up for a good time and for any adventure. I loved that about me too. Maybe it was seeing my grad school friends again this weekend and having some time to myself, but I realize I don't—we don't—have as much fun anymore. I know, I know, that's the price of being a grown-up, we have kids and responsibilities and bills, etc. But, Karl, I feel like we've come so far from the people we used to be. I feel like I've lost myself a little but . . . I also feel like I've lost you too. I can't quite figure out when this happened. It's a slippery slope. Maybe it's impossible to pinpoint that exact moment when your life shifts into something you never expected or wanted. I've been trying to trace the thread back from the beginning.

When I left for Paris after grad school I was every bit a writer. Sure I tutored wealthy Parisian offspring in English to pay the rent, but only because that gig freed up my afternoons and most evenings to sit in my small attic apartment and work on my novel. It feels strange to write that now. My novel! Remember when I was working on a novel? It seems like a different life, or a memory that happened to someone else.

Whenever I felt blocked, like I couldn't possibly get another word on the page, I wandered across the Pont Notre Dame to Shakespeare and Company to read the words of better writers than me in the hopes of being inspired to either write or drink the night away. In my twenties both of those options were desirable, and the drinking often led to writing, so I didn't have a preference for which one would come first. As far as bookstores go Shakespeare and Company was absolutely perfect, with its floor-to-ceiling shelves of used books and the air thick with the musty smell of fingered pages. I loved that they hosted a writer in residence every few months who got room and board upstairs in exchange for working in the store a few hours a day. I'd

*applied three or four times and never even received a rejection
letter. I didn't hold it against them, but I did maintain a morbid
curiosity about who they'd chosen in my place and I dreamed of
running into the lucky son of a bitch as I perused the stacks.*

*One of these nights I was tucked in one of the stacks,
breathlessly finishing* The Little Friend, *when the clerk informed
me the shop would be closing soon for a private event, an author
from the States would be giving a reading. I figure I'd keep
browsing until they kicked me out. I liked to pull things off the
shelf at random and read the last page of a book. You can tell
everything from the last page. You could read only, "So we beat
on, boats against the current, borne back ceaselessly into the past"
and know everything there was to know about* The Great Gatsby.

That was the first thing I said to you. Remember that?

*I felt you standing behind me and I turned around quickly
on purpose to scare you away. I expected a creepy old Parisian,
the kind who liked to grab my ass in bars and then pretend I'd
just bumped into their hands. I startled you. I thought you were
admiring me, but you merely wanted me to get out of your way.*

"I'm trying to grab that book," you stammered.

I stepped aside and you plucked Black Spring *from the shelf.*

*I said that line about the last pages of books and then
regarded the one you held in your hand. "It's his worst book,"
I said next. I felt confident saying things like that back then,
declaring that someone like Henry Miller had a worst book. You
humored me, maybe because I was wearing a blouse unbuttoned
one button revealing my flimsy black bra, or because you were
surprised to be flirted with in a bookstore. After a lifetime of
moaning about them, I missed American men.*

"I know. I happen to like terrible books." You glanced at
The Little Friend *in my hand. "I also happen to be in love
with Donna Tartt."*

I was undone by your smile.

The clerk began clearing the aisles then.

"I'm Karl," you said to me.

The clerk started asking you questions about where you wanted the chairs and the podium and the wine.

"Are you the author?" I asked.

"Far from it. I work for the publisher." You were very modest. I didn't learn for three more weeks that the publisher was your father.

You invited me to stay. I said I had things to do but I'd try to come back in an hour. I had nothing to do, but I knew from the start I might want to sleep with you, so I ran home to shave my legs and put on my best underwear and returned in the same outfit so it looked like I'd been running around the city being busy and doing important things. I can't believe I never told you that until now. I still have some secrets I guess, and I bet you do too.

You paid more attention to me that night than you did to your writer, and her irritation with both of us was palpable. As soon as I could I whisked you away to Le Select, hoping to impress you, but you'd already been there.

"Hemingway's favorite bar. I brought first dates here in my twenties to impress them with my ability to quote A Farewell to Arms," *you said as we ordered gimlets.*

"Did it work?"

"Never. French girls find me too American and they think Hemingway is a misogynistic pig."

"They aren't wrong."

"No, they aren't."

I delighted in teasing you.

My mother once told me that a man will reveal everything about himself in the first conversation he has with you. You only have to listen. You told me you wanted to work as an editor, that you wanted to travel the world searching for new writers with new voices, the kinds of people who needed to be

*published and were too often ignored. But you also told me you
loved the Upper East Side and your parents and that you felt
an obligation to make them happy. That's the part I should
have paid closer attention to.*

*We shut down Le Select, both a little tipsy, but not drunk,
and I thought about how I could ask you home without
you thinking I was a slut. You grabbed my hand then and
suggested a walk through the Tuileries. You only had six hours
until you needed to get to the airport.*

"Don't you need to get to your hotel?" I asked.

You nodded to a small backpack. "I travel light." I loved that.

*I'd never seen Saint-Germain so empty. I liked the way your
jawline looked in the flickering streetlamps. I wanted to touch
every part of your face.*

*"Let's race," I said to you, impulsively, as we walked into
the garden. "To the Louvre." It was my nerves. It struck me
that, in spite of my bravado, I was alone in the middle of the
night with a near stranger. A moody gray drizzle turned the
empty park into a Monet.*

*I removed my boots and placed them on a bench with a
thud. You looked at me like I was cute, but a little insane, and
made no move to take off your shoes. As soon as I straightened
up something sharp—a shard of glass—drove right into the
soft part of my bare heel. I screamed in pain and the look of
wonder disappeared from your face. I sat on the park bench
and without a word you lifted my foot into your lap and
expertly removed the shard while I blinked back tears.*

"You should have been a doctor," I said.

"It's easier to pick up women in bookstores."

*I'd been so independent for so long that something in me
enjoyed being a damsel in distress. Even in the dark I could
see a few drops of blood had dripped onto your pants, but you
didn't seem to mind. I pulled a scarf out of my bag and you*

tied it around my foot. You leaned close to me, hesitated for a moment, and then made up your mind to kiss me. I'd expected you to be shy. I was ready to be the aggressor, but you slid your palm behind my head and clasped at my hair with a brute force that felt like you were about to swallow me whole. As you moved your lips expertly down the front of my neck and unbuttoned my blouse, I reached down between your legs and felt you throbbing against the zipper of your pants. I was embarrassed by my gasp of surprise. I was, to be honest, a little caught off guard by what I found, how massive you are.

You frantically tugged my bra to the side and spent what felt like hours tracing my left nipple with your tongue, lightly grazing it with just the tips of your teeth, before continuing down my stomach in a trail of torturously slow kisses. Just as your lips got to the top of my lace panties, you paused and looked up at me. You smiled, teasing me, and I don't think I'd ever been more turned on in my life. Overcome with desire for you, all I could do was moan and offer one barely audible, but desperate, word: "Please."

Still looking me in my eyes, your breath and expression hungry and urgent, you gripped my thighs right above the knee and slid my skirt up to my waist as you ripped my fancy black underwear, the ones I'd worn to impress you, into two pieces and tossed them to the ground. I was so wet as you buried your face between my legs.

"Don't stop," I begged.

A jolt of electricity shot up my spine as you made the slowest circles with your tongue that wiped away any possible thought of who could be watching us. It didn't matter anyway. I didn't care who saw, or who heard. I screamed in shock and pleasure and felt a release inside me unlike anything I'd ever experienced.

We practically ran back to my apartment, desperate to make the most of our time before you had to leave. I pulled you through the streets as fast as I could because I couldn't wait to feel you inside me.

But once we were there you took your time, removing each item of my clothing with care and curiosity, devouring every inch of my skin with your eyes and your mouth, making me feel like the most perfect woman in the world.

Just when I thought I couldn't wait any longer you pulled me on top of you as if I weighed next to nothing and expertly guided yourself into me. I let out a slight cry. No man had ever filled me up like that. It felt like we fit perfectly as we grinded together, sweaty and focused, my nails pressing into your back, making half-moon indents that would remain for hours.

I came quickly, but you weren't finished with me yet. You flipped me over, gave me a fierce spank, and we were back at it again.

I wanted to do anything with you. Everything.

Karl, that first night together I'd never felt so close to someone, so satisfied. We pleased each other in every way we could think of for hours (and in ways I'd never trusted anyone to try before) and even though we were strangers it felt like our bodies had known each other forever.

At some point, I was aware of time again. "Don't you have to get to the airport?" I whispered.

"I'm not leaving you today," you said, and disappeared beneath the covers again.

I bawled when you left three days later, despite our promises to see each other again soon—for a proper first date. I didn't stop until I discovered you'd left me on my bedside table sticky notes inside the novel I'd been reading. In your surprisingly elegant handwriting were two lines from Andrew Marvell:

> *And your quaint honour turn to dust,*
> *And into ashes all my lust.*

That was the man I fell in love with, the hopeless romantic who made me come in a public garden, who left my underwear in tatters on a park bench, who skipped his flight home to hole up in my apartment for three days.

The woman you fell in love with was wild and crazy and adventurous and ready to change the world with her prose.

I want us to be those people again. I want us to get back there.

Ever since I got on this plane an old Edna St. Vincent Millay poem has been rattling around in my head. You used to read it to me back in the days when we still read to one another before we fell asleep at night:

> *I will come back to you, I swear I will;*
> *And you will know me still.*
> *I shall be only a little taller*
> *Than when I went.*

Love,
Kate

Chapter Four

My fantasy of the Suvarnabhumi Airport in Bangkok was nothing like the reality. In my ignorance of modern Thailand, I'd anticipated something exotic and chaotic. I didn't expect a run-of-the-mill, sleek and modern international terminal that could have been in Denver or San Diego, complete with a gleaming Dean & DeLuca featuring plastic containers of organic hummus, wasabi peas, and sea salt kettle corn, the likes of which I could have purchased a few blocks away from my house. I'd traveled halfway around the world to experience something new, something different. I said a quiet screw-you to the individually wrapped black-and-white cookies, even as I purchased three of them.

I turned on my phone and waited for the network to switch to a local carrier, but the no-service indicator remained stubbornly lit up in the left corner of the screen. In the past few years I'd traveled with this phone to London, Berlin, and even Hong Kong on work trips with Karl and never had a problem with coverage. I wondered if I could buy a phone card. The last time I traveled alone people still bought phone cards. That's how long it had been.

Because the McDonald's in the food court promised free Wi-Fi with a purchase, I bought a large coffee and checked my e-mail, hoping for a response from Karl and an encouraging message nudging me along this journey from Nina. My new messages were mainly spam, a reminder from the girls' school that parents should not, under any circumstance, send gluten-filled pastries for their children's birthdays, and an e-mail from my colorist at Sally Hershberger asking if I needed an appointment the following week. Nothing from Karl or Nina.

It had been more than forty-eight hours since I'd slept, and the adrenaline of embarking on this adventure had faded, threatening to be replaced by exhaustion or worse—regret. I had to stay in motion, to forge ahead. When I saw Nina and this magical zen center I knew it would all fall into place. I had come this far. I just had to keep going.

I made my way to the car rental counter, selecting Hertz, where I knew we were Gold Plus members.

"May I help you madam?" the clerk asked me in perfect English.

"I want to rent a car?"

"Are you certain?"

I blinked through my exhaustion, confused as to why he would ask me that. Was it because I was a woman?

"I am certain." I spoke slowly even though it was more than obvious that he could understand me.

He shook his head a little and smiled. "OK. It's just that American drivers hate driving here. Where would you like to go? Will you be leaving Bangkok?"

"I will. I'm going north, toward the mountains." I named the retreat center and pointed at a spot on the map that was encased beneath a thin sheet of fingerprint-smudged plastic on the counter. "I'm going here."

"Oh, you do not want to rent a car then." He shook his head with greater force.

"I do," I insisted.

"It's a terrible idea."

Well, here was the worst rental car agent I'd ever met. I glanced left and right at the other rental car counters, all with long lines of impatient travelers. Maybe there was a reason this one had no line.

"Why? It's a couple hundred miles. I'll be there in a few hours."

He ran his finger along the line I had just traced. "These roads are hardly even roads. Sometimes they turn into rivers. There are other roads, but you will never find them. Even if you knew which way to go it would take you seven, eight, maybe even as long as fourteen hours of driving. There will be no signal. No GPS. You do not want to rent a car."

"Does your boss know you tell people not to rent cars?"

The agent smiled cheerfully.

"Of course. We do not want you to get lost and die. This is what we call excellent customer service."

My first instinct was to reach for my phone and call Karl. I despised that instinct. I wished I could pinpoint the moment I became so dependent on my husband as a traveler. Before we met I had hitchhiked my way across Eastern Europe. I knew when to get in a car and when to pretend my gang of friends was just peeing in the bushes while we waited for a bus. And then I moved to Paris on my own and negotiated my own rent for a small attic room in the Marais that I could hardly afford on the pittance I made teaching English and waiting tables at the Au Coeur du Marais. I walked everywhere and fended off the advances of more than a few Frenchies who figured American girls were an easy lay. Self-sufficiency once came so naturally. I did not need to call Karl. And besides, why should he help me now when I had just flown thousands of miles away from him and our life together?

I decided to play the rental clerk's game rather than head over to the Avis counter and see if they felt like renting me a vehicle.

"OK, then how should I get there?"

"My cousin will take you," he replied matter-of-factly. "I can call him now."

Skepticism must have trumped the exhaustion on my face.

"He is a taxi driver," the clerk promised. "This is what he does. You will be safe, and he will give you a good price because you are my friend."

"We just met," I said.

"But we are already friends. Hold on while I text him."

I wondered how much it would cost for a taxi to drive me seven, maybe fourteen hours to a tiny mountain village. I excused myself to find an ATM where I withdrew the local equivalent of five hundred dollars.

When I returned a nearly identical man wearing crisp jeans and a green polo shirt stood next to the clerk. He had closely cropped hair that reminded me of a marine and kind brown eyes.

"This is my cousin Kasem. His girlfriend lives in Chiang Mai, so he drives that way often. He knows the roads."

"I would like to take you to the mountains," Kasem said, his smile wide and eyes shiny like a new penny. "I have my taxi outside."

"How much will it cost?"

"Four thousand."

It took me a minute to access the Thai currency in my brain. It was the baht. I'd just seen it written on the screen of the ATM along with the exchange rate.

"It's just over one hundred US dollars," the clerk said helpfully.

With nothing more to go on than gut instinct, I appraised him. Nothing felt off or particularly rapey about the clerk's cousin. We were standing at the Hertz counter, for Christ's sake. I was carrying a paper bag filled with Dean & DeLuca cookies and charcuterie.

"Let me text my husband and tell him I will be driving with you," I said. I reached for my phone and pretended to type a message and press send. "My husband always likes to know where I am."

Well that was a giant lie!

I finished pretending to text then asked where he was parked.

"In the taxi kiosk. Where is your luggage?"

"This is it." I pointed to my suitcase, which contained a pair of linen slacks, the wrap dress I had worn to the wedding, jeans, a button-down blouse, and a sweater, all of them worn and dirty from my days in Big Sur. I had no clean underwear. I'd wanted to buy some back at the airport in San Jose, but underwear is the one thing you can never purchase in an airport. Maybe I should mention that to Lois Delancey when I got home.

"How long are you staying?"

"Not long, maybe a week," I said as he grabbed the suitcase's handle from my hand and pulled it behind him. There was no reason to tell this stranger I hadn't purchased a return ticket yet.

"Everyone says they are staying for a week. You'll be here longer."

"I really can't. I have to get home."

"You have a husband?"

"Yes. He's meeting me. I texted him, remember."

"He'll want to stay too. It's very beautiful where you're going. You'll fall in love all over again."

"We're still in love," I insisted as Kasem popped the trunk of his car, saying it louder than necessary. As the Hertz clerk had promised, Kasem owned a proper taxi with official-looking Thai script on the side. I hadn't expected it to be a bright Pepto pink. A bumper sticker declared in English HONK IF YOU LIKE TO HULA.

"We went to Waikiki two summers ago," Kasem explained with a small shimmy of his hips.

"How long do you think the drive will take us?" I asked once I'd settled into the backseat.

"A couple of hours."

"Your cousin said at least seven." I tried to cover a yawn with my hand.

"A couple to get out of the city. It's rush hour. If you're sleepy you can nap." Kasem sipped from a tall metal travel mug. I realized too late that I'd left my large McDonald's coffee behind on the rental car counter.

"I'm fine."

Soon we were in bumper-to-bumper traffic on a freeway outside of the airport. Motorbikes carrying three or more passengers, sometimes women clutching small children, even infants, whirred dangerously close to my window. I checked my phone for service as we got closer to the city, but I still had nothing. No matter how kind and legitimate my driver appeared I was determined to stay awake.

However, despite my best intentions, the soft humming of the motor combined with my physical and emotional exhaustion lulled my restless body into a deep sleep. When I woke I was surrounded by an enveloping blackness. I knew I was in a car, but it took a moment of catching up to realize I was in a taxicab hurtling into the northern mountains of Thailand.

"You snore." The man in the driver's seat laughed.

I ticked through the things I knew about the present moment. This man's name was Kasem. We were driving to the Dawna mountains. I was in Thailand. I was going to visit Nina, a friend I'd only just reconnected with after twelve years. I had left my husband and daughters behind in the States.

I was fucking crazy. I once read a story about what happens to the synapses in the brain when a person has a mental breakdown. The mind tricks the patient into believing everything they're doing is completely rational. Even though the breakdown is obvious to everyone around them, they believe they are completely sane.

"I've been told that before." I squinted into the dark beyond the taxi. Karl reminded me of my snoring often, even after years of sharing a bed. Early on he'd recorded videos of me sleeping that he would play back for me as he told me I sounded like the most adorably constipated moose he'd ever heard.

"Where are we?" I asked Kasem.

"Not so much farther now. You slept ten hours." My stomach grumbled and I cursed myself for finishing all of my airport snacks the second I got into the taxi.

The road beneath the tires was bumpy and I was suddenly grateful for Kasem. It would have been madness to drive this alone, with no idea where I was going. I'd wanted to be adventurous, but driving these roads would have been reckless. I'd forgotten there was often a fine line between the two.

"Your girlfriend lives in Chiang Mai." I remembered this much from our introduction. "That must be hard, living so far away from one another."

Kasem laughed. "It is wonderful."

"Oh yeah?" I could smell my breath and tried to remember the last time I'd brushed my teeth.

"It gives us the chance to miss each other. I see her every other week. Time apart is a blessing. We have our own lives. Naw, my girlfriend, is very independent. We do our own things. When we come back together it is all brand-new all over again."

"That must be nice. It will be harder if you ever have kids. To be apart so much." This sounded uptight and preachy coming out of my mouth. I knew the words were meant to conceal my own guilt.

"We do have kids. We have two boys."

"Oh?" I tried to hide my surprise.

He reached his arm back toward me and offered his phone to show me the smiling faces of two handsome boys. I guessed their ages at about five and seven, not too different from my girls.

"They live with your girlfriend?" I asked.

"And her mother and her sisters. My girlfriend works as a tour guide. She also does treks and takes visitors, mostly Germans and Danes and the Dutch across the border. She's very adventurous. Like you."

"I'm not very adventurous." (*Well, I used to be,* I thought, *the old me.* But not anymore.)

"You're here in Thailand on your own."

"My husband is meeting me." Why was I bothering to maintain the charade?

"OK," Kasem said. He didn't need to tell me he knew I was lying. "I will write down Naw's number and her e-mail in case you need a guide. She can come down to you. She is very reliable."

"I'm only staying a week," I said.

"Just in case," Kasem insisted.

Suddenly Kasem slammed on the brakes, thrusting my head forward into the driver's-side headrest.

"Fuck!" I rubbed my forehead. I hadn't said the word *fuck* out loud since Isabel was a toddler and began parroting everything we said.

Kasem shifted the car into park right there in the middle of the road and twisted his head around to look at me with a mix of panic and concern. "I'm sorry! You OK? Are you hurt?"

I rubbed my head, expecting to find a cut, to feel blood, but there was just a sore spot. "I'm fine. What the hell is happening?"

"It won't be long."

When I peered through the windshield I expected to see the red taillights of another car. Instead I glimpsed dark shapes shifting slowly in and out of our headlights.

"It's just the elephants." Kasem sat patiently and began to peck at his phone. "They see me. They see the lights. We are safe. They won't charge. This is why it's bad for Americans to drive alone. Two tourists killed this year. They didn't know to slow down and just watch."

"What happened to the elephant the tourists hit?" Now that I knew what I was seeing I could make out each individual giant shape lumbering in front of us, silhouettes of legs and trunks and ears.

Kasem laughed again. "The elephant is always fine. It is like a fly running into a human."

"Are you sure we don't need to worry about them stepping on us?"

"They're smarter than we are."

I wanted to lean out the window and record a video for the girls. It was the way I processed most of the world these days, finding ways to give my own experiences to my daughters. But I didn't pick up my phone. Instead I sat frozen and just stared, admiring the giant beasts a few feet from the car. It was humbling and majestic. *This is why I came*, I thought. To experience this, to see things that were both new and awe-inspiring, to feel real emotions about something other than my children. The sight loosened the tension I'd been holding inside me. I felt free and unburdened.

Soon enough the road in front of us cleared. Kasem stopped texting and put the car back into gear, and we were on our way again. "Not much longer now," he said over his shoulder.

The next time Kasem stopped I knew we'd reached our destination, though there was no sign to mark the zen center. Just one tiny window that shone with a soft yellow light through the darkness.

"I'll wait until you are all organized," Kasem said helpfully.

I wanted to tell him not to wait, but I was afraid for him to leave me here in the middle of nowhere with no cell service in the middle of the night. In a country where I knew no one, Kasem now felt like an old friend.

"OK, just give me a minute to go inside and find out about my room? Thank you."

Nina must be here already. There had to be some kind of a clerk who would show me to her room. I imagined I would sink into her soft bed and we'd giggle about the turn of events that had reunited us on another continent.

I opened a flimsy wooden door to find a room lit by a single bulb hanging perilously by a frayed wire over a rickety wooden desk.

"Hello?" I called out softly. Then with more intention, "Is anyone here?"

I walked behind the desk and opened what looked like a back door to find a space no bigger than a closet. The floor shifted. Upon closer inspection I realized it wasn't the floor, but a blanket covering a small woman. She rolled onto her side and turned to look up at me. When she smiled I saw she was missing her left incisor. Her face was lined and puckered, like she'd sucked too long on a lemon and her features had stuck that way.

"You're here." She said it as though she were expecting me, and I took it to mean that Nina had already arrived and told this woman (maybe the night clerk?) that I would be coming in late.

"I'm here." I sighed with relief.

"Who are you?" she asked in the same tone she'd used moments earlier.

"I'm Kate Carmichael. Nina Galloway is my friend."

"Who is Nina?" The woman had yet to rise from her supine position. I heard someone open the door behind me and turned to see Kasem standing there with a worried look on his face.

I reached down to help the woman stand.

"My friend Nina is here already. She organized our rooms. She checked in this morning, or maybe yesterday." I realized I knew very little about Nina's itinerary and that in hindsight she and I hadn't discussed many details of our reunion here at all. Could I be at the wrong place? I pulled my phone from my pocket, but it was long dead.

"I don't know Nina. No Nina is here."

I turned to look back helplessly at Kasem. "Could we have the wrong place?" I asked him.

He shook his head. "This is the only place to stay within thirty miles and the only retreat center in this part of the mountains. This is the place you asked to be."

The old woman stood, stepped between us, and smiled calmly. She took my hand. Hers was warm and rough. She interlaced her fingers with mine the way a child would, squeezing the knuckles. "You want a room?"

A small part of me worried that something had gone very wrong. It told me to turn around and get back in the car with Kasem and pay him whatever it took to take me back to Bangkok or up to Chiang Mai, where I could get on a plane home.

I gritted my teeth. I was going to see this through . . . whatever this was.

"I do want a room." It was late and Kasem had been driving all night. It was only fair that I would pay for a place for him to sleep. "And a room for my friend too," I said.

"No, no," Kasem interrupted. "I am fine. You do not need to do that."

My actions were selfish. I wasn't ready for him to leave me.

"You're sure you want to stay here?" His concern only made me more nervous.

"I'm sure."

"Good-bye then, Kate. You can call me if you need me." He turned on his heel and walked out the door.

I looked back down at the small woman who hadn't let go of my hand this entire time. She'd begun gently swinging it between us like a small child. The night was warm, but her body was mummified in what looked like five layers of loud sarongs.

"I'm Kate," I introduced myself again, hoping she'd tell me her name in return. She merely smiled and let go of my hand. Then, with the brute strength of Atlas, she heaved my suitcase up over her head and disappeared into the closet where I'd first found her.

She kicked her blankets aside. There was another door leading out the back of the building.

"Come," she commanded without looking back at me.

It took every ounce of courage I had to follow the woman's small shadowy frame down a steep wooden staircase. We went down several stories and then stopped at a dirt path surrounded by tall trees.

An animal shrieked in the distance, a bloodcurdling sound like something being murdered, and I remembered Kasem telling me there were still tigers in these mountains.

My eyes adjusted only enough to see the woman's silhouette in front of me. After a few minutes on the dirt path she stopped at another stairway. We climbed up about ten steps to an elevated wooden boardwalk that stretched in both directions. She paused in front of a door.

"Here," she said. I imagined Nina inside the room, fast asleep in a beautiful handmade hammock, her willowy legs slung over the sides, a book open on her chest. She'd lazily open her eyes when I entered and rise to hug me. We'd laugh over the madness of getting here and she'd hand me her cell so I could call Karl and tell him I was safe. I'd tell him I loved him and missed him and I would mean it. I'd tell him the things I wrote in the letter on the plane. I'd try to explain myself and make him understand why I'd gotten on that plane. I could dimly imagine a point in the future when we would laugh about this—the time I ran away from home.

The woman dropped my bag on the floor, opened a door, and pulled a string hanging from the ceiling to light the room. Moths with the wingspans of dollar bills rushed in from outside to thump against the light, their wings making a sound as loud as the beating of my heart.

There was no Nina, no hammock. Just a thin single mattress on a hard wood floor. No dresser, no bathroom, no mirror. The only other furniture in the room was a wooden desk and a simple metal folding chair, the kind pulled out from behind the bleachers during school assemblies.

My joy at seeing the elephants stomp in front of our car dissipated. My thirst for adventure began to dry up. "Where do I shower?" I asked tentatively. I was too embarrassed to ask what I really needed to know, which was, Where did I pee? The woman tipped her head forward and let the suitcase tumble to the floor with a clatter. She grabbed my hand again and brought me back out onto the boardwalk, down the stairs, and back to the dirt path. We made a left and a right and came to an even smaller shack with a toilet that was actually just a hollowed-out stool perched over a hole in the floor. Flies buzzed around a roll of toilet paper on the floor. I must have looked completely stricken just then because the woman rooted around in the folds of her robe and produced an object. When she handed it to me I saw that it was a headlamp with REI emblazoned on the side of it.

I accepted it and flicked on the light. The soft yellow glow was an immediate comfort, though it did little but illuminate the path a few feet ahead. We retraced our steps back to the tiny room with its sad mattress on the floor. In the morning I could ask if there was some-place a little less rustic to sleep. *Stop it, Kate,* I admonished myself. *You're not some coddled Manhattan mommy who can't survive without room service and a Klonopin. You're better than this.*

I reached in my pocket for a baht but couldn't do the math to figure out a decent tip for a woman who had just carried my suitcase down what felt like twenty flights of stairs on her head. I handed her a sweaty, crumpled bill, but she shook her head and pushed the money away.

"Sleep now," she instructed.

The nap in the car had done little to ease my exhaustion, and the sooner I slept, the sooner it would be light and I could get my bearings and find Nina and call home.

I nodded to thank her and sat down on the mattress to show I intended to take her advice and go to sleep. She shut the door behind her, leaving the bugs, who seemed intent on burning themselves alive. I stood to pull on the string to turn off the light and sank back down on the mattress. It was more comfortable than it looked. Buried within the blankets was a thin pillow. I didn't bother to change my clothes. Something scurried in the corner, small nails scratching the wooden floor. It would be easy for anything to run right across my body and my face. A larger animal shrieked again in the darkness and I knew the flimsy walls wouldn't keep it out if it decided it was hungry enough to come find me.

I was too exhausted to care.

Chapter Five

It was still dark when I opened my eyes. Had I slept the entire day and into the next night? I felt the uncontrollable need to scratch at my arms and noticed nickel-size welts along my biceps, forearms, and the backs of my hands.

I looked up to see a fat ball of mosquito netting hanging from the ceiling that'd I'd missed last night. All I'd needed to do was pull it over me—a mistake I wouldn't make again. Something crept up my inner thigh. I slapped at it and discovered a wormlike creature with dozens of squirming legs. I let out a piercing shriek as I flicked it to the floor.

There was a little more light than when I fell asleep even though the lightbulb remained off. It leaked through cracks in the walls. Upon closer inspection those walls were moving, gently swaying, actually. I reached my hand out to touch one and found it soft. They weren't walls at all, but curtains shifting in the breeze. The light coming out from the sides was the sun. I grasped for an edge, flung open the fabric, and then fell to my knees in awe at the sight that awaited me.

The old woman had brought me down so many stairs that I assumed I was now on the valley floor. That couldn't be further from the truth. My hut was terraced at least twenty stories above a fluttering jungle canopy cut through by a silver river that wound like a snake through emerald foliage. My room was curtained on three sides, and as I flung all of them open I realized I was sleeping in little more than an elevated tree house lined by rickety railings. I'd never seen anything so spectacular.

I could see the roofs of other structures like mine above, around, and below me. There must have been thirty of them in all. Nina must be in one. The jungle began again just inches from each hut, like it was intent to swallow the man-made structures whole.

I opened my suitcase and took out my long linen pants and the freshest shirt I had. I'd need bug repellant. I had a brief thought that I could pick some up in the center's gift shop, like in a fancy hotel, and then I remembered the woman sleeping in a closet who led me to my room and realized I would likely be doing without bug repellant, sunscreen, and a daily green juice. A phone card, though, I had to get a phone card. How long had it been since I'd spoken to Karl? More than forty-eight hours. He must be frantic by now. The last thing he needed was me piling additional stress on his plate when he was already overwhelmed by Paradigm's finances. I had to at least let him know that I was safe.

There was only one path leading up. I paused to catch my breath every third set of stairs. No wonder that woman was able to haul my suitcase over her head on the way down. Going up and down these stairs all day would have her in better shape than Tracy Anderson.

When I finally made it to the top and opened the door to the lobby, the smell of coffee wafted deliciously into my nostrils. I noticed a simple Mr. Coffee filled with steaming brown liquid on a card table along with some kind of doughy pastry and a bowl filled with slices of Technicolored fruit. I had yet to see another person, despite the evidence that someone had been in this room recently enough to turn on the coffeepot.

I crossed the room and opened the second door to find a spacious dirt clearing. A bright pink car parked parallel along the edge of the trees. Either someone else had recently arrived or Kasem had spent the night here. I wandered over and found him curled into a ball in the backseat. He startled awake after I rapped twice on the window.

"Good morning," I said.

"Hello, Kate." He sat up and blinked his warm brown eyes.

"I thought you were driving back last night. I would have paid for a room for you," I said.

"I do not mind sleeping in the car. I pull over often for naps. I thought I should check on you this morning."

A warm blush crept up my neck.

"I think I'm going to be OK here. There's coffee and pastries inside. Come in and have something before you head back."

Kasem agreed and followed me inside. Together we loaded a plate high with what looked like cinnamon rolls, filled two mugs with coffee, and sat at a picnic bench in the sun.

"When does your husband arrive?" Kasem asked kindly. It took a beat to remember lying to him.

"Soon," I lied again.

"Why did you two choose here? Second honeymoon?"

I picked at the doughy pastry with my fingers. My nail polish was chipped and the tips of my nails had grown ragged from biting them. There was something spicy and exotic in the dough, maybe cardamom. It was delicious. Before I could ask Kasem about it I looked up and saw sexy Jesus emerge from the jungle.

OK, so it wasn't really Jesus.

But he did bear a striking resemblance to the Jesus I grew up with in my Sunday school picture books—a taller-than-average white man with thick flowing brown hair with a body wave. He wore loose white pants and a white button-down shirt, completely unbuttoned to reveal what had to be an eight-pack, beneath a long white robe. His face was long and angular with a Roman nose, wide-set eyes, and plump lips. Even Kasem couldn't take his eyes off him.

Behind sexy Jesus there followed a motley line of disciples, also wearing white pajamas. I scrutinized the crowd, hoping to find Nina, but the only one with a dark bob in the group was practically a teenager, with the unlined face and eager eyes of a girl who could be taking a gap year from one of the Seven Sisters schools.

Sexy Jesus grinned at me with his dazzling teeth as he took a few steps toward us and stretched a massive hand in my direction. When I stood I realized he wasn't just taller than average. He was freakishly tall, maybe six foot six or seven. His hand eclipsed mine.

"I'm Kevin," he said in a deep baritone with a crisp Midwestern accent. "I run the zen center."

Of course a Buddhist retreat in the Thai mountains was run by an American named Kevin who looked like the offspring of a professional basketball player and an L.L.Bean catalog model. He was probably from Michigan.

Kevin turned to the rest of the group. "I'll see you in a few hours." They each smiled up at him with the sort of glazed Jim Jonesy wonderment of someone who is truly dazzled by another human being or high on really good pot.

The pajama-clad disciples dispersed in different directions, but Kevin stayed.

"I'm Kate," I said. "I got here last night. Late. I'm meeting my friend Nina. Do you know her?"

Kevin closed his eyes, as if he were accessing the information from his interior hard drive. A devious smile played at his lips, and I couldn't help imagining Nina and Kevin fucking, her riding him on a dirty mattress in one of the huts, the floor swaying on the thin jungle stilts.

"She's the writer," Kevin said.

"You do know her," I said eagerly. "Is she here?"

"Not this week."

That sentence knocked the wind out of me. There had to be some kind of misunderstanding.

"Are you sure?"

"I'm sure. Everyone who is staying with us, except for you, was just at morning meditation. I'd know if Nina were here. She's pretty larger than life. One time during meditation she took off all her clothes and was buck naked when everyone else opened their eyes. We call her the nudist Buddhist. She was here maybe a year ago. She's definitely not here now."

What the hell was going on? Nina couldn't be so flaky as to promise to meet me halfway around the world and then bail. I wanted to believe that, but I knew Nina was definitely that flaky and absent-minded. Of course she would make plans to meet me halfway around the world and then bail. The Nina I knew twelve years ago would break plans at a moment's notice, usually when something better came along. One December she was so depressed she couldn't get out of bed. I bought her a plane ticket to come home to Wisconsin with me, since she had no family to spend the holidays with. The ticket cost me a week's tips bartending at one of those preppy rapey bars on Second Avenue, but she was my friend and I didn't want her to be alone for the holidays. Then she never showed at the airport. The night before she'd gotten invited to an ayahuasca ceremony in a Tribeca penthouse. I could have gotten a refund on at least part of the ticket had I known even twenty-four hours in advance that she wouldn't be using it. When I returned to the city after New Year's she promised to pay me back, but of course she never did.

"How long will you be staying with us, Kate?" Kevin asked me.

"A week, I think."

"I hope you stay longer than that." His teeth were so perfect I could see a bit of sunlight glint off a canine.

"I can't. I have kids," I said.

"How old. My boy is ten and my girl is eight going on twenty-seven."

"Are they here?" I looked around and imagined white pajama–clad children running barefoot through the forest.

"They're back with my wife in New York. I spend four months here at a time. They used to come more often, but now they're in school."

I couldn't help myself. I had to know how many degrees of separation were between me and Jesus of the jungle. "Which school do they go to?"

"City Day, in Greenwich Village."

Kevin must have been making a killing in this zen center. City Day was one of the most prestigious and most expensive elementary schools south of Fourteenth Street.

Penelope's kids, Atwood and Updike, went to City Day. There was no doubt that she and Kevin knew one another. Atwood was also eight, and Penelope made a point of knowing all the parents in his class, even as she rasped about them behind their back.

"All these West Village mommies and daddies are into polyamory these days," she had complained recently. "Open marriages are like the new 'hashtag' divorce. I have to constantly keep the other moms from leaping on Edward."

I found it hard to believe any downtown mommies in their right minds would want to see Edward naked unless they had a latent Keebler Elf fetish.

I didn't tell Kevin about our close degree of separation. Penelope was the last person I wanted to be associated with here.

"My kids go to Atherton," I offered. "Two girls."

Kevin nodded to acknowledge the coincidence but didn't ask any more.

"You've been to your room. Did Buppha share the schedule with you last night?" He pronounced it like Betty Boop. Boop-Ha.

Buppha must have been the old woman sleeping in the closet. I shook my head.

Kevin led me back to the small building with the coffee and pastries. Kasem curiously, or maybe protectively, followed behind me. We passed through a third door that I hadn't noticed this morning or the night before. This one led to a grand deck overlooking the verdant valley below. Red round cushions dotted the floor. In one corner was a shelf with regular-looking yoga mats and blocks and straps, in the other was a shrine to the Buddha covered in peeled oranges and necklaces of purple orchids. Wise-eyed monkeys lounged on the wooden railings.

"This is the meditation and yoga and dining space," Kevin said, swatting at the animals. "Make sure to keep the curtains in your room closed. The monkeys will ransack it. They're sneaky little thieves. Keep anything you don't want them to take in your suitcase. This whole place runs on solar, but we don't have outlets in the rooms. Feel free to charge up here."

I saw a pile of devices stacked on top of a single surge protector all competing for juice.

"My cell doesn't work here."

"It won't. The government just signed a contract with a new carrier and they're still hashing out the deals with local service providers. You can buy a local cell in the village."

"Do you have Wi-Fi?"

"Only up here. Not in the rooms. And it comes and goes. Our goal is to get you away from as many of the distractions of your everyday life as we can, but we understand most people can't go cold turkey and we don't want to shock your system," Kevin said. He continued with the logistics. "We usually start the morning meditation here at six thirty, but today we did a walking meditation through the forest instead. We always meet here in silence. Then there's breakfast. Buppha makes the pastries. They're not gluten-free. I've only had to start saying that recently. Now everyone asks. Humans need a devil. Sugar and gluten serve that purpose, I suppose. Don't get me started. Anyway, then there's unstructured time. There's a yoga class at noon and another at four and a dharma talk at five thirty followed by dinner and the nighttime meditation, which can last anywhere from two hours to four, depending on how you feel. The nearest village is an hour's drive away. It's not far, but the road is bad and windy. Did you bring a car?"

I nodded toward Kasem. "I came in a taxi."

"I have a truck. A few other guests have cars. We'll probably go into town on Tuesday together."

I needed a local phone. I couldn't go much longer without calling Karl and the girls.

But before I could ask if I could borrow his truck today, Kevin pulled his own phone from a pocket hidden in his robe to check the time. "I have to run and check on a few things with Buppha. Feel free to ask her anything you want. She speaks perfect English when she feels like it, but she gets a kick out of pretending she doesn't. She's definitely listening to everything you say." He paused like he wanted to say something else, then looked me directly in the eye in a way that made me feel naked and vulnerable. "It's great to have you here, Kate."

I'm sure he told all the guests how happy he was to have them. Still, his words made me feel special. He radiated the kind of charisma usually reserved for politicians and aging British rock stars. I wanted to spend more time with him. I wanted to tell him everything about myself.

Once Kevin was out of earshot, Kasem cleared his throat. "I can drive you to the village," he offered.

I nearly hugged him. "I'll pay you," I said. I picked at one of the welts on my arm until a trickle of blood emerged from the soft white center of the bite.

Kasem pushed my nails off my skin. "You can get something for that in town."

"Let me run back to my room and get my wallet."

There was no actual running to the room, more like huffing down the stairs. I sat onto the mattress to catch my breath and gather my thoughts. It finally sank in that Nina wasn't here, and I knew in my gut that she wasn't going to show at all.

I looked around the bare little room. When I first saw the room I couldn't imagine spending another night here, but now it felt perfect—the bed was comfortable, the desk was a sweet place to think and write. And, the view. My god, the view.

Maybe this wouldn't be the wild girls' adventure I'd thought it would be. Maybe it would be something else entirely, something I desperately needed—time alone to write.

I pushed the desk toward the very edge of the floor until it felt as though it would teeter off the terrace and into the jungle. Not two feet away a bright green bird with a black head and red crown twisted to stare at me. I knew a few things about birds. In grad school I had read the entire *Field Guide to North American Ornithology* when I was researching a story about two bird-watchers who got lost and had to survive in the wilderness for ten days. The characters spoke in parables about wood thrushes and scrub jays and evening grosbeaks. The story was told from the point of view of the birds watching the humans as they fell in love and then had fumbling sex in the forest, and in hindsight it was the hubristic failure of a first-term MFA. I didn't know the name of this particular bird. He was probably a male. The prettiest birds usually were. The females had simpler colors, easily camouflaged in the forest to protect them in the nest. This cocky bird was exotic and curious and refused to break our staring contest.

"I'll see you later," I whispered to him.

I rooted around in my purse for my wallet and my hand clasped my notebook, now stuffed with extra pages shoved deep into the margins, including my letter to Karl. I made a mental note to get stamps and envelopes and get it into the mail.

I arranged the notebook and papers neatly on the desk and weighted them down with my useless phone. Then, remembering Kevin's warning about the monkeys, I packed the papers back into a pile, zipped them into my suitcase, and closed the curtains.

Then I took a long moment to gaze out over the perfect stillness of the jungle. I kept expecting to feel guilty, like I was doing something wrong. When, in fact, everything about this felt right. I was filled with an all-consuming sense of peace, like I had taken my first deep breath in years.

I slid into the front seat of the taxi instead of getting into the back. As we drove, Kasem told me more about the history of the region. We were on the edge of the Thungyai Naresuan wildlife sanctuary, created to protect the area from international strip mining. As the crow flies we were less than thirty miles from the border with Myanmar, but it could take two or three hours to reach the border by car. The name Thungyai Naresuan means "big field," referring to the vast savannah that ran through the center of the sanctuary. A famous Siamese king once based his army here in the late sixteenth century to wage a war against Burma. Since then the border has been in dispute. The local people were called the Karen and they referred to this land as "the place of the knowing sage," because it had been home to ascetic hermits for centuries. When the modern Thai state was officially recognized at the turn of the twentieth century, both Thailand and Burma began to see the Karen as illegal immigrants. They'd been persecuted, threatened, and relocated on both sides of the border, but the Thai government eventually set up refugee camps for those escaping the worse end of the persecution in Burma, now Myanmar.

"It's a very beautiful place," Kasem said. "We are lucky the government decided to protect it. It's the most protected land in Thailand."

"It is beautiful," I agreed, and as if to punctuate the thought a brightly colored butterfly the size of my face flew in front of the car. We were driving maybe fifteen miles an hour on razor-thin switchbacks into the valley. I wished again that the girls could see this and felt a pain that I had no way to share it with them.

It took ninety minutes to reach the village, which was really a single road flanked by tin-roofed shacks and wooden huts on high bamboo stilts. I felt a small measure of relief that there wasn't a Starbucks, a McDonald's, or a Dean & DeLuca in sight. Beyond the buildings, green rice fields stretched out toward the rolling mountains. Kasem pulled the taxi onto the side of the road. I stepped out into a massive mud puddle, my foot sinking up to the ankle in thick slop.

"Oh no," Kasem said. "You have stepped in bull shit."

I should have been disgusted, but with everything that had gone wrong since I'd arrived, I found the idea of stepping into literal bull shit hilarious. I laughed, a deep laugh that shook my entire core.

Off to the side of the road I saw the actual bulls, lazily gnawing their cud and stupidly staring at me with their giant brown eyes. I dipped the bottom of my shoe into the puddle and tried to scrape the remaining shit off on a sharp rock.

"There will be a shop at the end of the road." Kasem pointed straight ahead. "You can buy thongs there."

Thongs? I was surprised at Kaseem's knowledge of women's undergarments. The truth was I hated thongs—butt floss, as I called them—even though I wore them every day. Maybe Thailand was a chance to escape thongs too. I could get some nice sensible granny panties. Either way, this wasn't something I needed to discuss with Kaseem.

"Have you been here before?" I asked, changing the subject.

He shook his head. "No, but there is always a shop at the end of the road. All the villages are the same."

Just walking down the street I could feel my face already getting red. Sweat dripped off every part of my skin. It had to be at least ninety degrees, maybe even close to a hundred. Higher up at the zen center, with the shade of the canopy, it was much cooler. In the village there was nothing to protect us from the unrelenting midday sun.

We walked side by side, dodging more piles of steaming bull shit. The shacks lining the street looked like they'd topple over if you blew on them with too much enthusiasm. Brightly colored tapestries flapped from clotheslines. Sometimes a curious child would peek around one of the doorframes. A group of boys, probably eight or nine years old, kicked a half-deflated soccer ball next to us as we walked. A family of pigs squealed from under one of the wooden structures, and a baby goat emerged to nuzzle my ankle with her mouth. A pack of filthy monkeys jogged lazily in front of us.

Up ahead, the last wooden house on the left bore a weathered sign for Coca-Cola above the door. Inside, a bored teenaged girl wearing thick eyeliner and a tight yellow Taylor Swift T-shirt manned the counter. Rough wooden shelves reached from floor to ceiling, piled high with canned fruits and vegetables, bottles of shampoo, toothpaste, toothbrushes, and six-packs of soda. I picked out a few basic toiletries.

Kasem pointed me toward a bin of flip-flops wrapped in plastic.

"Thongs," he said, and pointed to the shoes. He hadn't been talking about underwear.

A lonely can of OFF! bug repellent teetered on the edge of the shelf, but Kasem directed me toward an unmarked amber bottle on the counter.

"Tea tree oil, thyme and cinnamon, and rubbing alcohol." He listed its contents. "Trust me." He made eye contact with the girl and muttered something in Thai.

She nodded and pulled a locked metal box out from beneath the counter. Inside were tiny flip phones.

"You pay for the minutes," Kasem explained about these old-school flip phones. "You can get an iPhone or an Android in the big cities, but not out here. How many do you want? Two hundred minutes is good?"

"Two hundred should be good," I agreed.

As Kasem spoke quickly to the girl, she waved her hands and began to look cross. He shook his head and raised his voice and I felt bad for the girl, but she held her own, jutting out her chin and tossing the phones back into the metal bin and slamming it shut. Kasem relented to whatever she was asking for and asked me for the baht equivalent of a hundred dollars.

"I tried to get you a bargain, but you're very white," he said, shrugging his shoulders.

"I'm sorry about that."

"It's OK. There's nothing you can do about it."

"I should probably get sunscreen too," I added. "On account of my whiteness."

The girl made a sound that was half laugh and half snort and handed me a bottle of SPF 30.

"She speaks English," I said to Kasem.

"I do," she replied. I blushed and felt like an ignorant ass.

"Most of us speak English," Kasem explained. "There are so many British and American tourists coming to Thailand. You get the women seeking spiritual enlightenment. They confuse Thailand with Bali half the time. Then there are the men seeking strange sex and the couples looking for the perfect honeymoon, sometimes also seeking strange sex, and the rich people who want to pretend to be poor for a little while. English is taught in schools, even ones as remote as here."

"Thank you," I said to the clerk as I paid her and walked back out into the oppressive heat.

The scruffy monkeys had set up camp on top of our car. They seemed to laugh at Kasem as he shooed them away. They leaped back into the road when he started the ignition.

"I can't thank you enough," I said to him.

"You don't have to thank me. You looked like a person who needed help. When a person looks like they need help you have to help them."

Kasem fiddled around with the radio until he landed on a Thai pop station where the refrain of every song seemed to be *baby, baby, baby*. I stared out at the window into the dense jungle. I would need to wait a few more hours to call the girls on my new phone. My throat and stomach tightened as I realized how restricted my communication with the outside world had become. My message to Marley notwithstanding, my family had to be worried about me by now.

We exchanged an awkward hug good-bye when Kasem dropped me off. He scribbled his e-mail on a napkin and entered his cell number into my new tiny phone. It felt like the ending of a first date where you both decided you'd be better off as just friends.

"Good luck, Kate," he said. "Enjoy your time here. You deserve it."

He was so earnest that I was seized by the sudden urge to confess my earlier lies.

"My husband isn't coming. He was never coming," I blurted out.

Kasem's expression hardly changed. "I know," he said simply.

"Why didn't you say anything?"

He looked up to the clouds and flipped both of his palms to the sky. I noticed a small black tattoo in the middle of his left palm, a single word written in Thai. "Sometimes people need to say things. First you were scared. Then it made you feel good to talk about your husband."

I realized that was true. Talking about Karl, pretending even for a moment that there was the possibility that he would join me for a second honeymoon here, was a comfort in this strange place.

"I needed a break," I admitted out loud for the first time. Once I started admitting things, I couldn't stop. "I've been living a life that doesn't feel like my own. I needed to get away from my family for a little while to figure some things out."

Kasem took one of my hands in both of his. "You will. Remember what I said before." He flipped his palm back over and traced the thin black lines on his palm with his index finger. "This means 'space,'" he translated his tattoo. "Time is a blessing. Make the most of it."

I went back to my room and counted down the minutes until I could call home.

Once the sun kissed the horizon, I couldn't wait any longer.

Karl didn't answer on the first try. I had no idea what kind of weird number was coming up on his phone. I tried over and over.

On the fifth try he answered, his voice groggy. It was only 6:30 a.m. there.

"Katie?"

The second I heard Karl's voice my best-laid plans went to butter.

I blurted out the first thing that came to mind. "I'm sorry. I needed to get away."

"Kate, where are you?"

Thailand, I whispered in my head before saying it out loud. It sounded so absurd, even in a mental whisper.

"Thailand." Yup, it sounded as ridiculous as I had expected.

There was an audible choking sound on the other side of the line.

"You're in Asia? You flew all the way to Asia?" His voice rose an octave.

"I'm sorry," I repeated myself. "I came with Nina . . . Well, I'm meeting Nina," I whispered.

His voice rose another octave. "Nina? Crazy Nina? From Columbia?" Karl had never actually met Nina, only heard stories about her. "The one who almost burned down your grad school apartment? You up and flew to Thailand with her?"

"She just recommended it. She isn't here. And she didn't burn it down. Just her mattress. Only her mattress was on fire."

It was time to attempt to explain myself. I took a deep breath.

"I haven't been myself lately, Karl. I haven't been myself for a long time. I'm exhausted and run-down. I needed to do something just for me. I'm trying to reset." There was more, but I couldn't get it out. I felt crazy, practically bipolar. I craved time for myself even as I was desperate to be with my family. But those competing impulses were a part of being a mother and wife—the constant push and pull between two different identities.

"Can I talk to the girls?" I asked before he could respond, partly because I was afraid of what that response would be.

"They're still asleep. It's a school day. It's probably not the best time. I don't want to disrupt their day." Karl was back to being Karl, even-keeled, rational Karl. "Kate, I'm worried about you."

"Can I just have a little time?"

"Why are we talking about this now?" His voice was low and heavy with sadness. "Why are you telling me this after you've already gone?"

"I tried to call you. I tried to talk to you."

I heard a distinctive squeal in the background. The girls were usually good about not leaving their beds until 7:00 a.m. They each had their own night-light that stayed red until seven on the dot. When the light turned green, no matter what day of the week it was, they were allowed out of their rooms. "Daddy, you promised to make pancakes," Tilly whined in a bright falsetto.

"I hear Tilly. Please, let me talk to them," I whispered again. "I'll be fast."

I heard Karl tell Tilly to go get her sister. Once she was out of earshot he spoke quickly.

"Kate, I really don't know what's gotten into you. If you needed a break this badly, I wish you'd told me. We would have figured something out. Getting on a plane and blindsiding me isn't fair."

"I know," I said. He was right. What I had done wasn't fair. But maybe, just maybe, this was exactly what we needed—both of us— something dramatic to shake things up. The alternative was trudging along, maintaining the status quo, and that increasingly felt like it wasn't an option at all.

"Mommy, mommy, mommy." Both girls shouted to me in unison. They sounded so cheerful, so delighted to hear my voice. I wanted to tell them that I'd be on a plane and home by dinnertime. How could I explain to them that I was so far away? That I wasn't coming back soon.

"I'm putting the girls on now," Karl said. He'd shifted his tone the second they came into the room. "I'm putting both of them on speaker."

"Hi, babies," I said. Hot tears now rolled down both my cheeks. "I miss you."

"I miss you too, Mommy. How is Caleefornee," Tilly replied first.

"It was nice. It was very pretty. I'll send you more pictures. I found you a seashell shaped like a unicorn horn. I have it wrapped up in tissue, safe in my suitcase."

"Can I have it tonight?" I could hear Tilly clap her hands.

"Not tonight, baby. I won't be home tonight." I squeezed the edge of the desk, drilling my nails into the soft wood, forcing my voice to sound cheerful. "I'll be home in a week, maybe two. I have some work to do. But I'll talk to you while I am here. We can talk every day."

"You don't work, Mommy," Isabel said with a squeak. "You're not one of the mommies who works."

Before I could respond, Karl jumped in. "Of course Mommy works. All mommies work. Sometimes Mommy works at home, and now she is working away from home on a very special project."

I've never been more grateful to him as I was in that moment, for both acknowledging that what I did in our home was work and for explaining my absence to the girls.

"That's right," I said. I knew I couldn't keep this facade up much longer without my voice cracking. The key was making sure that Karl and I both sounded OK. As long as we could do that the girls would believe the world was exactly as it should be.

"Say good-bye to Mama," Karl said. "If you get the milk and the eggs out of the refrigerator I'll make you pancakes in just a minute."

The promise of pancakes facilitated a quick good-bye.

"I love you," I said.

"Love, love," Tilly yelled, already halfway down the hall.

"Love you, Mama," Isabel said, and I heard her kiss the receiver of the phone with a sloppy smack.

I heard Karl close our bedroom door. When he spoke again there was fear in his voice. "I still don't understand what's going on, but I understand you need time. Take the time, Katie. I love you."

"I love you too." I said it emphatically. I meant it.

But he hung up so quickly, I wasn't sure he'd even heard me.

• • •

I stared at the flimsy walls for more than an hour before a pain in my stomach reminded me I needed to eat. I thought about texting Karl. There was so much more I wanted to say, but I couldn't figure out how to craft a message on the ancient phone. Besides, no matter how concerned he had sounded, I knew Karl would find a way to pack his feelings away, to maintain the discipline needed to go on with his day. He'd just be getting to the office now, answering e-mails, preparing for the morning team meeting. I'd never known someone so good at compartmentalizing as my husband. The day his father died, he'd signed one of the most important authors of his career. He'd cried to me that morning, his head in my lap while I stroked his hair and felt his tears soak my thighs. Within hours he had negotiated a five-million-dollar sale. It was how he coped. We were similar that way. We both needed to keep moving.

I pulled my jaunty new headlamp down over my brow, adjusting the band to fit my skull, and began the journey up the stairs. The moist air clung to my skin. The thrumming and buzzing of insects filled the otherwise silent jungle. My muscles ached from so much climbing. It was the satisfying kind of ache, born out of moving my body with a distinct purpose rather than just jogging in place on a treadmill with episodes of *This Is Us* to keep me going.

The reception area was empty. I noticed a lone computer on the desk and remembered that Kevin said the Wi-Fi sometimes worked up here. I sat down and tried to remember how to turn on a PC and cursed Apple for reprogramming my brain. There was the faintest of signals, just enough to let me check my Gmail in super basic html mode. That was fine by me. There were only two people I wanted to hear from anyway.

A wave of relief washed over me when I saw Nina's name in my in-box. It took five minutes for the damn e-mail to load.

> Hey Katie. Got sidetracked! Ended up hopping a flight to Lamu with Alex. Crazy story there. Will fill you in later. Enjoy Thailand. Don't do anything I wouldn't do . . . lol.

I reloaded the e-mail three times to see if there were words I was missing, but that was it. Classic Nina. I felt like a fool for ever thinking she'd meet me. I'd been so desperate to be back in touch with her, to have a real connection with someone who knew me before I became some boring stay-at-home mom, that I'd forgotten all the reasons I'd lost touch with her in the first place. The truth of it was that Nina was terrible at being a friend and I had no reason to believe that had changed.

My need for food trumped my desire to send a scathing e-mail back to Nina. I wandered toward the meditation deck. I heard the sounds of dinner—wine being poured, glasses clinking. A long rustic farmhouse table, its surface covered in bowls of noodles, rice, grilled meat and vegetables, and sauces of every imaginable color, now took up almost the entire length of the meditation room. A line of votive candles sparkled like little diamonds along the walls. The meal had clearly been in progress for some time. Empty bottles of wine huddled in the center of the table. Diners' eyes were glassy, their jaws slack, their laughter slightly slurry.

"Kate!" Kevin's jovial voice boomed when he saw me. "Join us. Plenty of food. Plenty of wine."

I pulled a chair from beneath the table and let loose a primal howl as a lizard the size of a cat fell off the seat and onto my foot. Everyone else at the table thought this was hilarious.

"I didn't think there would be wine here," I said as I poured myself a generous glass. "I guess I thought a zen center would be all about abstinence."

Kevin chuckled. "Oh no, Kate. We drink. I like to say we pray hard and we play hard."

Now I understood why Nina liked this place. I helped myself to noodles and veggies and some kind of sticky pudding that I thought would be sweet, but was actually quite salty and spicy. I picked up snatches of information about the other guests. Some had only been there a few days, some for a few weeks. They were a motley crowd; everyone seemed to be escaping something or someone. I shouldn't have been surprised, right? You don't travel all the way to Bangkok and then drive to the middle of nowhere in the jungle if you're happy with your life.

Saul, a man about twenty years my senior with an enthusiastic gray comb-over and a Magnum PI mustache, explained that he was dodging an ex-wife who was, in his words, "stealing my money and my soul."

Prithi, a petite Indian woman with the most beautiful green eyes I'd ever seen, said she escaped an arranged marriage to a man she hardly knew. Thom, a stocky dead ringer for Mark Ruffalo wearing a Star Wars T-shirt with a Wookie on it, was mourning the failure of his start-up. Steven, a pudgy Korean in his twenties, hung his head and slurred, "I got fired for looking at Internet porn in the office."

The pretty, young maiden who I'd wrongly assumed was studying art theory at Vassar turned out to be slightly older than I thought and explained with a wry look why she fled the States in a single sentence. "I was Harvey Weinstein's assistant. Let's just say I had to get out from under him."

The old Thai woman from the closet shuffled in with a bowl of noodles almost as big as her torso.

"Boop, sit down," Kevin said, pulling out the chair next to him. "Take a load off." He looked at me. "Kate, you've met my mother-in-law, Buppha."

Buppha swatted him away and shook her head before returning to the kitchen.

"She's your mother-in-law?" I said. "Your wife's Thai?"

When Kevin first mentioned his wife was back in the West Village, I'd pictured a statuesque blonde in skinny jeans, a scoop-neck tee, and an oversize Fair Isle sweater clutching the hands of two equally towheaded children while walking down the street in camel suede ankle boots.

"She is. Well, half Thai. Buppha raised Aly all by herself. Her dad was an American who came here for the wrong reasons, and after Boop got pregnant he split and left her with the baby. She worked three jobs to put Aly into an international school and ultimately sent her to the States to William and Mary. Then Aly came back for her PhD." He clearly liked bragging about his accomplished wife and his fierce mother-in-law. It made me wonder what kind of tone Karl took when he talked about me.

He continued. "We met here. She was doing a PhD in botany and I was a fucking bum backpacking around Thailand. She grew up here on this mountain. We tried to move Buppha to New York, but she wasn't having it. After three months in the United States, Boop booked her own ticket right back to Bangkok and came back here. Aly, my wife's name is Aly, works for Body Botanicals in New York, extracting oils from plants for ridiculously overpriced lotions that promise to make you look twenty-five. That's why I come back here alone. She's really busy with work."

"So why didn't your husband come with you?" Perhaps he was emboldened by the wine or maybe he was just this blunt, but it caught me off guard.

There were plenty of answers I could give. I decided to start with the simple one, if not the entirely honest one. "He couldn't take off work."

"What does he do?"

The last thing I wanted to do was explain Karl's job. In fact, I'd recently grown to despise explaining his job. The second you admit your husband is a publisher everyone excitedly tells you they've written a book. Seriously. Everyone and their mother thinks they're going to write the next *The Goldfinch*. And then I'm in the uncomfortable position of having to dodge their next question, which is inevitably, "Do you think your husband wants to read it?" The answer was always no.

"He's in finance." No one ever asked questions about your husband being in finance. I changed the subject back to him. "Does Aly miss living here?"

"She comes back during the summers and holidays. I love it here more than she does. She's a big fan of air-conditioning and Shake

Shack." He smiled in a way that conveyed he thought Aly's affection for modern conveniences and chain restaurants was endearing.

"She helped me build this place, though. There was hardly anything here when we started. We built one room at a time for ten years."

"I'm impressed," I said.

"Thank you," Kevin said, clearly proud of what he'd done. "I am too. But what about you, Kate?"

I could feel two dozen eyes fixed on me. "What about me?"

"What's your dream? What are you running away from? What do you want to accomplish while you're here? Et cetera, et cetera." He waved his hand through the air as if to emphasize the infinite range of possibilities.

I suddenly drew a blank. I chose the simple answer:

"I just needed a break."

"Cheers to that," a sad-eyed woman in her fifties croaked with a thick Russian accent. "We could all use a fucking break."

I finished my glass of wine. Magnum PI Mustache refilled it. I looked at all the friendly faces sitting around the table, this intriguing random assortment of strangers, with their vast array of stories and secrets and desires and regrets.

Fuck it.

"Well, actually, that's not my entire story."

I got into it then. I told them how I needed a break . . . from my marriage, from my kids, from New York.

As I drank I got funnier, more animated. I told the story about Lois Delancey and the baby food. I admitted that I called her waterproof panties Stinx behind her back. I became a different woman, a woman I liked, one I would have wanted to be friends with.

"Have more wine," Kevin said. And I did. I already liked it here.

A few hours later I woke up in a jumble of meditation cushions in the corner of the room. There had been more wine, then some dancing, someone had pulled out a limbo stick. My head throbbed. I stepped over Prithi and the Mark Ruffalo look-alike, the two of them tangled in a chaste embrace. Someone had drawn a set of pert boobs on the Russian woman's forehead with a black marker. She lay faceup in the center of the room snoring like a donkey.

I'd flown thousands of miles to end up at adult sleepaway camp. I could have done this in the Berkshires.

I stumbled down the stairs to my room. My head throbbed. I dug into the bottom of my bag for a bottle of Advil and lay down on the thin mattress and closed my eyes, but sleep wouldn't come. I did everything I'd read about on Goop to will myself back to sleep—visualization exercises, counting backward from one hundred, alternate nostril breathing, picturing Gwyneth Paltrow doing alternate nostril breathing.

Finally, I stopped fighting it and resigned myself to being awake awhile longer. Kevin's question echoed over and over in my head: *What did I want to accomplish here?*

I rolled over, picked my notebook off the floor, and flipped to a blank page. There was just enough moonlight that I could see the faint lines. I've never been one for mantras, gratitude lists, or vision boards. I only read *Oprah* magazine when I was waiting for a teeth cleaning. But I figured, what the hell. I'm here in a zen center. I might as well just write down what I hoped I'd accomplish during my stay.

I chewed on the end of the pen until it became warped and soggy. What I wanted seemed so simple written out in front of me:

- *Be less cynical.*
- *Relax.*
- *Be happy.*
- *Reboot.*
- *Write.*
- *Remind your husband that he needs you.*
- *Be the hero of your own story.*

Chapter Six

Dear Karl,

Time is a slippery thing. It's as if I blinked and the girls had gone from infants to walking and talking and then telling me what to do. The days felt long, but the weeks and months pass in a blur. That's how it feels now. Impossible that I've been gone two months. But now, just ten days and counting, and I'll be with you guys. I can't wait to surprise the girls on Christmas Eve. Will they be more excited for me or Santa Claus do you think? He's tough competition. Remember when we took Izzy to Macy's when she was a baby and I'd put her diaper on backward and she peed all over angry department store Santa? At the time I never thought we'd laugh about it, but it seems hilarious now.

I've been buying presents for weeks now—a teak xylophone for Izzy, brightly colored silk pajamas embroidered with baby elephants for Tilly, coconut shell monkey statues and tiny hand-carved silver bracelets for both of them. Thanks for letting me know the tree arrived. I wasn't sure I'd be able to pick it out and have it delivered all the way from here, but that's the magic of the Internet. I'm sorry I'm not there to decorate it with you.

Last night I was thinking about our first Christmas together. You'd convinced me to come back from Paris for good and move into your West Village bachelor pad. We'd only been a couple, a transatlantic long-distance couple at that, for less than six months, but going back to New York with *you, snuggling in bed in your fifth-floor walkup, watching the snow pile up on the windowsill, and making love first thing in the morning made for a warm homecoming. You were so pleased to adopt my family's old tradition of forgoing traditional wrapping paper in lieu of covering presents with old newspapers and pretty ribbons we reused year after year. We did it in my house because wrapping paper was expensive and my mother was a champion at cutting corners in ways that didn't feel like a sacrifice. You thought it was adorable, and I loved you even more for that.*

I don't think your mother thought it was nearly as adorable. I remember the look on her face, like I'd handed her a piece of trash, when I presented her with her very first present wrapped in the Styles section of the New York Times. *It was that first edition of the autobiography of Alice B. Toklas that we had found in that antiques shop in Carré Rive Gauche. I was desperate for her to like me. Your dad was easy. Your dad liked everyone. Like you, he had an innate curiosity about other people. He'd talk to the dry cleaner for an hour and know the names of all his children. But Alyse, well, she was something else entirely. I never told you how intimidated I was the first time we walked through the imposing black door of your parents' house on Eighty-Second Street, how even my knees shook as I took in the grandest home I'd ever set foot in. I know plenty of women who would have died to live in that kind of house. All I could think was "this looks like so much work." Still, I wanted to run through the rooms, touch everything, smell everything, taste everything. I didn't want to do it because I coveted any of it. I needed to do it because this was the place where you grew up and I wanted to consume every bit of you. The house itself, though, terrified me, as much as your mother did. The formal Christmas dinner that afternoon, with the serving staff, the five courses, the brick-hard plum pudding, was nothing like the raucous family gatherings of cousins and friends and neighbors I'd grown up with, where Uncle Eddie played the accordion and someone always passed out on the couch. I don't belong here, I thought.*

I remember telling you that night that I couldn't imagine ever fitting in on the Upper East Side. You told me I'd never have to. You told me we'd never have a life like your parents. You wouldn't allow it.

But things change. We changed. In the end it did make sense to move uptown and into the house after your father passed and your mother moved to West Palm. It was so close to the good schools, the park, everything we needed as young parents. And then we painted the black door red. That was such a happy day. We worked hard to make that house our own, to make it our home, and I have cherished every Christmas we've had together since.

Still, looking back on that first Christmas, it was the first time I felt truly out of place anywhere in the world. And, if I am honest, that feeling never entirely went away. I feel strangely at home here, in my little box in the middle of nowhere.

The room I've been living in is basically empty. After a decade of filling three houses with more and more stuff, living with nothing lightens something inside me.

I don't talk to many people. I spend most of my days alone writing and reading. Yet I feel more like myself than I have in years. I think that's why two weeks have turned into two months. It's so cliché to say that I'm finding myself. You know how I hate to be a cliché.

Tomorrow I'm visiting a refugee camp for women and girls on the border of Thailand and Burma. No one calls it Myanmar here. It's like the new name gets all tied up on people's tongues. I've been so busy writing, I thought it would do me some good to do some good and volunteer for a few hours.

 I miss you all the time. I miss you in the moments between the seconds. I'll go hours, sometimes days, concentrating on something else and then realize I've still felt you with me the entire time. Thank you for giving me this time here. It's the best present you've ever given to me.

Love,
Kate

One week had turned into two, and then a month went by and I still hadn't booked a ticket home. In the blink of an eye it was nearly Christmas.

If I were a man leaving my family for a few months for an exotic adventure it would have been labeled a midlife crisis. "He'll come to his senses. They always do," people would say.

But for a woman? Well, I couldn't even imagine how harshly and gleefully Karl's colleagues and the school moms were judging me. Actually I could. I could see the moms clustered together at drop-off, hands around steaming travel mugs of Starbucks, a band of vultures devouring every last detail. They'd speak in horrified and disparaging whispers: *How could she?*

I couldn't blame them. Let's be honest, I probably would have joined in on the excitable speculation if I weren't the mom being burned at the metaphorical stake. From their perspective my actions looked completely unjustifiable.

But I knew well that their outspoken judgment only served to cloak their own insecurities and peccadilloes. In my time in New York I'd seen too many sordid affairs, blatant nanny abuse, bribery of admissions officials, secret pill addictions, and enough backstabbing to fill a stack of Danielle Steel novels.

None of us was above judgment, even as I imagined how sharp-tongued theirs would be. Which is why I had purposely avoided opening any of their e-mails. I'd seen the subject of one or two messages from Lois Delancey. The first: "ARE YOU HAVING A NERVOUS BREAKDOWN????!" And the second: "IT'S TOTALLY OK IF YOU'RE HAVING A NERVOUS BREAKDOWN!!!!!"

I knew Karl hadn't told a soul where I really was, he valued our privacy even more than I did. Yet I steeled myself for the clichéd *Eat, Pray, Love* comparisons—middle-aged woman on a quest to find herself in the Asian jungle. The thought of it made me laugh out loud. I hardly ate here. Buppha's noodles and puddings were filling and tasty, but not haute cuisine, even by Thai standards. Even though I now lived in a zen center I hardly prayed, and I was still complete shit at meditation. I could barely concentrate for more than a minute or two before I'd need to pull out a notebook and start scribbling ideas I'd like to write later in the day. As for looking for love, that wasn't my intent. Or sex. The last thing I wanted to do was fuck someone new. If anything I was on a quest to *Rest, Relax, Make My Husband Want Me Again*. But that wasn't a very compelling title. Besides, didn't Elizabeth Gilbert eventually leave that guy she fell madly in love with in Bali for another woman?

The cast of characters at the center changed every couple of weeks. Sometimes I'd partake in their sessions of laughter yoga, or the shamanic sound baths. I made my way to a couple of boozy dinners, but cut myself off before passing out in a corner again. One time I told Kevin I'd come to tequila Twister night, which was definitely a mistake. One night there was a foam party that reminded me of a bar mitzvah we once went to in New Jersey. But, for the most part, I did my own thing.

By this point I had settled into a comfortable routine and I reveled in the fact that I could wake up and have the whole day to myself. It was a luxury I'd almost forgotten how to enjoy. Most days I rose with the sun and went for a long hike through the jungle.

The saw-bladed palms of the forest engulfed me. Bright pink flowers erupted on vines, coating the thick trunks with strawberry frosting.
Fat caterpillars crawled over my feet. I wandered through the soft mist
of elaborate spiderwebs and didn't bother to wipe them from my face
or arms.

There's a real difference between starting your day with a quiet
walk in the forest and being assaulted by alerts on your phone. I felt
like my brain had simultaneously slowed down and rewired itself for
creativity.

After my hike, I'd find coffee, write for four hours, have lunch, and
write for another four hours.

I read books left behind by other guests. Long hours of uninter-
rupted reading, the joy of finishing a novel in a single feverish sitting,
those were other small pleasures I'd forgotten were even possible.

I was productive. I'd gotten plenty of words on the page, which
already felt like an accomplishment. But more than that, I actually
liked what I had written. I was proud of it, which felt like the biggest
feat of all.

When I mailed off the girls' Christmas presents in Chiang Mai, I
also sent off a stack of pages ripped from my notebook—four stories—
to an editor named Ben Hirsch at *Zoetrope*. I'd met him once at our
home during one of Karl's events and I remembered him telling me
he despised receiving submissions over e-mail, hated the added burden of printing everything out. He told me he never read anything on
a screen. I hoped he would appreciate my "old school" handwritten
pages.

I sent them using my maiden name, Kate McKenzie. I doubted
he would recognize my name and immediately connect it with Karl,
but I didn't want to take the chance. If I was going to get published I
wanted to do it on my own.

I knew it was a shot in the dark. Ben Hirsch probably didn't even
open his own mail and the stories would likely end up in a slush
pile and eventually the trash. But I was proud of the four stories I

sent. I'd written and rewritten them over and over, agonizing over every sentence. Three of them were things I'd started in grad school and never finished. One was something entirely new, and it might be the best of the bunch. It was a story about a middle-aged couple, constantly teetering on the brink of divorce, who are only able to fall back in love when they attend someone else's wedding. The protagonists move through various emotions over the course of the event—disdain, ennui, fear of rejection, desire, passion. The celebrations become like a powerful drug and they begin to crash strangers' nuptials just to get another hit.

Write what you know, as they say.

With just ten days left until Christmas, Buppha and I were the only ones left on the property, and our lives quietly orbited one another's. She still did most of the cooking, which seemed to make her happy. Kevin told me she liked having people to fuss over. She had her own apartment just down the road, but I would often find her dozing on the deck in a hammock. Her snores were soft like a kitten's.

I shook her awake on the morning when we planned to go to the refugee camp. Before Kevin left he'd praised the camp's director, a doctor named Mia, as one of the most brilliant and dedicated women he'd ever met. Even though Kevin was prone to hyperbole, I was excited to meet her. I longed to get out of my own head, to try to do some good. You'd think, with all our funds and resources, that it would have been easy to find a way to dedicate myself to something meaningful back home. I'd tried. I'd joined boards and organized fund-raisers. It always felt like we were moving vast amounts of money around without accomplishing anything tangible. I'd grown weary of the $1,000-a-plate fund-raising dinners where more than half of the money went to the venue, the dinner, the band, the photo booth, and the chocolate fountain. Last Thanksgiving and Christmas I took the girls to volunteer in a soup kitchen on far East Seventy-Third between Second and First. It was the first time they'd witnessed real poverty, and I was proud of the way they took it in and stood by my side, helping me dish out meals to the women and children. Before we left, Izzy handed her American Girl doll, the Kirsten, the one she'd begged to have for an entire year, to a little girl about her age. When I took the girls back for Easter, the doors were shuttered. Apparently the neighborhood homeowners' association raised concerns about the "kinds of people it attracted to the neighborhood."

Buppha sat up in the hammock, the early-morning sun streaming around like a halo, lending her a sacred air. I took in the smell of her. She always smelled the same, like sweat, dough, and a freshly peeled orange rind. She smiled at my outfit, a bright orange sarong. Buppha had given me three of her sarongs and showed me how to tie one into a skirt and another into a halter dress.

"I need more underwear," I had whispered to her.

She dismissed me by pulling up her skirt to reveal nothing beneath.

"Natural air-conditioning," she said, and erupted into a fury of laughter.

I made us both coffee and brought the mugs into Kevin's beat-up truck.

Buppha drove wildly down the mountain with a teenager's abandon and enthusiasm for being behind the wheel. She pulled the seat as close to the steering wheel as it would go, but her feet still barely grazed the pedals. We veered off the main road, the one with the switchbacks leading into the valley, and went the other direction, deeper into the range. The path became even more narrow and precarious. It probably wasn't meant for vehicles at all, but here we were.

She chewed on the end of a Red Vine candy that had come in a care package from Aly. Buppha adored Red Vines and Sour Patch Kids and consumed the candy like someone who still had all of their own teeth, which she didn't.

Buppha stopped the car at a tall and thick bamboo fence with broken beer bottles on the top meant to discourage outsiders from climbing over. An official-looking white sign with blue writing read

UNHCR, THE UN REFUGEE AGENCY. A less official sign, hand-painted on particle board in rainbow colors, read WELCOME TO NEW BEGINNINGS. The words were translated twice, once in Thai and below that in Burmese.

Kevin had filled me in a little bit on the refugee camps on the Thai-Myanmar border. Some of the refugees had been there for nearly three decades, but more arrived every day. The refugees lived in isolation. They were people without a country, and Thailand still hadn't made up its mind about allowing them to assimilate. Kevin had described the situation for ethnic Karens and Karennis in Myanmar as a slow genocide. Villagers lived in terror of the military coming to their town, killing the men suspected of being a part of the opposition, raping the women, and conscripting the children for service in the army. Hundreds of thousands had fled for Thailand and found themselves stuck in the camps, where conditions were dismal, but they no longer feared for their lives.

Buppha exited the car and smacked her palm flat against the gate. A stern-faced guard wearing khaki fatigues and a jaunty black beret, and brandishing an automatic weapon opened it. Buppha's eyes came to his belly button. She raised her head, spoke quickly, gesticulated wildly, and then pointed at me. I heard the word *American*. It pleased the guard enough to pull the gate open wider so the car could drive through. We parked among a chaotic mishmash of thatched-roof huts and lean-tos all built practically on top of one another. Some looked more permanent than others, with clotheslines strung between them. A few even had satellite dishes perched atop them with a tangle of power cables hooked up.

A line of a few dozen women snaked outside a structure with a red cross painted onto a white sheet that hung listlessly over the door. Each of the women clutched a wailing infant or had one wrapped in a sling over their shoulder. Some breast-fed as they waited. It made me think of the $300 raw-silk ring sling Alyse gave to me as a Christmas present when Isabel was born. In New York we carried our babies in expensive scarves as a status symbol, to prove we were good mothers who'd read all the right books about attachment parenting and baby wearing. These women wore their babies because they didn't have any other choice.

A group of little girls in ragged pink dresses and blunt pageboy haircuts played a version of hopscotch in the puddles along the side of the road. The sight of them made me miss my girls with such intensity that I wanted to grab them and press their small bodies into mine.

We parked behind the only two-story building in town, a cement structure painted bright blue with a corrugated tin roof. Buppha pushed open the door with both hands and strode down an empty hallway to a small office.

"Meet Dr. Mia Williams." Buppha said it like an instruction.

A woman a little younger than me, wearing battered jeans and a formfitting black tank top, stood up behind a metal desk. Her long red hair hung loose down her back, past her shoulder blades. She had the posture and flat chest of a runway model.

She greeted both of us in a bright Australian accent. "G'day. Welcome to the end of the world."

Out of habit I glanced at Mia's left hand and noticed she didn't wear a ring, nor was there the faint white line of someone who'd recently removed her ring. I don't know why it mattered to me if she was married or not. It was just something I was accustomed to noticing. I was again very aware of my own jewelry. I should have taken it off before we left.

"It's good to have you, Kate." Mia grinned at me. "Buppha's a good friend. I've spent many weeks up at the center. Kevin and Aly are the best. I need bodies to help, especially now. No one comes here during the holidays, and I have more work than I can handle. I'm always desperate for people who can help teach the women English and computer skills but now I need the basics. I need people to give out food and medicine. I'm a one-man band most days."

"I'm happy to help." I meant it. I didn't tell her that I would be another one of those people clearing out of the country for the holidays. I promised myself I'd help as much as I could until I left to go home.

"Great! I'll give you the tour."

Buppha held my hand as we walked, letting go every so often to greet someone she knew or to hand one of her Red Vines to a child.

"I keep telling her not to give them candy, but she doesn't listen," Mia said with intense affection.

Mia showed us around the hospital, a small building crammed with forty beds with barely an inch between them.

"We end up doing some triage here. There's one doctor besides me. We get too many women coming in after they've stepped on a land mine, blown their leg to bits, and still made it forty miles through the forest to cross the border. I run out of morphine on a weekly basis. I never have enough pain meds to help women through childbirth. We deliver a couple babies a week, and God help them if there are complications." She led me to a tiny back room with a single incubator.

"Just got this donated. It's a ten-thousand-dollar piece of equipment and most days I don't have the electricity to plug it in."

We went back into the street. A little boy with a dirty face gave me a shy smile and reached out to grab my other hand as he walked alongside us. Next Mia led us into another small building built from crumbling cinder blocks.

Inside there was a rickety table covered in brown cardboard boxes.

"Welcome to the new computer training room. This Hollywood actress, that one who adopted a refugee baby from Myanmar and then posed with him on the cover of *People* magazine like she was holding an Oscar, donated a hundred laptops to the camps. A year ago Google began a project to bring free Wi-Fi all along the border. I helped them with the logistics. It was a bureaucratic nightmare, as you can imagine. And while these computers are a nice gift, we probably don't have enough electricity to power it all."

"That's why you have me!" a tall white man said as he snuck up behind Mia and wrapped her in a hug. He looked much younger than she was, maybe by ten years. Intricate tattoos snaked up his taut muscular forearms. I picked out a dragon, a scorpion, and the word GRATITUDE. The man squeezed Mia and landed a wet kiss on her cheek. She leaned into his hug.

"This is Derek. My little brother. He's spending a few months up here to help. And he swears he knows how to install cheap solar panels and build a generator out of some chicken wire and a car battery to keep those computers going. If he doesn't I'm shipping him back to Oz."

Derek's bright blue eyes twinkled with a youthful eagerness. His floppy brown hair fell into them. He pushed it away with his right hand, which bore two copper rings, one on his ring finger and the other on the index finger. Around his neck he wore a necklace made of delicate white shells. I remembered something Nina told me a long time ago when we lived together: "Men who wear a lot of jewelry love to go down on you. It's just a fact."

Derek and Mia had the same high cheekbones and thick eyelashes. He wore cargo shorts, the kind with lots of pockets that no one ever puts things in, and a white tank top that read: EAT, SLEEP, RAVE, REPEAT.

I will never understand tank tops on guys. They're high on the list of reasons I'm glad I'm not in my twenties now, along with Tinder and vaping.

He was a pleasant cliché of a twentysomething backpacker. I caught his gaze traveling from my bare legs to my chest. I saw myself through his eyes—a pasty middle-aged woman wearing a poorly tied sarong and a floppy hat to keep the sun off her face. I felt ancient.

"Just you wait, sis. I've got skills." He did a little jig when he said it then stretched out his hand to shake mine, and when our hands touched he raised mine to his lips.

"Charmed," he said with a grin. Twenty years ago this gesture would have been enough to tempt me into bed with him. Now I just rolled my eyes in amusement.

Mia swept her hand around the room to indicate the boxes. "As you can see, we haven't done much with these yet. Learning computer skills could give the refugees a real chance at getting a job. But, the learning curve is steep. We're also hoping to help some of the newer arrivals set up social media profiles and e-mail accounts so they can get updates from back home and communicate with their families. We have a lot of women here who lost contact with their husbands and have no way of getting in touch with them. Some of them don't know if their men are dead or alive."

The last part of that sentence lingered in the air. My skin burned at the thought of not knowing Karl's whereabouts and I felt a stab of guilt that I had caused him a similar pain over the past couple of months.

Derek rubbed his hands together. "Let's get them out and plug them in."

"You do that, baby bro." Mia ruffled his hair. She looked at me. "Want to help him?"

I nodded and tried to hide my disappointment. I'd hoped to spend the day meeting some of the refugees, but I couldn't refuse. This was real work that needed to get done. I wasn't here as a tourist.

With my orders in place, Buppha set off on her own, a new package of Red Vines magically appearing from within the folds of her robe.

Derek and I fell easily into the conversational beats of getting to know one another. There was something about being in a foreign country, surrounded by complete strangers, that made it easier to condense your life story into talking points, even the parts you rarely discussed.

Derek told me how, before he came here, he'd been in the middle of getting a PhD in astrophysics.

"Really?" I felt like a judgmental bitch before the word finished coming out of my mouth. Why was I so surprised? Because he was fit, handsome, and covered in elaborate tattoos? I reminded myself that Neil deGrasse Tyson was probably something of a babe when he was in grad school.

My surprise didn't seem to ruffle him. "I've always liked the stars," he explained. "And I'm weird good at math. It's a little useless, now that the space program's going to shit, but I figure maybe I can work for Ricky Branson one day and get a bunch of richies to the moon for holiday."

"So you're on break from school?" I asked.

"I took the year off," he said, and proceeded to explain how he came here to take a break before going back to his family's cattle ranch in Australia.

"My mom died last year and Dad's selling the place now. It's been hard. With her gone I felt this duty to go home and help my dad. Even if it meant putting my life at university on hold," he said.

"I hear you," I said. "I'll bet it isn't easy. Your dad must be glad for the help."

Karl had stepped up in a similar way when his father died. Before Karl Carmichael Sr. had his first heart attack, my husband had promised me he was going to take a break, to take six months away from New York to spend just with me and the new baby. We researched apartments in Nairobi, not far from where Karen Blixen wrote *Out of Africa*. I'd slowed the pace of my own writing then, but I hadn't stopped yet. I told myself I'd keep writing after the baby was born. I'd write when she napped. Back then I thought babies napped all the time, not just for erratic thirty-minute intervals during which you could only accomplish one thing and that one thing was usually brushing your teeth or going to the bathroom.

But when Karl's dad had his second heart attack, and then the stroke, Karl took the big job he'd told me he never wanted. He became the publisher. Soon after that we made the move to the Upper

East Side. We never talked about that apartment in Nairobi again. In the years after that it seemed to me like we'd never even dreamed it was possible. Ten years later, Karl and I were essentially living his parents' life. We lived in their house. He ran his father's company. I even sat on some of the same boards as Alyse. In fact it stunned me how like Alyse I'd become without ever thinking about it. Actually, when I really thought about it, it horrified me. Our current life was the opposite of the one Karl and I plotted as newlyweds living in our first apartment in the West Village. But it had happened so gradually, like a frog in slow-boiling water who doesn't realize he's dying. The shape of our lives felt entirely out of my control.

Derek was eager to help his father keep their ranch alive, but lately it had become too much of a struggle. Competing with the large commercial farms was impossible.

"I just came here to clear my mind before going back. Get some perspective, you know?"

I did know.

He paused then. "There's also this girl back home . . ."

I laughed at that. Wasn't there always a girl?

He looked at me over the monitor between us, the final of the fifteen we'd set up over the last couple hours. "Looks like we're about done here, so that'll be a story for another time, eh. Let's call off and get a beer." He licked his lips as he grinned. His bottom two teeth were crooked in a way that made his face even more interesting.

"There's a bar here?"

He laughed at me. "It was a joke. I think I could round us up some piss-warm bottled water, though."

My throat was dry. "Anything to drink would be a dream."

"Wait here and I'll see what I can find." Derek had a slight hop in his step that would be exhausting if he weren't so adorable.

I walked out of the computer room and back into the blazing sun.

The shriek of a small child pierced me through my heart. It sounded exactly like Tilly had only a couple years earlier. Karl called the noises she made during her tantrums the "dolphin shrieks." Across the road a young woman stood with her legs splayed over a screaming toddler. The little girl lay facedown in the dirt, pounding the road with her tiny fists, her head bucking up and down into the air. The mother clutched the hand of a slightly older child. The child's other hand gripped one of Buppha's waxy Red Vines.

The woman met my eyes with embarrassment. "I said she must share the candy." She spoke slowly and deliberately like someone who had only recently learned English. I understood. All mothers feel the need to excuse their children's behavior, as if it's an immediate reflection of who we are and every choice we've ever made as mothers. How many times had I done it on the playground in the midst of one of Tilly's tantrums? Her terrible twos were also her terrible threes and into the beginning of her fours. She'd wail herself hoarse over losing a toy, not getting a turn on the swings, and once when a squirrel in Central Park ran away from her. I always apologized and made excuses no matter who was in earshot, most often a crew of Haitian nannies who had seen and heard the worst of all the children in Manhattan. Those excuses were more for me than anyone else.

I walked over to her. "There's nothing you can do. You have to wait it out. She'll get tired."

The woman had a round face and almond slivers of eyes. Her light brown skin was smooth. She was young, a couple of years past twenty. She wore faded sweatpants with a hole in one knee and a green T-shirt. When I stood closer to her I noticed a long pink scar down her cheek. Purple circles stained the skin beneath her eyes. "I'm Kate." I pointed my index finger toward my chest.

"Htet." She said her name shortly and quickly, *tet*, like it was punctuation rather than a word. Her eyes were flat as she watched the child continue to scream and I recognized in her the same exhaustion I'd felt in the first few years with my own girls.

"My youngest is four. It gets better," I promised. I remembered strangers telling me this when Tilly threw a fit at the park, in the grocery store, in the middle of Madison Avenue. I didn't believe them then. I wanted to tell them to fuck off. I knew the truth. It was never going to get better.

But just as I thought I had reached the end of my sanity, it did get better. "My daughter did this for three years and now she's wonderful." I sat down in the dirt and rubbed circles on the little girl's back out of habit. I looked up to see gratitude pass across the mom's eyes. The child twisted her head and pressed her cheek into the dirt to look at me. She'd expected her mom. Her mouth was set in a steely frown.

"What's her name?" I asked. The back rub worked its magic. Most kids behave better when they have an audience besides their mom. It happened each and every time Karl came home after I'd spent a day with two angry children. For him, they were angels.

"Cho," Htet said, and raised two fingers to indicate the girl's age. She nudged the other little girl forward and raised a third finger to show she was three. Cho's sister continued to watch the little girl on the ground with bored disinterest. "This is Chit. Means 'love.' Cho means 'sweet.' Not sweet now."

"Cho is a beautiful name," I said.

Derek appeared carrying two bottles of water and two amber bottles of beer. He approached the four of us and easily introduced himself to Htet. I pulled both bottles of water from his hands and handed them to the young woman. "You're welcome to the beers too," I said. I was pleased that Derek gave a small nod in agreement. His unhesitating generosity made me like him even more.

"Just water. They're thirsty. We waited six hours for medicine shots. Thank you."

Mothering was the hardest thing I'd ever done, probably the hardest thing I'd ever do. I'd done it under the best of circumstances, with nearly every resource at my disposal, and it still nearly destroyed me. I couldn't imagine doing it here in this camp, with no resources and the constant reminder that you had no real home.

Htet kneeled down and scooped her small daughter into her arms.

Cho's eyes were drooping, the candy long forgotten. She'd probably fall asleep in her mother's arms as they walked down the road.

"You're welcome." I paused then. I don't know why I had the urge to follow her, to help her, besides the fact that she was another mother and she looked like she could use a friend.

Instead I turned in the opposite direction. Derek and I walked side by side back to Mia's office, where I was hoping to find Buppha.

"It's the kids that get me," Derek said. "They break my heart. I can't imagine growing up here. But it's worse for them where they come from. The stories my sister tells me . . ." He tapered off and kicked a jagged rock down the dirt path with the side edge of his filthy flip-flop.

"You have kids?" he asked.

"Two. Both girls. Isabel and Matilda."

"Are they in Thailand too?"

"New York. They're back in New York with their dad."

"You still married to him?"

I was taken aback by the question. "Yeah, very much so." A note of defensiveness crept into my voice.

"But you're here all alone? Buppha said you've been here for a few months." He sounded surprised.

"A couple of months." It sounded surreal when I said it out loud. *Have I really been here that long?*

He paused and took a swig of beer, then grinned. "Hmmm, a marriage vacation. I like it."

I forced a laugh that sounded more like a grunt. "I don't know if I would call it that."

"I didn't mean to offend you or anything. I just mean that's cool that you two can deal with the separation." He paused for a breath. "That scenario didn't work out so well for Mia."

"Mia, your sister?"

"Yeah, her and her husband both joined up with Doctors Without Borders, but they got assigned to different places. She ended up in

Laos and he was in Somalia. They figured it was just a year. Right? What the hell. You can do anything for a year."

"So what happened?" I reached over to pull the other beer out of Derek's front pocket. The cap wasn't a twist-off so I walked over to one of the buildings and whacked the top off on the side of a piece of wood, the way I'd been taught when fetching beers for my dad and his friends as a little girl.

I was pleased that Derek's eyebrows rose, impressed with my skills. I took a long sip of the warm liquid. It tasted like a rusty penny.

"Her man fell in love with another doctor, broke her heart, and she never saw him again."

I stopped dead in the center of the road. "That's terrible."

Infidelity was something I never worried about with Karl. He was loyal to everyone in his life, almost to a fault. Still, Derek's story needled its way into my brain, and I couldn't shake the possibility that any man left alone for long enough would start to look at other women.

"What did Mia do?"

"She was devastated. But, she's in love with her work. She's been in different parts of Asia ever since. Laos, Vietnam. She's been here the longest, though, running this camp. My dad and I have been up here a few times visiting her. We joke with her that she's married to all these people now and she has hundreds of babies to take care of, but I know that it isn't the same thing. I think she's happy with her life and sad at the same time, you know?"

I did know. I knew all too well. I nodded, but before I could say anything else I heard a woman shouting in a distinctly American accent.

"Your Web page says we can visit between the hours of noon and five and we are only a few minutes late. I want to volunteer. I am offering up my services to you." The voice belonged to a tall brunette wearing expensive leather boots over skinny jeans and sweating through a silk pussy bow blouse. Her skin was pulled so tight across her face it looked like her cheekbones were wearing spandex. She definitely had a rich husband. Sure enough, that man stood in the mud behind her. He was a short and stout fellow who resembled a warthog with the confidence of a lion. He whipped off a pair of gold Cartier aviators and squinted at Mia, who was trying to shoo his wife back into the Land Rover with their small Thai guide. The American man pulled out his wallet to offer Mia a wad of baht. "Can my wife just walk around and take some damn pictures with your fucking refugees?"

Mia shook her head. "Sorry, sir. We've got strict rules to follow. I'm not supposed to let visitors in here after five. It's a liability issue. We'll lose our funding if we break the rules."

Just then the man caught sight of Derek and me. "There's some other Americans. If they're allowed in here why can't my wife take a few goddamn pictures. She's on the board of Feed the Children and she just wants to show the board members some goddamn pictures of some hungry goddamn children."

Mia motioned to us. "They're full-time employees. Maybe you can come back tomorrow. I can let you in at seven. You can spend the entire day here. I can put both of you to work. I could use the help."

"Tomorrow we're wheels up to Siem Reap." His face smoldered with the expression of a man willing to destroy someone when he didn't get exactly what he wanted.

The man's wife was now tottering after the little girls playing hopscotch, trying to corral them around her for a selfie. I attempted to cover the disgust on my lips with my beer bottle. I wasn't on a marriage vacation. This was what I had needed a vacation from. I needed a break from these kinds of people, the ones who thought a wad of cash could get them anything their heart desired, including selfies with the poorest people in the world.

The wife succeeded in taking a few photographs of the girls. They crowded around her, hoping to receive candy in return for posing. They knew this was a quid pro quo. Disappointment crumpled the children's faces when the woman strutted away, already scrolling through her photos to determine the best one for Instagram. Not that she noticed their hurt expressions. Her eyes lit up as she saw the line of women holding babies at the doctor's office, still snaking around the building. "They're perfect. I need pictures with them."

Now Mia physically stepped in front of her and pushed her back to her vehicle. "You have to leave. I'm sorry."

Seeing Mia's beleaguered expression, I decided to speak up. I knew how to deal with men like this.

"There are security cameras all over here. The last thing you want is for this video to go on YouTube, a video of you bullying poor aid workers so your wife can take a few pictures," I said in a strong voice that surprised me. I could tell I had unnerved him by conjuring one of the few threats he would take seriously: social embarrassment.

A group of four of the khaki-clad men with guns approached our group. I thought for a moment that the fat American man wouldn't know better than to back off. Thankfully, he had a modicum of sense and ushered his wife back to their massive vehicle.

But not without having the last word, of course.

"I have friends in the State Department," he said. "I can get you all fucking fired tomorrow for this. Don't think I won't be talking to your supervisors."

Mia rolled her eyes and looked as though she wanted to flip him the bird, but knew better. There was a moment of solidarity among all of us then, a moment where we all felt a little morally superior to those rich American assholes. It was the first time in a long time that I didn't feel like one of those rich American assholes.

Derek and I followed Mia back into her office. She took the half-empty beer from her brother's hand.

"It's getting worse and worse." She took a sip that finished it off. "First it was the volun-tourism, which I could handle, people paying lots of money to come here and help us build things. Even though they never built the right things. They'd build a school, but we have no teachers. They built a well where there wasn't any water. It was self-serving, but those people genuinely wanted to do good things, even if it wasn't for the right reasons. But these people. These are the worst. They want to come for five or ten minutes, an hour tops, and just take as many pictures of poverty as they can fit on their memory cards. They want to take selfies with the refugees so they can show their friends and colleagues back home. I want to scream at them: these refugees don't exist to be on your Instagram. But then some of them give us money, and money is the one thing we do need. The government really is cracking down. An American woman stayed after dark one night and she was harassed by some of the men."

"Is the camp dangerous?" I asked.

Mia sighed. "Yes and no. Anytime you have people in a hopeless situation there's an element of danger. There's mostly petty crime, the crimes of desperation. One of the teenagers could have plucked that fat bastard's wallet right out of his pants. And you know who that would have fallen on? The kid. She could have gotten a few years in jail because that man didn't have an ounce of street sense." Her face darkened. "It happened a year ago," she said quietly. "The girl, she was barely twelve, she drowned herself in the river instead of going to jail because she didn't want to be a burden on her mother. The wallet she stole was empty except for a driver's license and one credit card."

We were all silent then.

Derek sat down next to his sister and slung an arm around her shoulders.

"You can always come back to Oz," he offered. "If this is getting to be too much for you."

"And move in with you? Be the old spinster sister living in your attic?"

"We'd keep you in the basement," he joked. "And you'd only have to go in there when we had company."

I enjoyed watching the sibling camaraderie between them. My older sister and I had never been close. We were six years apart. Even though we never talked about it, my sister never understood why I was so desperate to leave Wisconsin, why I wanted to travel the world. Kelly taught the fifth grade. I'd seen her and her husband only a handful of times since I left for college. In my third-grade notebook I'd written, *I want a big life.* I didn't know exactly what that looked like at eight. Of course the irony is that I still don't know exactly what it looks like at forty, but the longing never went away.

Just then Buppha returned. She walked so softly, like an alley cat stalking a restaurant's back door, that I was always surprised to find her standing right next to me.

"Ready to go, Kate?"

I nodded and stood. My joints creaked. I extended my hand to Mia. "I'd really like to come back and help out. I don't want you to think I'm like those people you just shooed away."

"Of course," she answered. "You're welcome anytime. You're nothing like them. You stood up to that son of a bitch. If only we did have cameras. We can't even get enough power for the refrigerators. Half our vaccines went bad because we couldn't keep them cold."

The mention of the vaccines reminded me of the woman I'd met on the street.

"Do you know a woman named Htet?"

Mia squinted and tapped her fingers on the desk. "She has two little girls, right?" A look of recognition crossed her features. "She's been here for maybe six months. Quiet. Keeps to herself, not that I blame her. She's been through a lot."

"What's her story?" I asked.

Mia massaged her temples, as if the memory inspired a headache. "Her husband was attacked by the military police almost a year ago. He was badly beaten, three ribs broken, his skull cracked. I think they were farmers. Someone probably used him as a scapegoat. Htet nursed him back to health. Her husband got her and the girls across the border, but he knew they needed money if they ever actually wanted to leave. He was smart. You should see the old-timers in the camps. They escape hell on earth, but then they're stuck in purgatory with no money and nowhere to go. Htet's husband left them here and went to his brother in Bagan. That's on the other side of Burma. His brother had money. I think he drives taxis. Htet knew the trip would take a long time, but he had promised to be in touch. She hasn't heard from him. She has a name and an address for the brother, but that's it. No e-mail, no phone number. She sends letters to the brother and hears nothing back. She's devastated. She doesn't know if her husband is dead or alive. I worry she's going to waste away."

I'd spent the past ten years worrying about preschool admissions interviews, about selecting the right gift for the bat mitzvah of the daughter of an important editor, about losing those extra twenty pounds so I wouldn't be ashamed of my body at pool parties in the Hamptons, about whether the girls' food contained GMOs and whether it even mattered, about whether or not my husband still found me attractive and interesting. These were the nuisances of the one percent, maybe even the one half of the one percent.

Mia began to speak again and then closed her mouth. I watched her bite her bottom lip, as if trying to decide if she wanted to tell me something else. She exhaled as she told me the rest.

"Htet was pregnant when she came here. I don't think she even knew when her husband left them, but we figured it out pretty quickly. She was terrified of having the baby with her husband away, but hopeful about the child. She told me she had a dream it was a boy and that made her happy because her husband always wanted a son."

I knew what Mia was about to say before she finished the story and I wanted to stop her. I didn't want to hear the words out loud.

"She miscarried last month. There was nothing anyone could have done, even if we'd had a proper hospital. It was still early and it probably would have happened no matter what, but she hasn't been the same since."

Hearing Htet's story broke something inside me. I knew too well that you were never the same after losing a baby. I swallowed hard to keep my composure.

"That's terrible," I managed to say to Mia. "Is there anyone here she can talk to about it? A doctor? A therapist?"

"You're looking at her." Mia set her lips in a wry line. "I think she's ashamed. If we could find her husband it would make all the difference for her and those little girls."

I closed my eyes for a second. Mia reached out to grab my arm.

"Kate, are you OK?"

"I'm fine," I stuttered. "It's hard to hear the stories. I don't know how you listen to so many of them."

Mia rubbed at her eyes. "Their stories. Jesus Christ their fucking stories. I'm a vault of all of them," she said, her voice ragged. "But listening to them, writing them all down, is a necessary evil. It might help get us some cash to keep this place open. There's this documentary filmmaker from Los Angeles who wants to do something on refugees. I googled him. He seems like a big deal, won an Emmy a couple years ago. I had this long call with his manager. They want to know all the stories to see if this is the right camp to shoot in. If they do it we'll get some kind of grant, a million bucks. That money would be life-changing. But trying to write everything down is so much in addition to the day-to-day of running this place."

There are moments in your life when you know what you are about to do is exactly what you should be doing. I'd felt it the day I stepped onto Columbia's campus, even after taking out nearly one hundred grand in student loans to pay for an MFA program that would never get me a real job. I walked with pride, my chest puffed up through the Morningside campus gates on 116th Street ready to conquer the fucking world. A small plaque on the black wrought-iron bars read, MAY ALL WHO ENTER FIND PEACE AND WELCOME. It described perfectly how I felt in that moment, completely at peace with a decision that should have been crazy. I had the same feeling the day I turned around in the Paris bookshop and bumped into Karl. He was just a tall stranger blocking my way, but the same sense of calm and conviction washed through my body. My bones and skin and blood knew he was my person before my brain or my heart did. Hearing Htet's story I knew I wanted to do something more here than unpack boxes and turn on computers. This was something that would make a real difference.

"I can help. I can listen to their stories. I can write them down. It's what I do. I'm a writer." I hadn't said "I'm a writer" out loud in so long. Now, it felt true. "I know it's important. Listening and recording them. Let me write them down. I want to help."

The darkness from moments earlier passed from Mia's face and was replaced with astonished joy.

"Are you sure? It's a lot of work."

"I want to do it." I hoped I sounded as sincere as I felt.

"It needs to be finished by January fifteenth. It will be hours and hours every day."

I didn't have much longer before I was heading home, but I was a fast worker when I put my mind to something. "I want to do it," I repeated.

Those five words would change everything.

Dear Karl,

I tried to call you back after we got off the phone but you didn't answer. I understand why you didn't answer. I understand you need some time to process everything I told you. I can't imagine how I would feel if you called me three days before Christmas and said you weren't coming home.

I don't want to repeat myself here. But I can't tell you enough how much I need to be here right now. Volunteering in that refugee camp has changed me. I've been so desperate to find some meaning in my life outside of being a mother and a wife. This place has given that to me. Already, in my short time working there I feel like I've really helped change these women's lives. I'm actually making a difference. I can't imagine leaving this yet and returning to my life in New York, a life of such extreme privilege, when I know people here are still suffering.

There's one woman here. I didn't mention her when we talked. I wanted to. I wanted to tell you so much more, but then everything escalated and it was impossible. This woman's name is Htet. She has girls a little younger than ours. I've been helping her with her English, but more than anything I think she needs a friend. A month ago she miscarried a pregnancy. Her husband is missing. She has no one. Talking to her, trying to help her, has brought up so many of my own memories, my own pain, our pain. I recognize that particular kind of haunted look in her eyes, the grief of losing a child.

We never talk about it, Karl. Losing our second child. Our boy. We never talk about him like that. We never call him a child or a baby or a boy. We occasionally made mention of "what happened," but it was always something that happened to me, not to us.

I was brazen enough to feel "safe" at twenty-one weeks, that I was past the danger zone. I carried the baby long enough to hear a heartbeat, learn the gender, and see an inkling of the person he could turn into when we saw him on the ultrasound. Remember when we thought we saw him wave to us in our last appointment.

You were so delighted. "I think he's a leftie like me," you said.

You were so far away when it happened. In Frankfurt, at the book fair. I remember that because I started to feel strange pains at noon and I tried to call you and it was six in Germany and you were out to cocktails with Donna Tartt and Carolyn Reidy.

When you called me back I could hardly hear you and you couldn't hear me so I hung up. Then Izzy woke from her nap and I had no choice but to go to her even as I started to bleed.

I managed to get myself and Isabel into a cab to the doctor. I talked to the baby inside me the entire twenty blocks. "You're fine, little man. I'll keep you safe. It's OK, baby," I whispered over and over with increasing urgency. Izzy thought I was talking to her and she smiled and laughed. "I'm OK, Mama," she said.

Izzy wouldn't let me put her down. I couldn't lie on the table and hold her at the same time. A kind nurse finally took her away.

Then came the awful moment. The doctor waved the wand over my stomach and told me she couldn't find a heartbeat. I remember staring at the wall of my OB's office, her bulletin board covered in photographs of fresh new babies, some of them wrinkled and purple and straight from the womb, others photo-ready with their plump bellies and their gummy smiles. I knew Izzy's picture was somewhere among the bunch, but I needed to turn away from the bright eyes of all these living babies.

I never knew I could grieve someone so much I never met. The level of pain I felt astonished me.

One of our regular babysitters was able to pick up Izzy then and I was finally alone. There was no service in the windowless room, and I didn't know what I would tell you even if I could get you on the phone. I couldn't text. What would I text?

When we got the tissue tested and found out the fetus had a rare genetic disorder, the doctor tried to comfort me and tell me that the miscarriage was a good thing. That my body knew what it was doing. I hated her when she called the miscarriage a "good thing." It was like someone describing a "worthy earthquake" or a "benevolent five-alarm fire."

You were just as shattered as I was when you returned, and you did everything you could to try to make me feel better even as you grieved, but it felt impossible to completely share the

*experience with you. I can't help but feel that I started to build
a wall around my emotions then, that I started to shut you out.*

*I couldn't escape the feeling that the miscarriage was my
fault, that I was being punished, that I'd failed, that I'd done
something wrong.*

*And through it all I kept mothering. I couldn't stop
mothering. I wasn't allowed to stop mothering. Every time
I picked Izzy up and smelled her head and pressed my lips
into her soft downy hair I thought about that other tiny hand
waving at me from the grainy black-and-white screen. I muted
my pregnant friends on Facebook. I couldn't stand to watch
their bellies swell as they ticked off the weeks until their due
dates. I hated myself for despising their joy.*

*Before the miscarriage I still gave myself a couple of hours
every day to do something completely on my own while Izzy
slept. Mostly I wrote. Afterward I used that time to sleep, or
stare into space, or cry. Eventually that time was just folded
into the rest of the day and erased entirely.*

*I needed help that you couldn't give me. So we hired
Marley. I knew you didn't want a nanny raising your children,
but we needed someone. I needed someone. I told you it was
so I could rest, but that wasn't what I did. I left the house and
got on the subway. I just sat on the N or the R riding uptown
or downtown. Sometimes I'd switch to the PATH and go all
the way to New Jersey. I never got off the train, just watched
the stops go by. Sometimes I'd go to the movies and cry. Kind
strangers would hand me Kleenex. When I came home from
those trips I'd feel ready to mother Izzy again.*

*I don't know why I am telling you all of this, except that
talking to Htet and helping with her girls has brought up all
of these feelings I'd buried. And I want to be able to share these
feelings with you; I want you to be able to hear me, really hear
me. And vice versa.*

She's so brave, Karl. I want to be brave like her; to know that whatever comes my way, I can deal with it. And she is just one of hundreds of mothers here fighting for her girls. I'm honored to tell their stories. It's just taken longer than I expected to listen to them all, to write them down. I've started recording them too, in the hopes that it will make the project more appealing and help Mia and the camp get the money they need to keep going.

I met someone here who told me that "when a person looks like they need help you have to help them." Those words have stuck with me.

I can make a difference here. I have a purpose again. This won't be forever, but right now I need to stay.

Love,
Kate

Chapter Seven

I made my bed and now I had to lie in it. I made a choice to stay and now I had to face the consequences. The most excruciating of these was that my girls seemed more distant after I missed Christmas. Maybe they were upset that I'd missed the holiday or maybe they just realized that business trips didn't last this long. I clung to the hope that it was my imagination; that my guilt was coloring my perception, because dwelling on the alternative—that my kids would grow up to hate me—was too hideous to bear.

I could still see their days running parallel to mine. When I opened my eyes I saw Tilly sneak to her sister's bed and nip her on the shoulder to tell her it was morning. Izzy would be awake but lying on her belly, sketching on a pad, or reading a chapter book. She told me she reads chapter books now! She was the good one. She was Karl. Tilly was me, the old me before I became their mom. She wanted to move the second she opened her eyes. She was never satisfied with being in one place. As I wrote my first sentences of the day I could see Tilly roll her eyes as Marley reminded her that she had a Japanese lesson in the afternoon. I rolled my eyes with her. Who teaches a five-year-old Japanese? Why couldn't I just let them be kids? When I pulled the string to turn off the light in my room at the zen center at night I heard them recite their quiet prayers.

When we spoke they still told me about their days and repeated that they loved me and missed me. But their enthusiasm for our conversations was gone. I didn't know how to get it back. Some days I was able to tell myself they'd hardly remember these months without their mother. On my worst days I felt my betrayal like a knife through my heart.

I'd hoped the time and space would lead to long phone conversations with Karl, the kind of connection I'd been craving from our early days. With each call I buzzed with anticipation to hear his voice. I desperately wanted to talk to him for hours, to tell him everything about my days, my writing, how bit by bit I was figuring out how I wanted to live again. But he grew short on the phone and the last time we'd spoken he'd broken down in tears.

"I don't understand any of this, Kate. I wanted you to have your time, but this is too much." He choked on the words.

"I'll be home soon," I promised, even though I knew it sounded empty.

"I don't think I can talk to you anymore," he croaked. "You can talk to the girls. You should talk to the girls. But it's too painful to talk to you."

I was shocked. Was he saying and doing this to punish me, or was I just being that cruel to my husband that he had to cut off communication with me? I didn't know. The impulses to be sympathetic versus infuriated competed within me. I also tried to put myself in Karl's shoes. Would I understand if he needed this, this space and time? I liked to think so, but the truth is I didn't know. The fact remained, though, that I'd been gone for so long at this point, I needed something to show for it. I couldn't go home with my tail between my legs. I needed to prove to myself, to Karl, to the girls that this time away had been worth something. And I didn't feel like I was done yet.

Other times I'd whisper to myself. *Go home now. That's how you can fix this. It might be the only way you can fix this.*

But a strange combination of both inertia and purpose kept me rooted.

The documentary guy from Hollywood pushed his deadline.

"I can't look at anything for another month," he'd written in an e-mail. "Don't bother to send it before then."

I wanted to use every second of extra time.

For eight hours a day I listened to the refugee stories. We sat on overturned milk crates in a small room off the camp kitchen. Smells of festering shit wafted through the air. The camp's septic system often failed. I swallowed hard and pressed my tongue to the roof of my mouth and forced myself not to gag.

I wrote with a blue Bic pen as I listened, my fingers flying across the page. I'd never been a journalist, or even that interested in nonfiction. It felt different from fiction. These stories already existed. They were waiting for me to tell them.

There was one story in particular that got me: Aung's. She was a tall, thin woman with deep slash marks on her forearms, neck, and left cheek that had faded to dark pink welts. The left side of her face, shoulder, and arms were wrinkled with scar tissue. In halting English Aung told me her story, her tone filled with a mixture of suffering and something else . . . pride. As she recounted her tale I understood why. It all happened so quickly, she said—the soldiers arrived, suddenly, descending on the village like a swarm of angry bees. They had quickly separated the men from the women, rounding up some forty women in the local temple, including Aung and her daughters. That night, scared out of their minds and unsure of what awaited them in the morning—they hatched a desperate plan. Aung snuck out and set a small fire as a distraction. It was both reckless and brave, but it worked. When the guard ran to put out the fire Aung helped each of the women shimmy through a tiny window at the back of the temple and run into the woods. Over the next two weeks she led this group of women hundreds of miles to safety. She smiled as she said this: "We made it." None of the women knew what happened to their husbands, brothers, and sons, but they suspected the worst, even as they held out hope.

I reached for her hand, marveling at her bravery and wondering if in the same position I would be able to call for the same courage. I suppose we don't really know what we're made of until we're tested, and here this woman was tested in the most awful of ways.

Over the next few days, I heard so many horrible stories of violence and terror, but what stuck out to me was the hope and resolve. These women were . . . fierce. They were survivors.

I gripped the woman's hand in mine. There was a moment of heavy silence. I wanted to care for Aung in some small way, to give her comfort, but all I could think to do was offer her food. I asked if she was hungry. Her arms were thin, the bones of her shoulder blades protruded through the back of a yellow smock dress. She nodded, grateful to take a break. I heated up a can of refried beans and served us both in plastic bowls we placed on our laps. The thick lard coated my throat and warmed my insides.

Before she left me, Aung gave me a shy smile. "Telling what happened is all I can do right now. I can tell you my story and I can wait."

Later that afternoon I looked for Htet and offered to spend time with her girls to give her a much-needed break from mothering, the same gift Marley had given to me. I thought it might help me clear my mind from the horrors of the stories.

That first time Htet dropped her girls off with me a couple weeks earlier she had clutched them and hugged them like she was terrified she'd never see them again. I had planned to tread carefully with her daughters, allowing them to watch cartoons or play by themselves with plastic dolls with too big eyes and porn-star makeup that came over in a recent donation from some toy maker in Dallas. But as soon as their mom was out of the room the girls wanted to braid my hair and play on the computers. Htet returned just as I had pulled the two of them into my lap to read a tattered copy of the Berenstain Bears I'd found on a shelf outside Mia's office. I expected her to shoo her daughters off my lap and chastise me for being so intimate with them. But the woman who walked into the room after a few hours away from her children had the beginnings of a smile on her face. She was clear-eyed. She'd obviously washed herself and brushed her hair and maybe taken a nap. If she wasn't on the verge of feeling happy, at least she was content. She fussed over Cho's new braids and kissed Chit on her pink ear. Since then, spending time with her girls was often the highlight of my week.

But today Htet didn't want me to take the girls. Instead, she asked if I could help her with something on the computer.

"Of course," I said, trying not to let my disappointment show.

"Let me leave the girls with a friend. I meet you there."

It was late in the afternoon and the sky was turning a hazy rose. At one point, I would have taken a picture and posted it to my twenty-three Instagram followers. I know that @AllAboutThatBush would have liked it. Now I paused in the middle of the street to simply enjoy it. I made my way to the building with the computers. It was empty. I sat down and checked my own e-mail before Htet arrived.

For months I'd been careful with my e-mails. I avoided opening anything from the other mothers from school who kept sending nosy messages with subject lines like "JUST CHECKING IN" and "LET ME KNOW IF YOU WANT TO TALK." I knew that whoever got my side of the story would use it as social capital at drop-off and cocktail parties for months.

So I don't know why I actually clicked on Lois Delancey's e-mail. That woman never minced words. Her e-mail was short and sweet.

Look who Karl took to the Public Library benefit . . .

My heart skipped a beat. I didn't want to open the photograph attached to the e-mail. I could delete it now and pretend it never came. I knew the subtext of Lois's single line: Karl took a date to the benefit. Karl was moving on.

I couldn't help myself. I clicked.

Of course it took forever to load with the slow connection. I buried my head in my hands as I waited for the picture to download.

"Hello, Kate." I heard a quiet voice behind me and twisted my head to see Htet.

I turned away from Lois's e-mail and stood up, glad for the distraction. She took a seat next to me. "I want to know if you can help me with something."

"Of course, what is it?"

"You have been helping people put messages on the Internet, yes? To find their people?"

As other women here told me their stories I had helped some of them set up e-mail addresses and Facebook accounts to try to contact their lost husbands.

"Maybe I could do that? Try to find my husband?" She asked this shyly, but with a quiet desperation.

As Htet and I had gotten to know one another, I'd learned some of her story in her own words. I never pushed her for details she wasn't ready to share.

"I have Naing's brother's address and his name. I have never met him. He is a half brother. He was not at our wedding. They were not close, but Naing thought he might help us with a loan. That is why he left us to go find him."

"There are a couple things we can try," I said.

I opened a browser on a new computer, abandoning my own e-mail, forcing myself to forget the photo loading on the screen. I turned my attention fully to helping Htet.

"We can google his name and address and see what comes up in public records and social media." Myanmar's public records were sparse, but I'd had some luck with other refugees looking for relatives. Sometimes we got lucky if the name wasn't common. More and more people were adding addresses to their Facebook profiles.

Htet handed me a wrinkled piece of paper with rough block-lettered writing.

"Have you used Facebook before?"

Htet shook her head. Mia had told me twenty-two million cell phones had been purchased in Myanmar in the past two years and that social media was booming. But Htet was from a poor family in a poor village, so her answer didn't surprise me.

"We can use Mia's account," I said. I'd assiduously avoided log-ging into my own Facebook for the same reason I avoided reading most of my e-mails.

"Let me do a search for your brother-in-law's name and address." Htet cracked her knuckles and knotted her hands into nervous cat's cradles. I typed the information into the search bar. As the results loaded on the page I heard Htet gasp behind me. She pointed a bony finger at one of the photos on the screen. I clicked to enlarge it. She squinted and brought her face just a few inches from the screen.

"I thought it was my husband," she said.

"You did?"

"Must be his brother. They look the same. Eyes and the mouth are the same. This man has different hair. Fatter nose. Fatter chin. It must be him."

I friended the stranger with the striking similarity to Htet's husband. I made a cursory examination of his account without making a big deal about it to Htet. He hadn't been active in a few weeks and all of the writing was in Burmese, but a month earlier he had posted a few photographs. In one he was flanked by two large-breasted cocktail waitresses at what appeared to be the Thai equivalent of a Hooters. In another he flipped the camera the bird with both hands in front of a large golden Buddha.

I don't think this is the man who is going to save your husband. I kept the thought to myself.

"We can send him a message," I said to Htet. "Like an e-mail." The keyboards on the laptops were multilingual, but typing anything longer than a name and an address was beyond my capabilities. "Do you want to write something?"

"What should I write?" she asked in an awed whisper, as if I had just performed a magic trick.

"It can be very simple. We can just ask if your husband is still with him. That's all. We don't need to ask anything else." Htet nodded and began to type with two fingers on the keyboard. I turned away to give her some privacy. When she was done she asked me how to send it. I moved the cursor to the required button and sent the message into the ether.

"When will he get it?" she asked.

"I don't know," I replied honestly. "It all depends how often he checks his account, but it's a start. I'll tell Mia you sent the message and she will keep checking on it for you."

Htet's lips wavered as she broke into a slow smile.

"We might hear from him soon," she said.

"We might." I didn't want to get her hopes up.

I only remembered Lois's e-mail once Htet had left. The photograph had probably loaded by now. What would I see when I opened it? Karl, dashing in his best Armani tuxedo, standing next to a beautiful Young Lion, one of the 40 Under 40 recipients, a brilliant young poetess with the legs of a giraffe.

I pulled a breath into my belly as I moved the mouse to wake the computer screen.

My cheeks flushed hot. I stared hard at the picture. Karl was still the handsomest man I'd ever seen.

Standing next to him in front of a loud step and repeat on the library steps was Isabel, an enormous smile revealing a newly missing tooth. She wore a shiny purple dress and pretty pink shoes. She looked so proud to be all dressed up and out to a fancy party with her daddy. Karl grasped Izzy's tiny hand in his giant right one. His left hung at his side. He never knew what to do with his hands in pictures. I could just catch a glimpse of the camera's flash off the gold of his wedding band.

I placed my palm on the warm screen and closed my eyes.

Seeing that picture of Karl and Izzy at the library became fuel to work even harder and faster to finish the interviews so that I could get home.

But it also pushed me to focus on my own writing. I indulged in a fantasy about next year's public library benefit where I would walk in on my husband's arm and he'd proudly tell people: "This is my wife. She's an author."

I hadn't heard back from the editor of *Zoetrope*, but I hadn't really expected a response. It was enough for me to send the finished stories out into the universe. I'd finally begun to tackle the start of a novel. I'd spent most of my life dreaming about writing a book. It was daunting and sometimes humiliating. I'd started it at least twenty times, getting through five or ten pages and then ripping them to shreds.

Over the past few months I had become fast friends with Mia and Derek. I confided in them. I shared copies of the stories I'd sent to the literary magazine with them. They were honest. Some of it is great, they insisted. "But some of this is real crap, Kate. Don't show this one to anyone." At least Derek said it with a droopy smile.

I continued to be surprised that I'd formed more real connections with more people here in a few months than I had after years on the Upper East Side.

When Derek grew sick of sleeping on Mia's couch he took over one of the rooms in the retreat center, the one just thirty feet from mine. We had coffee together, sometimes breakfast, and took the occasional hike through the jungle where our hands would occasionally brush against the other's arm or hip.

I could hear him at night as he inhaled and exhaled, as he stripped off his shirt and unbuckled his pants, as he let them fall to the floor.

My body tensed when I heard him roll onto his own mattress. I tried not to listen.

One night we lay on the deck as he pointed out obscure constellations. He rattled off his knowledge of the orbits of asteroids and comets the way most men in their twenties rattled off baseball or soccer statistics. I enjoyed his description of a four-dimensional cosmic play being acted out by forces much larger than anything we could comprehend.

We felt like locals, wiser than the mere tourists who checked out of their lives for a couple of weeks, the ones who would soon return to their desks, their SUVs, their Starbucks, their alimony payments, and their flushable toilets.

"When are you going back?" I asked him. His stay so far seemed as open-ended as my own. He'd finished the solar panels on the computer lab. I don't think anyone was as surprised as he was when they worked. Next he installed some on top of the medical center and the kitchen. The aid work was addictive because it was never finished. There was always more you could do, more that needed to be done.

He tipped his head back, stretching his neck, his Adam's apple pointing to the sky. "I hate that question. What if I said never? I'm just never going back."

"You'd be lying. Tell me more about the girl back home . . . your girl." Derek talked a lot, often too much, about a lot of things, but he'd been tight-lipped about the lady he'd mentioned to me the first time we met.

"I don't know if she's my girl anymore," he said quietly.

I didn't say anything else. I hoped my silence would encourage him to keep going. I loved hearing stories about other people's relationships. Who didn't? But as an aspiring writer, I'd always been a collector of tidbits from other people's lives, a thief of other people's joy and pain.

"OK. Here goes." He sighed. "It sounds like a bad movie when I say it out loud."

"Welcome to my life." I allowed a wry laugh.

Derek released a long exhale before he launched into his story. "I feel like Zoe has always been my girlfriend, even before she was my girlfriend. She grew up in the next town over. That was still sixty kilometers away. When you talk about living in the middle of nowhere, you're really talking about where I'm from. I first saw her in church. She was in the front row because her pops was the pastor. There were nine of them in all, the pastor's kids. Eight boys and Zoe. She was the youngest. My dad saw me looking at her one day. I was staring. My mouth was probably open or some shit. She had these red braids that ran all the way down her back, right to the top of her butt. I wondered if she could sit on them. I wanted to pull one. Not in a mean way. It was just how I thought about touching her when I was a stupid ten-year-old boy. So my dad caught me looking and he told me to go on over and talk to her and I told him to shut right up. Then I apologized because that just wasn't how I talked to my dad, but I was embarrassed that he caught me looking at a girl when I was supposed to be busy thanking God. When the sermon was over my dad went up to talk to the pastor and he dragged me next to him. That's when I stood close to her for the first time. Her hair was even brighter up close. It took all of my willpower not to grab one of those braids right then and there. The pastor was a real nice guy. He knew my dad and he asked if he could teach his girl how to ride horses. Mia was out of the house and in college by then and my mom missed having a little girl around, I think. My dad said yes and that's how Zoe started coming to our house twice a week. As we got older she started coming all the time. We played together at first. We were pals. And then when we were fifteen or so I kissed her on a class trip down to Ayers Rock. We were sitting in the back of the bus. Nothing good ever happens in the backseat of a school bus."

I smiled and remembered that my own first kiss was also in the green vinyl seat of a yellow school bus. Tommy Miller's mouth had tasted like the Doritos that had gotten stuck in the spaces between his braces. He darted his tongue in and out of my mouth like a lizard trying to catch a fly. Four years later I would actually lose my virginity to Tommy Miller's brother Ryan, who was two years older than us and in his freshman year at the local community college. Ryan was one of those impossibly good-looking guys who you start to hate after talking to them for more than five minutes. But I wanted to lose my virginity before I left for college. I was convinced I *had* to lose my virginity before I left for college or else.

I don't know why, but the consequences of not doing it seemed dire in my mind. Ryan was lifeguarding at the community pool with me that summer. I invited him down to my parents' finished basement under the guise of listening to the new Alanis Morissette CD. He awkwardly shoved his hand down the front of my pants during the chorus to "You Oughta Know."

He blushed at "go down on you in a theater" . . . and then I went down on him in my parents' rec room before we moved on to the awkward and fumbling sex.

I remember thinking, when he was on top of me, that his penis did the exact thing his little brother's tongue had done years earlier. He screwed with a perfunctory in-and-out motion not unlike the tongue of a lizard.

Afterward we watched *The Breakfast Club,* but only up until the scene where Emilio Estevez admits to taping Larry Lester's buns together. I always cry a little at that scene and that freaked Ryan out, so he decided to go home. We high-fived good-bye.

Derek kept talking in the way that guys in their twenties do about a girl they really like, maybe even love. "After that Zoe and I were going steady. Then we both went to uni. I ended up at UNSW and she went to Queensland. They were a short plane ride or a long drive away, but we stayed together during freshman and sophomore years." He paused then.

"What happened?"

"Then I fucked up."

"What'd you do?"

"I was just a stupid kid. I got drunk and kissed someone else. Then I got drunk and had sex with someone else. Then I got drunk and told Zoe about it. I thought I was doing the right thing. She told me to fuck off."

"How long ago was that?"

"Six years." His breath was shaky.

"So what's happening now?"

"Now she lives back home, doing her training to be a farm-animal vet. When I went back to help out my dad we met up again at the bar and we got to hanging out. First just one night a week and then two and finally she let me call her my girlfriend again. But then I left."

I turned to him and rolled my eyes, now exasperated by his story. "Why'd you leave?"

"I got scared."

"Did you tell her that?"

"No. I told her I wanted to ride a motorcycle through the Thai jungle."

"Very mature."

He flipped his palms over in surrender. "I'm a sad sack. I got spooked. If someone had asked me a year ago if I thought I'd be back living in my hometown, sleeping in my childhood bed, making my dad breakfast every morning and trying to win back my high school sweetheart, I'd have said fuck no. But life is ridiculous."

I agreed with him: life was ridiculous. "Do you want my advice?" I asked.

"No." He chuckled when he said it. "I get enough of it from Mia, doing the big-sis thing. I just want to think it through myself, you know?"

Before my friendship with Derek, it had been years since I'd been alone for longer than a few minutes with a man who wasn't Karl or my doctor. Men and women back home were never this intimate unless they were sleeping together. The unspoken boundaries of how the sexes interacted on the Upper East Side were downright Victorian.

"Want to come with me to a rave in Lombok on Friday?" he asked as though the idea just occurred to him and as though I was absolutely the kind of person who would enjoy going to a rave. I thought back to the molly on the beach in California. And then I thought about the brutal hangover.

"No. I think I'm good. But thanks for asking."

Sometimes, when Derek looked at me, despite what he'd told me about Zoe, I knew without a shadow of a doubt I could fuck him if I gave the right signals. I knew it the same way I'd known I could sleep with Karl the second he bumped into me in that bookstore. I thought about what it would be like to be with another man after all these years. Would I even enjoy it? I tried to imagine it once—his huge hands with their neatly clipped fingernails gripping my breasts as I pushed myself down onto his lap.

The thoughts didn't turn me on. Instead I felt an intense wave of shame as I remembered the anguish I'd felt at seeing Lois Delancey's e-mail, those moments when I thought Karl had moved on. The sad truth was that I couldn't blame him if he did. I'd given him every reason. What was a man supposed to do when his wife left and refused to come home?

"Come home, Katie," he had begged the last time we spoke on the phone. "It's time. We need you. We miss you." It was rare for Karl to show this kind of emotion. I'd craved it for so long, but now its intensity frightened me. There were so many reasons to go back. I was a mother. My place was with my children. I was a wife. My place was with my husband. And yet . . . and yet . . . my time here still felt unfinished.

"I'm not ready," I whispered. "I'm sorry. I can't come home yet."

Chapter Eight

In my dream I wandered through our house on Eighty-Second Street. I peeled open doors to find rooms I hadn't known existed. At first I felt a burst of delight at each undiscovered space. Eventually, it became a terrifying labyrinth. Rooms vanished inside new rooms. My heart filled with dread every time I turned a corner or opened a door. There was one final door. I knew it was the last. I don't know how I knew that but I did. I clutched the brass handle and tried to turn it but it wouldn't move. It glowed bright in my hand, burned my skin. I couldn't stop touching it. I turned back the way I came and realized there was no longer any other way out. I was trapped.

My heart thumped furiously against my ribs when I woke, dripping in sweat. There was a heavy weight on my chest.

I opened my eyes and realized I wasn't alone.

A straggly gray monkey squatted on my sternum. To his credit, he was as surprised to see me as I was to see him. He released a blood-curdling shriek that echoed off the valley walls below my room. He flailed his arms and pounded his chest, but made no attempt to get off me. I recognized him from the pack of macaques that patrolled the perimeter of the property like furry foot soldiers.

It was always fun to watch the new guests turn into giddy children when they saw a monkey. They stuck out their tongues and crouched on the ground to make clicking sounds with their mouths like they were calling a dog. The creatures' utter disinterest in them only served to make the humans love them more, the schlubby guy who never returns your phone calls. Sometimes one member of the pack would steal a baseball cap or a pack of cigarettes while the guests took pictures with their iPhones. I could imagine their cheesy Facebook status updates: "Just Monkeying Around in Thailand. LOL."

"They bite, they have fleas, and they're smarter than some people," Kevin warned me one day early on. "Don't touch them. But I get it. They're cute bastards."

I wouldn't call the one crushing my chest cute. He was mangy and beaten up. When he opened his mouth his lengthy yellow fangs dripped with drool. A gash covered over in white scar tissue turned his mouth into a sneer.

Don't move. He'll scratch off your face. I slowed my own breathing and widened my eyes. We began a staring contest. The pronounced ridge over his soft brown eyes furrowed, like he was trying to figure out what to make of me. After a few minutes that felt like an hour he blinked twice, stood, and leaped out to my railing and into a nearby tree where he turned away from me. I was already forgotten.

My knees wobbled as I got out of bed, yanked the curtains shut, and fell back onto the bed. I bent over and hung my head down below my knees to slow my heart rate. I could still smell the monkey's rancid breath as I tried to shake the feeling of how close I'd come to having my face disfigured. I was nauseated and frazzled as I pulled on a bathing suit and a pair of jean shorts for a day trip to Chiang Mai.

Rappelling down the side of a three-hundred-foot waterfall was Derek's idea. "It's the most fun we can have with our clothes on," he'd said flirtatiously. Everything Derek said sounded flirtatious. He couldn't help it. I really should have said no. I had writing to do. I wanted to go to New Beginnings. I didn't come here to leap off waterfalls.

But there was a part of me that wanted to be the kind of woman who said yes to things like rappelling down a towering cliff over a torrent of rushing water. I wanted to be brave and open-minded. It was the kind of thing Nina would say yes to without batting an eye. Goddamn Nina. Her leading me here felt like a dream. It felt like yesterday and a dozen years ago at the same time. I'd heard nothing from her since that single e-mail about running off to Lamu. A petty part of me hoped she'd get herpes.

Mia had a rare day off, so the three of us piled into her beat-up Camry and drove north toward the Doi Inthanon National Park in the foothills of the Himalayan range. We sang along to some eighties anthem rock songs I'd forgotten I knew all of the lyrics to. Then "Kokomo" came on the radio. We giggled and turned the volume even louder.

"My first sex dream was Tom Cruise in *Cocktail*," Mia said. "I wanted to go to Kokomo, wherever that is . . . get there faster, take it slow, have him go down on me for hours."

"There was no one sexier than pre-Scientology Tom Cruise," I agreed. I smiled to myself. Before Izzy was born Karl and I spent a long weekend in Aruba. We hardly got out of bed except to have dinner at the Dutch karaoke bar on a pier that stretched into the ocean. Our out-of-tune version of "Kokomo" had gotten the crowd clapping on their feet.

"I still wouldn't kick Tom Cruise out of bed now," Mia said.

"I think he's too short for you. He'd come up to your boobs."

"Who knows. I might like that. It could be quite useful."

I was so happy as we drove, with the windows down, the wind whipping my ponytail into my face.

We pulled off on the side of the road to have lunch at a no-frills café and ate BBQ pork skewers and *laab*, a mincemeat, offal, and blood salad that I never would have dared to order at home. I had two helpings.

"Thanks for helping Htet with her girls," Mia remarked as she slurped down a mug of boiled deep-fried noodles.

"I'm happy to do it," I replied to Mia. Her praise made me feel good. "It makes me miss my girls less." Derek and Mia both got quiet. They never probed. Both of them had their own stories they didn't want dissected and analyzed.

I leaned back into my seat and watched the two of them pick food off one another's plates. I pushed the bloody mess in my bowl around with my fork and thought about the time my well-meaning father took us to visit the famous Usinger's sausage factory, thinking it would be something his daughters would appreciate. "Important stuff, seeing how the sausage gets made," he joked. My sister threw up on the cement factory floor. But I loved my father for taking us there. My takeaway from that day was that life and death were messy in very different ways.

I finally asked Mia the question I had been avoiding. "Do you think Htet's husband is alive?"

She sighed loudly. "I wish I could say yes, but . . ." She got quiet.

"What will she do? What will happen to her if he really is dead? If he wasn't able to get any money to help their family?"

"She'll stay. Or she'll go back to Myanmar and try to find work. Where she's from women aren't valued much more than domestic animals. When they're here we try to train them to sew, to do hair, to repair small electronics, things that can get them a job if they go back. Too many of the women are scared to ask for those kinds of jobs. Many end up forced into sex work, or worse."

I shuddered to imagine what was worse.

Three hours later I was wearing a thick nylon harness that felt like a chunky diaper and looking out over a steep drop below. I'd been clipped to a rope, secured at the top of the waterfall by a competent-enough-looking man named Bo who chain-smoked the entire time he gave us his safety demonstration. He was slightly bowlegged and had a shock of black hair that stuck up straight in the back. He was Thai, but his English came out with a slight Southern drawl.

What we were doing was scary, but not dangerous. I couldn't imagine Mia scared of anything, but tears rolled off her cheeks when she contemplated the twenty-seven-story drop below us.

"Tiny children do this," Bo teased Mia. "You're too old to be scared."

I took a step closer to the ledge. I was ready to do this. Maybe that morning's encounter with the macaque had made me more fearless than I would have been on any other day. Without turning back, I let slack into the line and stepped into the abyss. For a few seconds I was weightless. I closed my eyes and allowed my body to hurtle down the falls. Cool water poured over my head and down the back of my neck. I turned my face into the stream and let it massage my eyes and lips. I was blinded.

For a beat I was blessedly alone. All by myself in the middle of a waterfall, and it felt the way people who were more religious than I was might describe a slice of heaven.

"Keep it moving, Carmichael!" I heard Derek first, then looked and saw my friends beginning their descent above me. Their harnesses were clipped together at the hip. They were making a tandem drop. Derek held tightly to the rope with one hand and clutched his sister around the waist with the other. I could see him whispering words of encouragement into her ear. I bent my knees and pushed off the rock wall, letting myself drop another ten feet, then another, then another.

A sharp rock jutted out from the wall. Someone—presumably a lovesick kid—had spray-painted it: I LOVE YOU D. It reminded me of how Karl had once carved C+K beneath his mother's grand mahogany dining room table when I teased him about being such a mama's boy at age thirty-seven.

As I looked down to see how far I had to reach the water the sun caught the fine blond hair covering my legs. I'd given up on shaving in the complicated outdoor shower. Looking at my legs now made me laugh and think about the thousands of dollars I'd spent in the past decade to make most of my body as bald and smooth as Bruce Willis's head. I'd never been much for waxing until I spent time in locker rooms after expensive workout classes du jour. I didn't wax for my husband. Karl liked a little bush. He said it reminded him of the first sticky-paged *Playboys* he stole from his next-door neighbor Erik Epstein in the eighties. I'd always maintained that women waxed for other women or if they were trying to have sex with another woman's husband.

My eyebrows had begun to fill in too. I noticed them in the rear-view mirror on that morning's drive. I'd forgotten how unruly they could be without regular shaping, but I liked the way they gave my face an unfinished look, or as Kasey in Karl's office would say: I now had a strong eyebrow game.

My feet dipped into the chilly pool. I wore a bright orange life jacket so I wouldn't be yanked to the bottom. I held fast to my rope anyway as I paddled away from the fury of the falls.

Adrenaline surged through my veins as I contemplated where I had begun at the top of the cliff and I felt a wild sense of accomplishment.

It was late when we set back out, so we grabbed a bunk room in a hostel about ten miles from the falls. Yes, a hostel. I was a woman who had almost exclusively stayed in the Four Seasons for the past ten years and now I was excited about sleeping in a bunk bed in a ten-dollar-a-night rat trap. This is what happens when you live on a mattress on the floor for months—your expectations are drastically lowered in a way that a single bunk bed in a hostel *feels* like the Four Seasons.

The hostel had a bar, as most hostels do, that served one Thai lager on tap and tequila shots for less than a dollar. The special of the night was a cocktail called a "Sticky Sex on the Beach," despite the fact that we were miles from the ocean. A fun and little-known fact is that the Thais love karaoke. They're terrible at it, but they love it just the same. Even the ones who don't speak any English will belt out an enthusiastic, if off-key, rendition of "Welcome to the Jungle" any night of the week, and most bars and even restaurants had invested in some kind of cheap karaoke machine.

I got us a round of Sticky Sexes—when in Thai, as they say—and returned to the table where Derek and Mia had settled themselves with some fellow Aussies. They'd never met, but within minutes they were best friends, throwing around slang like *bogan* (a redneck) and *fair dinkum* (genuine) and *stubbie holder* (those foam things you put around beer cans).

"You don't see many American ladies traveling on their own at your age, mate," remarked a young guy named Noah with curly white-blond hair and equally pale eyebrows and eyelashes. He puffed on an electronic cigarette, which reminded me that fake smoking was never going to be as sexy as real smoking.

"You don't know my age. How old do you think I am?" I teased him.

"You're at least thirty," he said with actual conviction.

"Thirty-one, actually," I said.

Derek winked conspiratorially and stood to get another round. He came back with three pitchers and a tray filled with golden amber shots.

"Oh no." I waved it away. "I don't do tequila."

"Spoken like a real grandma," Noah said as he tipped the liquid into his mouth and shook out his scruffy curls. He looked pained, like his mother had just crashed his favorite indie film festival.

I quietly passed my shot over to Derek, who took it down in a single gulp.

"They don't have 'Kokomo.'" Mia thumbed through the laminated song catalog for the obligatory karaoke machine. "But they do have 'Dancing Queen' and 'Mamma Mia' and well, the entire ABBA repertoire. Who wants to be the Christine Baranski to my Meryl Streep?"

I raised my hand, finished my Sticky Sex, and sashayed Beyoncé-style to the stage with Mia.

The place was packed with a crowd of unwashed backpackers half our age. We had them on their feet and cheering by the time we got to "Fernando."

Derek handed me the pitcher and I drank from it without bothering with a glass.

When we went back to the table he nudged his sister. "Should we do it?"

She shook her head. Mia's eyes were glassy and her speech was getting a little slurred.

"Come on, Mee. We can do it. This crowd would love it."

"Nope. Out of practice. Can't do it."

"Can't do what?" I leaned over to them and pushed Noah's hand away as he tried to hand me another shot.

"Mia and I can do the lift from *Dirty Dancing*," Derek stated with confidence, in a voice that told me he knew I would find this impressive.

"Mia brought me out to med school for a weekend when I was a teenager and we did it for the entire med school class. It's like our thing."

I shook my head. "No one can really do the lift from *Dirty Dancing*. It's physically impossible for anyone except for Swayze."

"I'm better than Swayze," Derek insisted.

Noah was listening in. "I'll bet you twenty bucks you can't do it, mate."

"Come on, Mia," Derek pleaded. "Now we have to."

She placed her head on the table and murmured into her hands. "I'll puke if we do the lift."

"You can't do it," Noah said.

"I'll do it with Kate then," Derek said. "Right?"

"No, no, no."

"Oh, it's easy. Let's go."

Before I knew it the dulcet strains of "I've Had the Time of My Life" began playing. Noah and an equally pale, nearly albino girl sang along loudly. News of our grand attempt rippled through the room and someone had pushed the tables and chairs out of the way, clearing a path toward the stage. The bartender did away with the pretense of a kamikaze shot and handed me a tumbler of vodka. I took a swig and began to sway.

You're the one thing, I can't get enough of . . .

All eyes were on me. Cell phones were raised in the air.

I wasn't old. I just climbed down a waterfall. I was getting drunk in a hostel with a bunch of twenty-year-olds.

Derek nodded. I took off slow, running toward him. The crowd began to chant my name.

KATE, KATE, KATE, KATE!

He caught me perfectly on my pubic bones. I spread my arms wide as I balanced in the air. We did it. We did the goddamn lift from *Dirty Dancing*. Derek began to twirl. The crowd screamed. I was having the time of my fucking life.

We didn't get back to the retreat center until noon the next day. I put my bag in my room. I was in pretty rough shape from the night before, with hand-size bruises on my hips and a lingering desire to vomit. I went upstairs to check my e-mail on the center's computer before planning to sleep it off for the rest of the day.

Then I saw it. An e-mail from Ben Hirsch. The subject was simple: "Your Submission."

I clicked on the e-mail and began to read.

Dear Ms. McKenzie:

Thank you for submitting your four stories to *Zoetrope*. Your pieces show promise. I regret to say that three of the four that you sent are simply not ready for publication. The fourth however was a gripping story and incredibly well crafted. You have all the elements of a memorable piece here, though they may not be in the right order just yet. I am attaching a PDF of a marked-up copy of your story and several suggestions for revisions. If you are interested in reworking this piece, I think it could be ready for publication in our summer issue. Please let me know how you wish to proceed.

All the best,

Ben Hirsch
Senior Editor
Zoetrope

I sat stiffly on one of the meditation cushions. For a brief moment I forgot that Ms. McKenzie was me, it had been so many years since I'd been Kate McKenzie. I read and reread the e-mail five more times, and the words still didn't feel real. When I mailed that package I never expected an actual response.

I pinched myself hard on the thigh. I was awake. I was a little hungover, a little nauseated, but I was awake. It was true. Someone wanted to publish me. Not just someone, but *Zoetrope*.

I hit reply to respond. Then I closed the browser. I didn't know what to say.

I felt elated and petrified at the same time.

That one story, the one that showed promise, was the story of the couple whose marriage was crumbling, the ones who attended strangers' weddings.

Was I really comfortable putting something like that out into the world? It wasn't Karl and me. It was fiction.

Instead of writing to Ben Hirsch I began an e-mail to Karl. It was brief and filled with exhilaration. I gushed. I told him I loved him and missed him and wanted him to read what I had written.

I needed him to be proud of me. I craved his approval. When we got married, I knew he'd chosen me over all those girls he'd dated in his twenties and thirties because I challenged him, pushed him outside his comfort zone. I had lived a life before I met him. He once told me I was the smartest woman he'd been with, and to me, that was far greater praise than telling me I was beautiful. I was never going to be boring. But then things changed. I changed. Being published would make me interesting again, would show Karl that I still had my own life. But, most important, it would show him that I'd actually accomplished something while I was away.

Still, I regretted the e-mail the second I hit send. It was all wrong, tone-deaf and juvenile. Unfortunately, there was no getting it back.

I returned to Ben Hirsch's e-mail and opened the PDF. The page was filled with notes and scratch marks. Entire paragraphs were covered over with an X. Every word of praise from his e-mail disappeared from my mind. All I could see was my ravaged manuscript.

It was impossible. I couldn't do this. I was fucking stupid to think that I could.

Submitting anything to be edited is like removing your clothes in front of a stranger you desperately want to like you. I felt raw and exposed and completely out of my league.

I read the document over and over until the red of the changes became a murderous blur. I had to walk away from it.

By morning my trepidation at having to make so many edits had faded to slight unease and was even ready to give way to excitement. This was the kind of challenge I had wanted.

I bounded up the stairs filled with excitement and anticipation for the day. Sticky dew clung to the railings. I liked the way it felt on my fingers as I ran them along the smooth wood.

I didn't even bother with coffee before I opened my computer to see if Karl or Hirsch had responded.

I should have had the coffee.

The first e-mail in my in-box came from the law firm of Goldberg, Lynch, Aster. Instantly I knew. I couldn't bear to read it word for word; instead I let words and phrases come at me from the screen like I was being punched: "divorce" "custody" "deserted her children."

I pictured Karl sitting in a glass-walled law office overlooking downtown Manhattan on one side and the Empire State Building on the other. His mother may have been sitting next to him, her spine straight as a flagpole, her smile perfunctory and cold as she detailed how her son's wife had abandoned him and their children. I thought of how Karl must have felt when I didn't come home from California, and then when I didn't come home from Thailand. I thought of Karl begging me to come home the last time we spoke. I heard myself tell him no.

The facts would make me seem like a flake, a madwoman, an idiot, a middle-aged fool who'd gone on a walkabout, someone unfit to raise children.

I could hear Alyse say in her tight efficient voice: "She was always a little off. Different, you know. She's from Idaho."

Wisconsin, you bitch.

I stared at the screen, my mouth slack, my eyes dull. I heard blood pulsing at my temples. I reminded myself to breathe so that I didn't pass out.

I had deluded myself into thinking he'd never do it. But who was I kidding? I had been gone for almost six months.

Love can last indefinitely through space and time and a long separation. A marriage needed more. It required work, effort, and sacrifice from both parties to keep it alive. I thought about that Gabriel García Márquez quote about marriage: "The problem with marriage is that it ends every night after making love, and it must be rebuilt every morning before breakfast."

You had to be there if you wanted to rebuild it. I wasn't there.

I closed my e-mail as if I could make it go away. Floating geometric shapes from the screen saver danced from side to side, taunting me. I held my hand up away from me, staring at my ring, as I used to do a thousand times a day when Karl first proposed. And then my wedding band, which I hadn't taken off since the day we got married and I became Karl's wife. I was Karl's wife until just fifteen minutes ago, now I was something else. I was in limbo between two different lives. I felt paralyzed. I didn't know how to go back, and I was terrified of moving forward.

Go home. I said it again for the hundredth time. *It's time to go home.*

But now there was a new voice. *Do you have a home to go back to?*

Chapter Nine

I went straight back to bed and didn't get out for two days. I didn't need food, in fact the thought of it sickened me. Nausea kneaded my stomach into a hard knot. I stared at the ceiling while hot tears rolled down my cheeks. My body created a permanent imprint in the cheap foam mattress. I pushed the tattered quilt off my legs. Sweat dripped all over my body. For a brief moment I wondered if I'd come down with a fever, but I knew that wasn't the case. My body was simply reacting to the complete and utter destruction of my life. For the first time since I arrived I longed for the old comforts of home, my linen sheets and down pillows. My heart was heavy with shame. I clenched my fists and dug my nails into my palms hard enough to draw blood. I fought sleep as long as possible. It was a peace I didn't deserve.

Buppha knocked on my door the first night. I knew it was her because Buppha always clicked her tongue and shuffled her feet when she came to my door. There was no lock. She could have just walked in, but she must have heard the despair in my voice when I called out to her, "I'm sick. I need to be by myself, please," because she left without another word, though I knew she'd be back.

The next afternoon, Mia came, but she didn't leave when I yelled to go away. She walked right in and sidestepped around the piles of books I'd been using as furniture. Guests always came to the retreat center with leisurely reading material—historical novels, weighty biographies, lots of Pema Chödrön. They inevitably left the books behind to make room in their suitcases for teak elephants and silk pajamas. I especially enjoyed coming across a book published by Paradigm. I'd flip to the acknowledgments and beam with pride when I saw another author praise Karl for making their dreams come true.

I'd used one pile of books as a nightstand and another to hold coffee and a pitcher of water. A third held photographs of the girls I'd printed off my phone and framed in cheap plastic frames from the Chiang Mai market.

"Do you want to talk?" Mia sat on the bed and pushed my damp hair from my face. She didn't flinch at my puffy eyes or the tears coating my cheeks.

I didn't want to talk, but I didn't have much of a choice. I had to get the words out of me. Keeping them inside allowed them to fester. I spoke quietly, letting the tears come again. I had a hard time saying the word *divorce* out loud. No matter what had happened in my marriage, no matter how little Karl and I spoke or how tense things had grown between us, divorce was never the way I saw this ending.

I was so stupid. How could I have been so fucking stupid?

Mia scooched down onto the mattress, pulled my legs over her lap, and leaned her back against the wall like we were teenagers listening to CDs in my bedroom.

"I never told you about my divorce." Mia sighed when I was finished and closed her eyes. She gently massaged my ankle with her thumb and index finger. I was grateful for her kind touch.

I wanted to hear her story. It's one of the more true clichés that misery loves company. "You never told me. Derek mentioned it once."

She gave a low snort. "Derek has his own narrative about the end of my marriage. Men in Aussie are still so masculine. Even the good ones. My little brother can't wrap his head around the idea that maybe what happened wasn't so cut-and-dry. Maybe I wasn't the victim."

"What happened?" I asked quietly, my throat raw from the sobs.

"Tim and I met in college. We dated forever, all through med school, and then we got married the day after we graduated. It felt like the next step. I'd never been with anyone but him. He was the first guy I slept with. Hell, his was the only penis I'd ever seen. Everyone loved Tim. I told myself I'd be insane if I didn't love Tim too. He studied so long to be a pediatric surgeon, he was eager for our lives to finally settle down. He knew he could get a position in Sydney or Melbourne, or Adelaide. We both grew up on farms out in the bush and he wanted all of the nice trappings of a good life in the city, a fancy house with a garage and two cars. Maybe we'd join the country club. I wasn't ready. Maybe I'd never be ready for that kind of life. At that point we'd been together so long it seemed absurd that we hadn't already discussed these fundamental differences. We both assumed we wanted the same things without ever discussing it."

Her story reminded me that Karl and I *had* discussed the kind of life we wanted to lead after marriage and children. Looking back, I thought I had been honest. In hindsight, he was the one who had wanted something completely different.

Mia continued. "I wanted it to work. I agreed to start looking for jobs in Melbourne. It seemed a little more bohemian than stodgy Sydney. My condition was that we join Doctors Without Borders for a year first. 'When else in our lives will we be able to travel and do good in the world?' I said to Tim over and over again. 'Soon we'll have two kids and a tennis club membership and the best thing in our lives will be the Melbourne Cup.' He agreed, even though it frustrated him to have to put his life on hold. I even suggested we ask for different locations, thinking it could be exciting to have two separate adventures before we came back together and started the 'forever' part of our lives. The truth was, I just wasn't ready for that life . . . or to let him go. I felt like I was buying time. He went along with it. Tim was a marathon runner. He always trained for the long game.

"I went to Laos and he went to Somalia. I'd never left Australia at that point. I went straight from the farm to college to medical school. The things I saw in Laos, working with the poorest of the poor, terri-fied and shattered me, but making a difference in their lives, giving women birth control so they didn't have to be slaves to pregnancy, dressing the burns of a baby who had leaned too close to the fire, exhilarated me. I knew very quickly that I couldn't go live in a three-bedroom split-level and drive my Subaru and host a fish fry on Sunday nights for the ladies in my book club when I could be saving lives. I also learned during that year that I didn't need to be with Tim. He'd been a part of me since I was a child and I didn't know I could ever live without him. I was still too chickenshit to call things off. Thankfully he did it for me. When I told him I planned to re-up with DWB for another year he told me he needed to start his real life. During the last few months of his contract he had met another woman, an American ophthalmologist who wanted all those things he wanted. They were engaged within two months and married in six and now they have three little boys and a dog and a cat and a three-story Victorian in Coogee."

My body trembled as I saw the similarities to my own marriage. Mia's thirst for adventure was the end of her marriage. But there was more than that. There was the gap in expectations. There were the missing bits of information that we withheld in order to fall in love. I'd never lied to Karl. I'd lied to myself.

Until I met Karl, I never thought I would get married. I didn't think I wanted kids. But Karl changed everything I thought I'd wanted. I was so in love I was ready to toss out my old romantic notions of a nomadic solo existence. I allowed myself to be swept off my feet and domesticated like a wild mustang who walks right into a rancher's pen and asks for a saddle and harness. For more than ten years I allowed Karl to call the shots, to determine where we lived and how we lived. I became a person I hardly recognized. And where had it gotten me? I'd short-circuited. I'd run away and blown the entire thing up.

"Do you regret it?" I finally asked.

"Sometimes," she said honestly. "I traveled all over Asia, and for a while I held on to this fantasy that maybe I would meet another doctor too and maybe we would get married and have kids of our own. I thought I would have kids someday . . . and then I just didn't. I married the guy at the right time, but he wasn't the right guy. Then there are days I'm happy I don't have to go through so much of the pain mothers go through. I was selfish with my marriage. I don't know how selfless I could be as a mother. It's confusing."

"Are you happy?"

She drew in a breath. "I'm fulfilled. I'm content. Sometimes I'm happy. I know it's hard for most people to imagine, though. Even Derek, who loves me more than anyone on the planet. A lot of people look at me and see a woman in her late thirties without a husband or children and they think that I missed out on something. They think I must be a tragedy. They can't understand how I could possibly be happy."

I remembered how I looked at her ring finger when we first met, how I'd tried to make a snap judgment about her life based on whether she had a husband and children like me. "I don't think you're a tragedy," I said, propping myself up on an elbow.

"I don't think you're a tragedy either." Mia smiled at me. "I think you're going to be OK no matter what, but I know you can't see that now. Want a little bit of unsolicited advice, now that you've listened to my sad sob of a story?"

"I do."

"Come to the camp tomorrow morning. Keep doing your work. It helps puts things in perspective."

I nodded slowly. "I'll think about it."

"There's one other thing I know about divorce that could be helpful."

I cringed again at the word.

"It's a legal gray area when someone files for divorce and serves you over e-mail. Technically you need to know you are being served. I was the one who ended our marriage, but it was ultimately Tim who filed for the divorce. I was traveling when he did it and didn't know for three weeks. Until I responded there was nothing he could do to move the proceedings forward. My advice for you right now is to take a deep breath and take your time figuring out how to respond. You don't need to make all of the decisions right away."

It wasn't much, but it was a small relief. I'd been crafting responses to Karl in my head for the past forty-eight hours. I imagined e-mailing, calling, getting on the next flight. I imagined being angry and scream- ing and blaming him. I imagined hurling myself at his feet and beg- ging for forgiveness.

I'd hit pause on my life for so long. Now I felt paralyzed.

I didn't make it to the camp the next day, or the day after. I stayed in bed until I finally had to eat and drink.

Then I walked. I hiked for hours up and down the rolling hills.

I strayed from the path and walked until I knew I had to return or I'd be lost in the dark. I imagined getting lost and Karl getting news that I'd disappeared in the jungle, my body discovered weeks later by trekkers from Bhutan, Glasgow, or Indiana. It would become the top story on cable news networks that couldn't get enough of stories about missing white women. I'd be a martyr. Then Karl would have no choice but to love me forever. His new wife would speak of me only in hushed and reverential tones. They'd keep all my photos in the house. I'd haunt them.

However delicious the fantasy, I couldn't stay out there. For one, I was a little afraid of the dark. Also: the tigers. Rangers had spotted one just half a mile from the center the week before. He'd been much larger than they expected. For years the government had thought the tigers were nearing extinction in these forests, now they believed they were merely in hiding. They'd been chased farther and farther into the jungle by the massive development in the country and now they moved in the shadows. The rangers existed to protect the tigers, not me. No one would come to my aid if I screamed. I flinched as the monkeys leaped from branch to branch a few feet above my head. Even the rodents frightened me as they skittered behind my heels. I kept my small narrow Maglite dark in my pocket, afraid of what it would illuminate. I made my way back up the mountain to the center by the time the moon crested the horizon.

I lay awake most of the night. My defenses were shattered. I had to call Karl. I'd promise him anything. I'd beg him not to make any more decisions until we spoke in person. *Don't talk to the lawyers again. Let me explain myself. I love you. I need you. I need us. I can fix us.*

I decided to wait until the two hours between the time the girls went to bed and when Karl usually went to sleep. I got out of bed at seven in the morning and stared into the jungle for an hour. At eight I went up the stairs, where I knew I'd get the best reception.

I tried Karl's cell first. It went straight to voice mail. We kept a landline in our kitchen and his office. I tapped in the house number from memory.

In all the scenarios I'd run through, this was not what I expected — a woman answering my phone. She was out of breath, as if she'd run to catch it. Her hello contained a confident smile. Her voice was sweet and curious.

I didn't say anything.

"Hello?" she repeated, just as energetically.

I knew she could hear me breathing. Finally, I spoke. "Who's this?"

"I'm Lena."

Chapter Ten

I was speechless. Who was this woman?

"I'm the babysitter."

She sounded older than our usual sitters, who were in their late teens or twenties.

"Actually, I'm not the babysitter. I work at Paradigm. In marketing. But I'm the babysitter tonight. The regular sitter fell through. Karl should be home soon. Do you want to leave a message?"

"No message," I said in a near whisper, and hung up the phone.

I felt silly for jumping to conclusions, for imagining the woman behind the sweet and curious voice as a stand-in for me, an easy replacement. Did I really believe Karl would already have a new girlfriend living in our home, answering our landline?

Still, there was a stranger in my home, a babysitter I'd never met. I'd become completely disconnected from my children's lives in such a way that I no longer even knew who was taking care of them.

I needed to leave here. It was time to go home.

I began to make the arrangements. I looked up flights. I could fly from Chiang Mai to Bangkok to Hong Kong to New York or I could drive to Bangkok and fly from there. Which ticket I bought depended on transportation. I'd have to ask Kevin if he could drive me. Or I could hire a taxi. Of course, Kasem! I could call and see if he would be available to drive me to the airport. His words, the first advice I'd gotten from my very first friend here, had rattled around in my brain often since he left me here. It would be nice to tell him that I took them to heart.

I went in search of Kevin to find out if he could drive me, but neither he nor Buppha was anywhere to be found. I remembered Kevin was leading a laughter meditation session in the jungle for another few hours. For such a free spirit, he followed an incredibly predictable schedule.

I'd need to say good-bye to Mia. I grabbed the keys to Kevin's truck off the hook in the kitchen and drove down to New Beginnings.

At the camp gate I nodded a polite hello to the guards in their khaki uniforms and black berets. They knew me now. I was just a regular. I parked and walked to Mia's office, surprised to find her desk was empty and more cluttered than usual, as if she had left in a hurry.

I set about trying to find her, making my way down the dirt road, taking in the camp for what could be the last time. A group of women in their twenties played cards on an overturned cardboard box. One of them plucked the feathers from a recently killed rooster as she contemplated her next move. A breeze blew the smell of blood and death toward my nostrils. Flies buzzed hungrily around the carcass. An old woman dunked her family's laundry in a dirty plastic bucket. Her shriveled hands furiously wrung water from clothes. Behind her a younger woman, not more than fifteen years old, cradled a fragile newborn who wiggled and squeaked. The new mother looked up and met my eyes. Her expression was filled with a fiery intensity. Her taut muscles clenched as she held on to that baby with everything in her body. Life continued in the camps. Despite the hardship and suffering, it was miraculous and powerful. I remembered something my mom said to me once when my dad lost his job and she took on so many extra hours working as a nurse at the hospital that she hardly had time to eat or sleep. "Courage is grace under pressure, Katie," she said. "We discover who we truly are when things are the toughest."

I needed to be that pillar of strength for my own daughters. I didn't need to enroll them in the "right" junior yoga classes or make sure they had enough playdates with the children of the masters of the universe. It probably didn't matter if their eggs were GMO-free and organic and came from a chicken named Fred who lived an idyllic life in a cage-free coop on a roof in Brooklyn. What mattered was that I could show them what it meant to be a strong woman.

I stopped in front of Htet's hut. Faded rainbow prayer flags fluttered off the doorway. Her home was just a dusty platform raised a few feet off the ground and covered in a delicate straw roof. A narrow ladder led the way to the front door. I called out to her and got no response. Cho appeared the second time I called her mother's name.

"Kat," she shouted down at me with a wide gap-toothed smile. She'd never called me Kate, had always liked the sound of Kat better. Sometimes she meowed when she said it. "Ma in bed."

I began to turn away. "I'm sorry. I don't want to wake her up."

"Not asleep. Just in bed."

Something in the child's tone told me that I shouldn't walk away. I placed my hands on the sides of the ladder and looked up at Cho. "Can I come in?" She turned her head to glance behind her and whispered something in Burmese then waited for a response.

"Come."

I'd never been inside Htet's house, or in any of the houses in the refugee camp. It felt like an unspoken line that volunteers shouldn't cross. The three of them lived in a single room, not entirely unlike the one I stayed in at the retreat center. There was no clutter; the floor was swept clean. Small shelves held everything the family needed. Their few items of clothing were neatly folded and stacked alongside three plates, three forks and spoons, three bowls, and a single pan. A bucket in the corner held water for washing. A second was covered by a board, which I knew was used as a toilet. There were two mattresses, one for Htet and one for the girls. They each held a pillow and a quilt. Htet lay on one now, her face turned to the wall where I could see she had taped an old picture of a family of four. Chit's lanky body stretched long next to her. The little girl stroked her mother's fine hair with her delicate hands.

Cho wrapped her arms around my calves. "Mommy doesn't feel good." Tilly still did this to me when I walked in the front door after being out of the house for a couple of hours. She would open her mouth wide and make like she was devouring my leg, whether it was bare or in a pair of jeans, her sticky saliva dripping down me. Cho's grip was looser than my daughter's, less insistent. It was similar, but not the same. I think a dozen children could grip my leg in what they thought was a similar way and I would be able to pick out my own daughter's grip every time.

"Htet?" I said tentatively, feeling like an unwanted stranger, unsure whether I should stay.

The woman made a small groan as she rolled over.

I sat cross-legged on the floor next to the mattress.

"Are you OK? Can I get you something? Do you need a doctor? I can try to find Mia."

Htet shook her head. When she sat up I noticed dark circles beneath her eyes and a gash along the side of her head, still caked with dried blood.

I immediately went into mom mode. I couldn't help myself. "Chit, can you take your sister right outside the front door to play for a few minutes?"

Htet's eyes widened with terror at the idea of letting the girls out of her sight. "It's OK," I whispered. "I will be able to see them right outside the door. I won't let anything happen to them."

Once the girls were out of earshot I asked what had happened. Htet was hesitant, but I kept pushing. It was another woman in the camp who struck her. She thought Htet had stolen her food. She clubbed her on the side of her head with a hot pan. The rusty edge sliced through Htet's skin. The girls saw the whole thing.

I reached out and touched her skin right above the scar and leaned in to get a closer look, hoping it wasn't already infected. "Did you tell anyone?"

Htet shook her head. "I don't want anyone to think I'm causing trouble. We can't get kicked out. We have no money."

"But that woman attacked you."

Htet turned her frightened eyes on me. The whites had begun to turn a murky yellow. "It doesn't matter. I would still be seen as a troublemaker." She paused then and I let the reality of her statements sink in. This wasn't a world with a clear system of crime and punishment.

Her slight shoulders shook. "We need to leave here. It's not safe. I want us to have a home again. I need to find my husband."

I didn't need to tell her that leaving here now was a bad idea, that taking the girls back to Myanmar was a risk, that leaving them here alone made them even more vulnerable. I'd come to say good-bye, but that would only emphasize that I had a freedom she didn't, that I could get on a plane tomorrow and go back to my life while hers remained in limbo.

We sat in silence for five minutes. I listened to her rasping breath and rubbed circles on the small of her back. Finally, she looked right into my eyes.

"Can you help me find my husband, Kate?"

"We're trying. I can keep sending messages to your brother-in-law. I'll go now and send another one."

She shook her head, slowly at first and then faster.

"No."

"No?"

"No. Can you help me find my husband? Can you go across the border?" Her face was now set with a steely resolve, her jaw tight.

It was clear that this wasn't the first time she'd had this idea. "You can go. I cannot go. It isn't safe for me to leave my girls. But you can go. It would be easy for you to go." Her determination made her more beautiful. Her cheeks were flushed, her eyes shining.

"Please," she begged.

I didn't know what to say. Then she said out loud what we both knew was true.

"You are a rich white woman. You would be safe. You would just be another American tourist."

I looked out the door at Chit drawing a tic-tac-toe board for her little sister in the dirt. I blinked away thoughts of what would happen to those little girls if they grew up here. The situation in the camp got worse every day, and Mia told me weeks ago that funds from the UN and donations from nonprofits were being diverted to the kinds of refugees making headlines—Syria, North Africa. Most people didn't even know there was a refugee camp on the Thai-Myanmar border. When the funds ran low the food got sparse, the services slowed. When the septic tank overflowed and there weren't resources to fix it, people acted out, Mia explained once as she lamented the situation as a pile of tinder that could light up with the tiniest spark.

Htet would do anything for her girls. If she had to she would cross the border tomorrow and sell her own body for enough money to keep them safe and fed and out of harm's way. She'd allow the soldiers to slit open her throat if she thought it meant, for one second, that her daughters would have a better life without her.

I could say no. It would be so easy to apologize and tell Htet it would be too much for me. That it would be a dangerous journey for me too, even with all of my privilege. I could say that, and she might hate me for it, but I could leave and we would never see one another again. I would be just another person who had disappointed her. But that's not what I was going to say. I didn't want to say yes to be a hero. I wanted to say yes because it was the right thing to do. When you see someone who needs help, you help them. It could be the one good thing that came out of blowing up my life. I would do this for Htet and then go home to face the music.

The crisp confident voice that came out of my mouth didn't belong to the woman who had left New York with a single rolling suitcase for a fancy wedding in California. It didn't belong to the mother who slumped down on her kitchen floor, depressed and distraught at a family calendar that left her out. It didn't belong to the wife who lay awake staring at the ceiling, silently begging her husband to hear the words she was afraid to say.

"I'll do it."

I had to keep moving. Once I committed myself, I had to keep moving. If I stopped it would all be over. I'd find one of a million reasons why I couldn't cross the border to Myanmar to search for a total stranger.

I forced my mind to remain blank as I drove back up to the retreat center and walked down the stairs to my room. I threw my few belongings into my black suitcase. I didn't have much. For months I'd worn a rotation of three outfits and Buppha's sarongs. I'd gotten a little attached to forgetting about underwear. I wheeled the suitcase onto the boardwalk.

I'd need help. I didn't want to do this alone.

I knocked on Derek's door.

"We're going to Myanmar," I said by way of greeting. I quickly filled him in on what I'd promised Htet. Saying the words out loud made the entire situation seem more insane. To his credit, he didn't even blink.

"Let me get my passport."

Derek tried to help me with my suitcase as we made our way back up the stairs.

I batted him away and lifted the thing over my head the way I'd seen Buppha do when I first arrived. "I've got this," I said.

I was stronger than when I got here and the bag was easy for me to lift, but I didn't take into account that I was still something of a klutz. My toe caught on one of the last wooden planks and I wobbled. It was me or the suitcase. It fell from my hands and tumbled down the rickety stairs. The suitcase landed at the bottom on its side like a tipped-over turtle, fully intact save for one of the wheels, which had flown into the jungle.

"Well, that's a goner." Derek leaned over me as I attempted to salvage the bag. "I've got an extra duffel you can have."

He ran to his room to get the new bag. I repacked, and we carried on.

I should have been amazed that no one told me what I was doing was ridiculous, but I was among the kinds of people who didn't just talk about doing things. They actually did things.

We called Mia to get her take. She agreed that it was Htet's best chance to either find her husband or gain some kind of closure. "Sometimes it's a relief to be allowed to let go of hope," Mia said with wisdom gained from years on the front lines of the refugee crisis. "Sometimes the hope is just a noose that keeps you from living the rest of your life."

Kevin helped us organize our travel. It would be easiest to fly to Myanmar through Chiang Mai. Americans were no longer allowed to cross the Thai-Myanmar border on foot. Even with a guide, entry was only valid through one of the three international airports. The good news was that it took less than twenty-four hours to apply for a visa online. We got the process started before we left the retreat center.

"Do we have any idea where the hell in Myanmar we're going? It's a big country," Derek asked as we drove to Chiang Mai, a lopsided smile forming on his face.

"Well, we have an address for this man named Nanda, Htet's brother-in-law, in the city of Bagan. He's a taxi driver."

"Should we hire a guide once we're there?"

"Actually, we already have one."

I ended up trying Kasem again. This time he answered. I expected he would recommend a local guide in Bagan. Instead he insisted his girlfriend, Naw, accompany us. He was planning to stay home to be with their kids anyway. He swore she was the very best guide for tourists looking to go from Thailand to Myanmar and began to tick off her many awards and accolades. I told him he didn't have to convince me.

Naw wasn't what I was expecting when we met her in the lobby of a hotel close to the airport. Kasem was a small man, you might

even call him puny. His girlfriend, meanwhile, must have weighed at
least three hundred pounds. She had a black bowl cut and dimples
that puckered her round cheeks when she smiled. She ran through
everything we needed to know about the next few days of travel. Naw
would fly with us from Chiang Mai to Mandalay. We'd drive to Bagan
and track down Htet's brother-in-law and be back in Thailand in a
few days. From there I'd continue to Bangkok en route to New York.

The hotel was less than fifty bucks a night. I'd booked just one
room for Derek and me in an attempt to be as frugal as possible. I'd
stopped using my credit cards, the ones that belonged to both Karl
and me, after I bought my first plane ticket to Thailand.

I hadn't thought about it in years, the fact that Karl was the only
person in our house making any of the money. The independent
feminist version of myself in my twenties would have been horrified
to learn that the forty-year-old me had no income to speak of. I did
have a little money of my own. When my dad passed away, he'd left a
modest inheritance, including our childhood home, to my sister and
me. By then I didn't need the money, but I took my half and put it in a
small savings account in my name. It was mine and mine alone. Why
had I done that? Did I have a premonition, just a couple years into my
marriage, that at some point I'd need a safety net? I didn't think so. I
think the amount just seemed paltry compared to the accounts with
so many zeros under Karl's name. I didn't think my little savings mattered. At the time I thought I would maybe use the money to surprise
Karl with a trip. I had never imagined that I would one day use that
account to fund a life in Thailand or a journey across the Myanmar
border to search for a near-stranger's husband.

Once we settled into the hotel, I stayed in the shower for almost
an hour, turning the water as hot as it would go until my skin turned
a ruddy pink. I used an entire miniature bottle of conditioner in my
hair, rinsed it out, and then used another. I lathered my legs, from the
ankle up to my ass, in thick coconut-scented lotion.

I stared into the mirror at my naked body. My stomach, thighs, and butt were newly lean from walking everywhere and several bouts with what the locals called Thai Tummy, excruciating diarrhea every visitor gets at least once. My stomach wasn't exactly flat, but it was flatter than before. My breasts still resembled floppy pancakes. I used to love my boobs. I grabbed them now from below and lifted them back into place, pulling the skin on the sides tight toward my back. They really did used to be wonderful boobs, the kind men stared at through a tight white T-shirt, bright perky globes impervious to gravity. That was before they were ravaged by breast-feeding and pumping, before the nipples became elongated like an old cow's or a street dog past her prime. When I let them go they wilted unceremoniously back toward my stomach. Most women in our social circle had their breasts and stomachs taken care of after their last child. I knew a few who had it done on the same day as their scheduled C-section. They called it the triple-crown. If I'd stayed I probably would have gotten around to fixing things eventually. Now I stared at my limp breasts, strange nipples, my tributaries of fading stretch marks, and appreciated the work my body had done to birth and feed my children. My postpartum body repulsed me at first. Suddenly I was fiercely proud of it.

I emerged from the bathroom still rubbing my hair with a towel.

"Should we order room service? I'll pay for it?" Derek asked in a childish voice, as if he were asking his mother for an ice cream.

"Sure. I'm too tired to go out to get anything. What do they have?"

"We definitely need a cheeseburger and french fries."

He was right.

The cheeseburger came on a hard little bun with a shiny yellow square of melted American cheese, a soggy piece of iceberg lettuce, and a sweaty tomato. The ketchup was too sweet, the meat overcooked, and yet it was the best burger I had ever tasted. The room service burger reminded me of my second date with Karl. He'd flown back to Paris and booked a room at the George V off the Champs-Élysées. He was definitely trying to impress me. I tried to keep my cool as I carried my ratty overnight bag into the grand gilded entryway of the most expensive hotel in Paris. I'd googled the rooms and knew the flower arrangements alone cost more than my rent. Three bell-hops in adorably absurd outfits rushed to relieve me of my pack. They called me Madame Carmichael like I was already Karl's wife.

"Are you trying to tell me something?" I shot him a sly smile.

He blushed. "I'll tell them your last name. I'm sorry. I should have . . . already . . . done that."

I placed my hand on his arm. "It's OK. It's funny."

"Do you like the hotel?" he asked stiffly as we rode together in the elevator to the room.

"It's lovely. I come here all the time," I lied.

By then Karl and I had been e-mailing and texting for nearly a month, some short and sweet, others long and earnest about our lives and our families. We talked enough that it didn't seem strange to pack a backpack, leave my attic studio, and spend a weekend in a hotel across the city with him. We weren't children. I was about to turn thirty. It didn't seem crazy until we were in the elevator of a fancy hotel and he was frowning at me.

I could see the hurt in his eyes so I grabbed his hand then. "I'm just kidding." The smile returned to his face. It gave me a sharp thrill in my belly to have that power over him.

We got out of the elevator on the top floor. Once we reached our room, a suite with a balcony and magnificent views of the Eiffel Tower, I could no longer keep my cool.

"Jesus Christ. Does your publishing house put all the editors up like this?"

He shook his head and looked bashful again. "I paid for the room. I thought you would like it."

That was the first time I realized that Karl had money, real money, and that even though he was frugal and sensible by nature, he was also used to being surrounded by very nice things. At night, we lay naked on the floor of the balcony, watching the tower twinkle on the hour. Their room service menu had every delicacy from every corner of the globe, yet I chose to order burgers and fries. I wanted Karl to know that was the kind of girl I was, a girl with simple tastes. For a long time, those were the best burgers I had ever tasted.

I felt Derek's eyes on me as I ate and I purposely didn't turn to look at him. When I booked the room I didn't think twice about the close quarters, but sitting here, my hair still wet on my shoulders, wearing nothing but a thin terry cloth bathrobe, I wondered if perhaps I had given him the wrong impression.

"How does Zoe feel about this trip?" I tucked my legs beneath me. I could hear Derek inhale and think about what he wanted to tell me. He didn't have to. I knew.

"You didn't tell her you were coming, did you?"

He took a swig from an amber-colored bottle of beer and began fiddling with the remote control.

"When was the last time you talked to her?"

"I called her a few days ago. I told her I was coming back soon." Derek and I had that in common. We both kept telling the person we loved that we would be home soon. We both kept disappointing them.

"What did she say?"

"She told me not to bother and hung up the phone." He smiled a melancholy smile and folded his long arms across his chest. "She deserves better than me. Now I've buggered off on her twice."

"What are you going to do when you go back? Do you want to be with her?"

"She's the only girl I've ever wanted to be with. I'm just a stupid ass is all. I'd ask her to marry me tomorrow if I thought she'd say yes." Humility radiated out of him. Derek was one of the good ones. I had no doubt about that. Men in their twenties were still children. It was one of the reasons I always counted my blessings that I got Karl at thirty-five. He was fully cooked at that point.

He shrugged. "I'm doing a metric shitload of positive thinking. Part of me wishes we were keeping the farm. Then Zoe and I could run it together. She could take care of the animals. I could do the business.

I never wanted that before, but I think I want it now. I wish you could come see the farm before it's all gone. We'll be out of it by the end of the summer, but it's a place I think you'd love. It's beautiful in a different way from here. When the sun sets in the red desert it looks like the entire earth is about to ignite in a big ball of flames. Then you go to sleep and it's all still there in the morning, prettier than you remembered it."

"Where will your dad go?" I pictured an old man puttering around a big empty farmhouse, packing up his belongings to prepare to spend the rest of his days in a retirement community, one of the nice ones with tennis courts and uncomplicated yoga classes.

"He has a few irons in the fire. He can't sit still very long. I'm not worried about him. He'll be fine. Maybe he'll get laid a lot."

"Gross." I threw a pillow across the room at him, and it hit him in the side of the face with a comical thud.

Derek got up and went into the bathroom. I heard him brush his teeth and wash his face. When he came back it was clear he'd been thinking about something else.

"Maybe I do just need to suck it up and propose. It's going to take a grand gesture to get her back. How did Karl propose?"

Talking about Karl was painful now, but this was one of my favorite stories to tell, and I couldn't resist having a fresh audience for it. There was something so affirming about recounting your own happy memories to someone new. I glanced for a second at my bare ring finger, at the thin white line where my rings had been. I'd removed them both and left them with Mia for safekeeping before we left for Myanmar.

"He proposed in Paris."

"That's romantic." Derek's voice was becoming slow and hazy with sleep.

"It is. Do you want to hear the rest?"

"Of course I do."

"So, he proposed in Paris. I was living there at the time. I woke up one morning in my little apartment in the Marais. It was tiny. Picture the kind of apartment a kid straight out of college can afford and then cut it in half and take away the kitchen and add a bidet and that was my Paris apartment. I loved it even though I could reach the hot plate where I boiled coffee from my bed. I woke up because I heard a swift knock on my door and looked over to see a thin white envelope slip below the crack."

"What was it?"

"It was a riddle."

"Karl proposed with a riddle?"

"No. He proposed with a scavenger hunt. A literary scavenger hunt that took me all over Paris. It sent me to Oscar Wilde's grave, George Sand's adorable little cottage in Montmartre, and then to Dingo Bar, where Hemingway met Fitzgerald for the first time. There was a clue inside a copy of *From Paris to the Moon* at the American Library on rue du Général Camou. He even convinced a guard to let me climb under Marcel Proust's bed at Musée Carnavalet. At the end he was down on one knee in the very obvious Bar Hemingway at the Paris Ritz."

"It sounds like something out of a movie," Derek murmured with awe in his sweet young voice.

"It does," I agreed. "But movies usually have happy endings . . ." I let my voice fade into an awkward silence.

Had I said that on purpose to end the conversation? I wanted to explain everything—that I still loved Karl, that I couldn't imagine being with any man other than Karl, that I wanted to lock the two of us in a room and force us to say all of the things we'd been too exhausted to say to one another over the last few years.

Derek wanted more. "Why'd you leave him? He sounds like a great guy."

"You left Zoe," I reminded him, perhaps too quickly.

He wasn't about to let me off the hook. "Yes, but I'm young and stupid. And we aren't even engaged, much less married. And we don't have kids."

I didn't have the energy to explain what made me leave.

I was in a yoga class once back home that was being taught by a celebrity yogi. She had perfect hair, glossy lips, millions of Instagram followers, and her own line of moisture-wicking yoga bras. She wore a T-shirt that said MY HORMONES MADE ME DO IT. For the rest of the class I made a lengthy list of all the things I thought my hormones had made me do over the past twenty years. I'd never thought that *Run away from your family and live in a jungle hut* would be one of them.

"I think I'm having a midlife crisis," I said instead with a rueful laugh.

"Aren't you just supposed to buy a Ferrari and start shagging men half your age?" he asked.

"Why do you think you're here?" I laughed, then he tossed my pillow back to me, and I turned out the light. "Good night, Derek."

He scooted down beneath his own comforter and flicked on the television to an American cable news network. After months without a television I was startled by the brassy voice of a female anchor with too-pink lipstick and false eyelashes that resembled miniature Chinese fans. She cataloged the day of terrible news in a sharp staccato. A plane stuck on a tarmac for nine hours leads to a passenger revolt. Millions of Americans will be out of a job by next summer. Mother dies while saving daughter from stabbing. Man kills eight in mass shooting at mall in Minneapolis.

"It's hard to go back to reality," Derek remarked.

I unwrapped the foil on a bar of sea salt chocolate I bought in the hotel lobby and bit off the corner. "Turn it off and keep the world at bay just a little longer." I crawled deeper beneath the crisp white hotel sheets, which still smelled faintly of bleach, and put my cheek against the cool pillow. "We need to try to get some sleep. Who knows what tomorrow will bring."

Chapter Eleven

We gave Naw the aisle seat and I cringed for her when the thin young flight attendant with her hair in a perfect high bun fastened together with blue chopsticks brought her one of those seat belt extenders for extra-large people.

Naw must have seen me wince because she grabbed her belly roll with both hands and shook it up and down. "More of me to love." She laughed and the flight attendant laughed with her, and I felt silly for being embarrassed for her in the first place.

The flight was just over an hour, faster than the shuttle from New York to D.C. Derek fell asleep before we even took off. Now he snored next to me, his head dangling from his neck and a thin line of drool dripping onto his T-shirt. Naw finished an entire crossword puzzle in English and I scribbled in a notebook. I hadn't touched the story for *Zoetrope* since I'd gotten the e-mail from Karl's lawyers. I'd managed to conflate the two events in my head, souring the excitement and acceptance with dread and failure. I hadn't even responded to Ben Hirsch.

I cataloged things based on before and after I read the e-mail where my husband asked for a divorce. Ben Hirsch's kind note about my writing and the possibility that I could be a real writer was a Before. Htet asking me to find her husband—that was an After. Right now I could only focus on the things that came After. Before, I was a wife and mother, a woman with a family. After . . . what was I?

Everything that happened from the moment we landed in Mandalay felt like a dream, or something that happened to someone else, recounted to me in colorful detail. In hindsight it's hard to imagine it happened to me at all.

Pasty tourists swarmed the airport. "Dutch and German," Naw explained. "The Germans wear the packs around their middle. The Dutch are taller and better-looking. Neither of them smile much. You'll see some Americans. As soon as the junta relaxed its grip, the American tourists trickled in. They're loud and constantly on their phones."

Naw swiftly fetched our rental car. No one at the airport rental counter batted an eye as she flashed an official-looking tour-operator badge issued by the Thai government and approved by the Myanmar authorities. We pulled onto a modern toll road with sparse traffic and after about thirty minutes found our way into downtown Mandalay proper.

Child monks in crimson robes, their heads shaved nearly bald, strolled the streets next to men in neat suits talking on Bluetooth earpieces and women wearing American-style skinny jeans and tight sweaters. A line of nuns in bright pink caftans over saffron pants begged for food near a bus stop.

The neat grid of numbered roads surprised me.

"Most of the modern city was built after the British took over. They made it very orderly and proper," Naw said, wrinkling her nose at the word *proper* and the memory of colonial conquest. "The British love their rules. I once dated a British backpacker who folded my panties into little triangles for me while I slept." She rolled her large brown eyes with a smirk.

I thought of a semiautobiographical George Orwell essay I'd read back in college about the time he spent as a policeman in Burma during the waning years of the British Empire.

"Lower Burma, I was hated by large numbers of people—the only time in my life that I have been important enough for this to happen to me," Orwell wrote. He was just Eric Blair back then. He wouldn't acquire the pen name of George Orwell for a few more years. He was a scared kid looking for adventure in a place that should have killed him. In the essay, the narrator, probably Orwell himself, or at least a close facsimile, is required to kill a formerly tame elephant that went on a spontaneous rampage and killed a villager. The elephant's suffering at the narrator's hands is meant to symbolize the long and drawn-out suffering of the native people at the hands of the colonial government. Orwell wants the destitute villagers to like him, to see him as a sympathizer rather than as an invader, but his position and his white skin branded him a hated outsider. I recalled Orwell's quote often when I backpacked in poor countries in my twenties. I felt like a cheap voyeur, collecting mental images of poverty.

Now, here I was, trying to help Htet as an outsider thinking my privilege could save her. I wondered whether I was on a quest to shoot a proverbial elephant.

Naw snapped me out of my reverie. "I'm getting you a snack here in the city. We have another five hours or so to Bagan. We could also take a ferry, but that's double the time and the river's low right now and you can't afford to get stuck. But it's pretty when you have the time for it. You'll do it next time you come."

I didn't tell her there probably wouldn't be a next time. She expertly eased our car into a parking space between two rusty bike rickshaws.

We dined in a building that had the look of an old colonial ballroom with massive French doors that opened onto a stunning orchid garden. We shared platters of giant dumplings, sticky rice, and a paste of fermented fish. Naw ate the way the locals did by rolling the rice and paste into a small ball with her right hand and popping it straight into her mouth. I tried to imitate her, but the rice kept coming apart in my fingers. I surrendered to using a knife and fork.

The drive to Bagan was largely unremarkable. Ever the tour guide, Naw asked politely if we wanted to pull off to inspect a temple or two, but I declined. We were determined to meet Htet's brother-in-law before dark.

"I get it," she said as she waved her hand in the air. "You've seen one giant gold Buddha, you've seen them all."

I must have dozed because the next thing I remember the car was stopped on the side of empty road.

I rubbed my eyes. "What's going on?"

"Get out of the car. You've got to see this," Derek said.

I gazed through the windshield at a sweeping green plain dotted by squat leafy trees. Ornate red spires thrust through the low scrubby canopy. There had to be at least one hundred temples, inflamed by the late-afternoon sun. A herd of skinny white cows meandered in front of our car, urged along by a woman wearing loose clothes and a large straw hat to protect her from the sun.

Derek scrambled onto the roof of the vehicle to take at least seventy pictures.

"This place is un-fucking-believable," he said. "I've got to bring Zoe back here."

Talking about the girl the night before had loosened something in him. It's as if he had brought their relationship back to life by recounting their past. I would have liked to do the same with my marriage.

We had to stay focused on our mission. I grabbed Derek by the elbow and pulled him back into the car. "Come on, we've got to hurry if we're going to find Htet's brother-in-law before dark."

Twenty minues later we arrived at a dilapidated two-story apartment building about four kilometers outside of the ancient city, in an alley behind a low-priced hostel. The building appeared abandoned with its broken windows and graffiti-covered walls. It's peeling exterior may have once been a bright blue, but now it was closer to a dishwater gray. The only sign of life was a washing line strung from a second-story window hung with child-size T-shirts, jeans, and a stained white nightgown.

Inside, a heavy stench of decay and cigarette smoke soaked into the cement block walls and ragged wall-to-wall carpet. I tried to breathe through my mouth, which let the smells linger only on my tongue instead of inside my nostrils. A single fluorescent beam flickered like a strobe, sending ominous shadows across the walls and ceiling.

The stillness in the apartment building sent shivers up my spine. I heard a clanging at the end of the long dark hallway. My eyes traveled the length to see a hunched-over creature covered in rags dragging a metal cart that had lost a wheel. On closer inspection I saw the long face of an old man. He cursed and spat at his wretched cart and disappeared into a door at the start of the corridor.

"Let's ask that man if he knows the guy who lives in apartment 202," I said to Naw. I didn't want to stay in that hallway a second longer.

Naw's left eyebrow lifted in a skeptical arc that seemed to say, *I don't think the natives are going to be friendly,* even as she made her way toward the old man's door. She knocked once and received no answer. She knocked a second time and whispered something in Burmese to the closed door. As Naw raised her hand to bang a third time the man answered. From my place behind Naw's back I could see that the old man was probably completely blind. His cloudy eyes stared straight into Naw's ample middle and didn't blink. She grabbed his small wrinkled hand in her meaty palm and I saw her slip him some local currency as she continued to ask questions I couldn't understand.

After a quick back-and-forth their conversation came to an end. Naw bowed her head gently to the man who could not see her and let him shut his own door. She beckoned us to follow her back out into the street.

"He told me his neighbor isn't the kind of man we want to meet late at night. I took that to mean he's a nasty drunk. He is a taxi driver, like Htet said. So I think I know where we can find him. If we go there now we have a decent shot of catching him sober on the job."

I hugged Naw then. "We couldn't have done this without you."

She flashed a toothy smile. "No. It would have been a bad idea."

We got back into the rental car to make the drive into the ancient part of the city. From previous visits with tourists Naw knew that the taxi drivers hustled for their fares outside the Ananda Temple, a grand structure from the eleventh century.

"They need to hustle for fares. Since electric bikes came to town everyone gets around on their own. No one takes a car when they can pretend to ride a bike," Naw said.

We parked our own rental car just outside of Old Bagan and walked to the temple. I was unprepared for the sheer magnificence of the massive ancient structure topped by a glowing gold spire.

"My god," I whispered.

"Nothing else like it in the world. Enjoy it now before all these temples get overrun like the ones in Thailand. The ancient legend about this place is that a group of monks came here from what would today be called India and showed the king a vision of the most grand Himalayan temple that had ever been built. The king re-created the temple he saw in the vision. When it was finished he supposedly had all the architects killed so they could never make anything as beautiful ever again," Naw said. "Men are stupid like that. Greedy bastards, most of them."

She pulled a plastic container of sweet tamarind flakes from her pocket and offered them to me. I pinched a handful of the flakes between my thumb and index finger and let them dissolve on my tongue as I batted at the mosquitoes whirring peevishly around our heads.

"These mozzie bastards are worse here than in the swamps back home." Derek smacked the back of his neck with a dull thwack. "And it's way hotter than I thought here."

"You need water too." Naw bent at the waist to purchase a plastic bag of water from a boy who couldn't have been more than ten years old. He had three dozen of the Baggies, all tied with a tight knot in a dirty red cooler, the same kind my dad used to fill with Hamm's to drink at the beach. I know I looked helpless cradling the bag in my hands, like a little girl who had just won a goldfish at a carnival. Naw showed us how to drink, lifting it above her head and poking a hole in it with her car key so that the water dribbled into her mouth.

The three of us walked in a horizontal line to the temple. An agitated scrum of taxi drivers gathered just outside the entrance, pouncing on tourists as they exited the temple.

"Driver, driver."

"Tours for you."

"Lowest price in town."

"Those bikes aren't safe. You need driver."

"Do you see him?" Derek asked me as I squinted to look at each of them.

I tried to recall Nanda's features from his Facebook photos. He'd been wearing dark aviator glasses and a baseball cap. He could have been any of these men. I shook my head.

Naw approached the group with her swaying hips and air of authority and chatted up a tall reedy man with a mustache that dripped toward his lips. After a few moments she turned back to us.

"Nanda was here. We missed him. He just took a German couple back to their hotel in New Bagan. They think he'll be back in about fifteen minutes." She shrugged. "Do you want to see the temple?"

Derek could hardly contain his excitement. I paid the small entry fee for the three of us. I tried to conjure some enthusiasm as I flicked through a pamphlet written in English that explained the history of the temple. If I were here on any other day, I would have spent hours examining the intricate frescoes depicting the life of the Buddha and inspecting the ancient glazed terra-cotta tiles. Now I was too distracted to take it all in. For a minute or two I found myself absorbed by the beauty of the ancient place before remembering we were there to learn whether a man was alive or dead, news that would change my friend's life forever. Before fifteen minutes had passed I ushered our small group back out to the entrance. I didn't want to risk missing Nanda a second time.

Htet's brother-in-law hung on the edge of the scrum and chewed on the end of a fat cigar. His long greasy hair hung to his chin and a scar across his upper lip gave his mouth the impression of a perpetual sneer. "That's him," I whispered to Naw. Our rudimentary plan was to separate him from the group of men, to behave like a typical taxi fare, and ask him our questions once we were in his car. Naw negotiated with him for a minute before he separated from the pack and silently took the lead to his parked car.

The second I was in the back of Nanda's unmarked white car I felt the same unease that jangled my nerves in the man's apartment building. He took out a lighter in the shape of a naked woman mounting a hand grenade and relit his cigar. Once we were on the road for a few minutes Naw asked him a question from the front seat. He glared at her. I could see his eyes smolder in the rearview mirror. Without warning he slammed on the brakes so hard my head crashed into the back of his seat and ricocheted off the window.

"Get out," Nanda screamed in English. "Now." He spun around in his seat, his entire torso now in the backseat, and thrust the glowing cherry of the cigar just an inch from my eye. "Who are you?"

His body buzzed with fury and perhaps humiliation, shame that these tourists would have the gall to get into his car and interrogate him. "I'm no one," I whispered, choking on the cigar smoke rushing into my nostrils. "I'm no one."

"Calm down, man," Derek said; his normally calm drawl was frantic.

In the hot glow of the cigar I could see Nanda's other hand held a blade, a short fat piece of metal with a jagged edge.

Derek smacked the hand holding the knife away from my face. My fingers trembled as I tried to undo my seat belt and unlock the door. Nanda's foot must have hit the gas pedal then because we shot forward.

I was blinded by a flash of hot white light from headlights belonging to an oncoming car.

Time slowed. In my spotty vision I saw my girls' faces. Isabel, Matilda. They were just babies. Izzy, Tilly, I saw them turn into toddlers and then little girls. And then Karl. His mouth was set in a grim line, staring into the distance. His eyes flickered to meet mine. "What are you doing?" he mouthed. What was I doing? I'd finally crossed the line between adventurous and reckless. I could be killed. I might never see my girls again.

I heard the sick crunch of crumpling metal and the screech of shattered glass. Our vehicle spun like a top into the center of the road. My head slammed into the window again. I heard Naw screaming before everything faded to black.

Chapter Twelve

Karl. He was right there in front of me when I blinked my eyes open. He looked younger than I remembered, happier, well rested. His gray eyes twinkled as he gazed down at me. I smiled up at him, but the harsh fluorescent lights hurt my eyes. I tried to reach to touch his face, but I couldn't move my hand more than a few inches. An IV was buried in the soft flesh above my right wrist joint. My left arm was too heavy to lift.

"You're OK, baby," I heard my husband whisper as he reached down to touch my cheek. I turned slightly to rest the weight of my face in his palm. "You're going to be OK. You need to rest."

Everything, including my eyeballs, throbbed. My pulse quickened. How did I get here? Where exactly was here?

I could hear an angry monitor beeping and buzzing next to me, the sound fading in and out, along with voices that sounded far away. My eyelids felt so heavy, I couldn't keep them open. *Stay awake, Kate,* my own voice screamed in my head. I tried to conjure my most recent memory, but the pain in my head was too intense.

I wanted to see Karl's face again, but I couldn't bear the bright lights.

I tried to speak, but no sound came out. What I wanted to say, but couldn't, was "Forgive me."

I needed to sleep. We'd talk when I woke up. Everything was going to be OK. Karl was here and everything was going to be OK.

There was no sign of my husband the next time I opened my eyes. Instead I saw Derek, asleep on a blue plastic chair next to my small hospital bed. His snores were loud and gruff. Stiff white sheets were tucked tightly around my hips and abdomen. The rickety metal bars on the sides of the bed shook each time I shifted my weight and I worried the entire thing might collapse. Mercifully, someone had turned off the overhead light. From the soft yellow glow from the hallway lights I saw I was in a simple, but clean, hospital room.

I craned my sore neck to see if Karl was out in the corridor, but there was only a nurse talking in hushed tones to a short, solid man in army fatigues. His jacket was decorated with patches and badges and flags that signaled he was important. He carried a large gun and had the bearing and authority of military personnel. Slowly, the details came back to me. We were in a car crash. A man threatened me with a knife.

I remembered the girls' faces flashing before me in the car, that moment of sheer terror when I was sure I'd never see them again. The monitor next to my bed beeped louder as my breathing and heart rate grew more and more agitated.

I could feel rough bandages wrapped around my skull. I remembered seeing Karl's face. If he was here then I must have been here awhile, at least two days, maybe more. That's how long it would have taken him to fly from New York. I had no idea how long I'd been asleep or how injured I was. I gasped as I noticed my left arm was covered in a plaster cast from the wrist to the elbow. I checked the range of motion in my right wrist and arm. It seemed normal except for the twinge of pain from the fat IV. I wiggled my left foot, then my right. Thankfully, both legs seemed to be in working order.

"Derek." My voice came out in a raspy whisper.

"Derek," I said louder and more insistently, but not so loud as to bother the nurse and the man outside my door.

His whole body jerked when he opened his eyes. It seemed to take him a moment to remember where he was.

"You're awake!" He pulled his chair closer to the bed and grasped my uninjured hand. A low cry escaped my lips as his fingers jostled the IV needle. He pulled back and clasped his hands in front of him, clearly nervous he'd hurt me if he touched me again. "Thank god, you're awake. We've been so worried."

"What happened? Where are we? Where's Karl?"

"Karl?" He blinked once and shook his head, then glanced nervously at my angry heart rate monitor. "Karl, your husband?"

"Yeah. Karl my husband."

Derek fussed with my sheets, making sure they were tucked around me. "He's probably still in New York. I wanted to call him for you, but I didn't have a number. Your phone is dead. I couldn't go through it."

"No. He's here," I said. "I saw him. He was standing right where you're standing. It wasn't that long ago. He was right there." I sounded as desperate as I felt.

"He's definitely not here, Kate." Derek was certain. "You banged your head hard. The doctor says you have a concussion. Maybe you dreamed about him. I'm sorry. I know you want your husband to be here."

"No." My voice shook on the single syllable. "He was here." Even as the words came out of my mouth, I knew Derek was right. A wave of disappointment washed over me. I'd imagined Karl. I'd imagined his kind eyes, happy eyes, his gentle hands.

"He seemed so real." I let my skull sink back into the hard hospital pillow. Karl didn't even know I was in Myanmar.

Derek's brow furrowed with concern. I noticed for the first time that his left eye was black and purple. It was the only injury I could see.

"Is that a police officer in the hallway?"

"Yeah," Derek said, folding his hands in his lap like a schoolboy. "He's going to want to talk to you. We told him he couldn't until the doctor gave the OK."

"We?"

"Naw and I."

Of course. Naw. She'd been in the front seat of the car when we crashed. "Is she OK?"

"She's fine. I think she's getting a coffee. She's been here the whole time, bossing the nurses and doctors around."

"And what about Htet's brother-in-law?" I couldn't remember his name in that moment. Why couldn't I remember his name?

Derek kept his voice low. "He's in jail, Kate."

"For the knife?"

"That didn't help. But, no. The bloke was drunk when that other car hit us. His headlights were off. He drove into the other lane. He's damn lucky no one was seriously injured. You got the worst of it. The window shattered when you hit your head. You have a concussion. They think it's just a concussion. There's no MRI machine here. We should get you to a place where you can be properly checked. Your left wrist is broken from trying to brace against the impact. They don't think it's a bad break. It should heal pretty quickly."

"How long will Htet's brother-in-law be in jail?" It scared me that I still couldn't call up his name. "Why do the police want to talk to me?"

It suddenly dawned on me that I'd come into a foreign country to question a man about the whereabouts of a refugee I knew very little about. My disappointment at Karl not being there turned quickly to relief. The last thing I wanted was my husband to know how careless I'd been. I stared above me. A brown water stain formed a Rorschach blot on the popcorn ceiling.

"Don't worry, Kate. None of us are in trouble. They probably want to make sure you're not going to press charges. Americans love lawsuits. You sue McDonald's when your coffee isn't the perfect temperature," he tried to joke. "Close your eyes and get a little more rest and I'll go out to find Naw. She talked to the cop more than I did. They won't bother you if they think you're asleep."

I needed to know more, but sleep sounded delicious and inevitable.

"Just a few minutes," I whispered, my eyes already closed. "Just a few minutes."

The next time I woke, Naw was snoring gently in the chair next to my bed. She wore a dark teal velvet embroidered top that reminded me of my grandmother's couch back home in Wisconsin. I swiveled my head to the other side of the bed expecting Derek and released a cry of fear.

I stared directly into Nanda's intense black eyes. He was close enough to the bed that he could reach over and grab me, that he could finish what he'd started in the car.

"Help," I rasped. I struggled to sit up. The room was too small. I was too injured. I couldn't escape.

Naw startled awake. The man who tried to kill us continued to sit there, looking intently at me. My brain flashed back to the memory of the smoldering tip of his cigar, the glint of the knife.

"Kate, Kate . . . you are OK. You are OK." Naw's hands were on my shoulders, trying to press me back into the mattress. Nanda's eyes softened and he looked almost frightened.

"Kate, this is Naing. This is Naing. This is Htet's husband."

When I gasped for air a sharp pain assaulted my ribs, like something was broken. Naing? She said it again and then again. The insistent monitor beeped to remind me to try to stay calm. "You're alive?" As I looked at him again I noticed that his features were softer than his brother's. His hair was shorter. His clothes were worn but neat. Naw spoke to him in Burmese. Whatever she said made him smile and when he smiled he looked nothing like his brother.

"His English isn't so good," Naw explained. "But he wants to talk to you. He wants to hear about Htet and his girls."

"Where has he been?" I tried to focus on Naing and Naw at the same time so as not to cut him out of the conversation.

"He's been here," Naw said. She placed a hand on my good arm and gave it a strong squeeze. "He's been driving a taxi, same as his brother, and selling roasted nuts to tourists on the side of the road."

"But why hasn't he responded to any of Htet's letters? She thinks he's dead."

Naw spoke again in Burmese, her words getting faster, her hands gesticulating wildly, hugging her arms around her body at one point and rocking softly from side to side, perhaps to imitate an intimate hug. Naing hung his head and wept. Naw pulled him toward her and pushed his face into her massive breasts in an embrace. They stayed like that for a few minutes.

When she finally turned to me both their eyes were wet with tears.

"His brother never gave him any of Htet's letters. He didn't know how to get in touch with her. He knew he needed money if he wanted to go find her. He has been working and saving and paying his brother money for rent. His brother didn't want to give it up so he hid the letters from him and said he never heard from Htet."

"Does she know?" I was yelling. "Does she know now?"

Naw shook her head. "Not yet. Derek hasn't gotten through to Mia yet. But Naing is scared. He is ashamed. He is ashamed he didn't do more to find them. He is ashamed he gave up hope. He is worried she will not want him."

"No," I yelled. "No. That's not it at all. She wants you. She needs you." It wasn't lost on me that I felt the exact same way. I'd been gone too long. Too much time had passed. My family didn't want or need me anymore. But then I thought about Htet and how desperate she was just to have all of them together again, how it was slowly destroying her to have him gone. "You need to go home. Will you go home?"

Naw translated for me. I saw Naing's expression change. A flicker of something, maybe hope, crossed his eyes. I couldn't believe it—it was the happiest of endings. We found him. Naing was alive; Htet would get to reunite with the husband she worried she would never see again.

I collapsed back on the bed, exhausted and in pain, but it was all worth it to imagine Htet's reaction, how happy she would be to learn her prayers had been answered.

I finally felt like my time here had been worth it.

"Katharine?" A heavily accented voice said my name.

"Yes," I said without opening my eyes.

"I am Dr. Duwa. I want to speak to you about your condition."

"My wrist is broken," I said. "They told me. When can I go home?"

"Your wrist is broken. And two of your ribs are cracked. You also have a concussion, and I am concerned you could have some internal bleeding, but we do not have the resources to check. I would like to recommend that you be sent to a bigger hospital that can give you an MRI." His English was impeccable.

"I can do that back in New York. I am going home to New York." I opened my eyes. Dr. Duwa was a short, thin man with a small head, a wide nose, thick gray hair, and Coke-bottle eyeglasses. He wore a starched white doctor's coat and pants that were just an inch too long for his legs. His stethoscope was slung around his neck like a scarf. He looked down at a clipboard in his hands.

I continued. "If you can give me my chart and the results of any tests you've taken here I'll check into a hospital as soon as I get home," I said. "Where's my purse? Did someone get my purse out of the car? I have my insurance card. Let me give you my insurance card."

"Katharine." The doctor paused after each of the syllables in my name in a way that let me know he was about to tell me something I didn't want to hear. "A nineteen-hour plane ride is not a good idea for you in your condition. I am worried about possible swelling in your brain. That swelling could be made worse by a prolonged change in pressure."

My heart raced and my stomach lurched.

"I have to go home." Panic crept into my voice.

The doctor shook his head and scratched his left eye with a long bony finger. "Perhaps if it were a shorter flight or if you could go directly. I am most concerned about the takeoff and the landings. From here to New York there would be at least two, maybe three flights. And one of them would be long, almost twenty hours. I cannot tell you what to do. I hope maybe you will listen to your husband. I have been talking to him."

How could this doctor have gotten in touch with my husband when Derek couldn't? "No! You talked to my husband? You talked to Karl?"

Confusion crossed the doctor's face. "I talked to Dirk." He looked out into the hallway, and I knew he meant Derek.

"Derek isn't my husband." My voice rose by several octaves and I realized I sounded like a madwoman. "My husband is Karl."

He cleared his throat. "I talked to the man who is with you. I am not saying there is no risk, but there is much less of a risk with a single, shorter flight. He said that he could take you to Darwin, Australia. You can drive to the airport from here and take one plane. There is a good hospital there, a modern hospital with excellent doctors. They can check you. It is still not ideal, but it would be better. Less risk."

Now that I'd had the chance to see the room, I could tell that it was more of a clinic than a proper hospital. He was right. I couldn't stay here. I could see Derek just outside the door, his expression sheepish, like a hound dog caught chewing his master's shoe.

My head ached beneath the bandage. Whatever pain pills they'd given me had worn off. I thanked the doctor. It was useless to argue with him. I caught Derek's eye and gave him a pleasant smile I hoped would soothe his nerves and persuade him to help me make a plan that would get me back to New York.

"Come back in," I called out.

The doctor, clearly still confused about my relationship with this much younger man, averted his eyes in disapproval but quietly left to give us privacy.

Derek spoke quickly, nervously. He kneaded my sheet with his hands, arching and flexing his knuckles. The sound of them cracking was surprisingly more pleasant than the indignant beep of the monitors. "I had to say I was your husband, Kate," Derek explained in a rapid staccato. "Or they weren't going to let me stay overnight and we didn't want to leave you alone."

"And Australia? You want to take me to Australia. Was that part of the ruse too?"

His features hardened. "No. I was serious about that. You can't fly around the world by yourself right now. Come home with me. I've already checked with Mia, and she agrees with this doctor. My sister is the most badass woman I know, and if she thinks it's risky to let you go all the way back to the States right now, I believe her. You can talk to her if you want. We can call her right now. My uncle Bob is a doctor at Darwin Private Hospital. He'll get you to the right people who can check you out properly. You can heal and then you can travel back to the other side of the world. You don't want to go back like this."

It made sense, even though I didn't want to admit it. What if I got on the plane to New York by myself and something in my brain burst? What if I just passed out with no one to care for me? My wrist was broken. My ribs were cracked. I could hardly lift a finger, much less carry a bag. I would need help to get anywhere.

Then there was the other option. I could call Karl and tell him what happened. I could beg him to come here to get me, to take care of me, to nurse me back to health. He'd have to say yes. He'd have to forget everything that happened between us. He'd have to get on the plane.

No. I couldn't do that.

I didn't want him to know that I'd put myself in danger, that I'd been irresponsible and reckless.

"I need more medication," I whispered to Derek. "I hurt. Everything hurts."

He grabbed my hand. His palm was warm and surprisingly soft, his fingers almost dainty like a young girl's.

"Think about it. Come home with me. We'll take care of you. You'll get strong and then you can go home and face all your demons in fighting shape."

A nurse walked in then and plunged a syringe filled with clear liquid into my IV. Her eyes narrowed when she saw me, and I imagined her eavesdropping and thinking I was a nasty American causing lots of trouble for lots of people.

"Morphine," she said matter-of-factly. I tried to say thank you but she turned away from me and made a sound like a grunt as she exited the room.

"They aren't shy about giving you the good stuff here." I mustered a smile at Derek as the meds hit my bloodstream.

"We've got even better drugs in Aussie. I promise you. Come on, Kate. Say yes and you can have everything checked out properly within twenty-four hours. You can be in a real hospital with real medication and real doctors."

"This looks pretty real to me." My words were beginning to slur.

"This isn't a real hospital. They only built it to fix bumps and bruises for tourists who fall off their bikes."

"Are you sure you're not just trying to lure me to Australia to try to set me up with your frail old widower dad?" I suddenly thought this was incredibly funny and began to laugh, which caused my ribs to ache.

Derek smiled, but he didn't laugh with me. In fact, his expression got twisted and strange just as I mentioned his father. He stroked my head as my eyes began to close.

"I'm not certain you're his type."

Chapter Thirteen

The phone rang at two in the morning.

At first it didn't wake me. I thought I was dreaming, but when I opened my eyes I saw the screen beaming in my dark room.

KARL—OFFICE

It was my old phone, my iPhone, the one I'd brought with me from New York, the one that had ceased to properly work in Thailand. It worked here. I didn't remember turning it on. Derek must have done it for me.

I managed to grab the phone off the nightstand and place it on the bed next to me. I poked at the speakerphone button. I didn't have the dexterity to get it to my ear.

"Hello," I spoke loudly down to the phone.

"Kate." Karl's voice sounded so clear he could have been standing next to me. "Kate, what's going on? Are you all right? The insurance company called. They said there was a car crash in Myanmar."

Dammit. The insurance card. Of course someone had called the house.

"What the hell were you doing in Myanmar? They said concussion, cracked ribs, internal bleeding. I've been trying to get ahold of you for two days. I called the embassy in Thailand. I called that retreat center. I talked to an old woman named Buppy, but she wouldn't tell me anything. I nearly lost my mind. How could she not tell me what happened to my own wife?"

Those three words. *My own wife*. They brought on an intense surge of love for this man. Hearing his voice was all I had wanted since I woke up in that hospital. I didn't want him to worry. I wanted to come back to him stronger than when I left, not like this, not broken.

I realized then that Karl and I hadn't spoken since the e-mail from his lawyer. I swallowed twice and hoped my voice sounded normal.

"It sounds worse than it is. I'm fine. I promise I'm fine. I went to Myanmar to help a friend . . . it was part of the aid work I've been doing. I was in a small car accident, but I'm OK. I didn't know the insurance company would call you. I never thought they'd call you. I didn't want to worry you. Do the girls know?"

I heard a rustling sound behind him and I tried to think about the time difference, but the calculations made my head hurt.

"No, no. I didn't want to upset them. Where are you now? This phone is working again? I tried the other one, but it didn't work. I've been leaving voice mails."

My husband was the only person on the planet who still left voice mails, and in this moment I loved him for it.

I was embarrassed and a little ashamed to admit I was somewhere new, an entirely new continent, in fact. "I'm in Australia. In the Northern Territory. They had to get me to a better hospital to run tests. Mia, one of the doctors I worked with at the refugee camp, knew people here. The doctor in Myanmar didn't think it was safe for me to travel all the way back to New York alone."

The line was silent. I could hear his inhales and exhales. He sounded as nervous as I felt. I found that slightly comforting.

"That's good. I'm glad you went somewhere they could take care of you."

I wanted to tell him that I needed him here to take care of me, that I had planned to fly home to New York before we got hit by that car. I wanted to tell him that we didn't need to get a divorce, that we could work things out, that we could start all over again if he would just give me a chance.

But, that's not what I said.

"The doctors here say they don't want me to travel a long distance for about a month. My concussion was worse than they originally thought. The broken ribs make moving around painful, and my wrist is in a cast." My voice faltered. "I'm falling apart."

"Kate—" He stopped.

"Karl—"

"There's something I need to tell you."

There's something I need to tell you too, I thought. *I love you. I miss you. I'm ready to come home.*

"I'm . . ." Karl started. "No. Now isn't the right time for this kind of conversation."

What had he been about to say to me? Was it "I'm sorry" or "I'm still in love with you"?

Then he said the last thing I expected him to stay. "You should stay as long as you need to get well. We can discuss everything when you're in better shape."

My voice cracked. "I know we have a lot to talk about."

"Stop. Your health is the most important thing right now. I can have Dr. Sullivan speak to your doctors there." Dr. Sullivan was our family's concierge doctor. We'd been with him for the past decade. He'd seen me through three pregnancies, two births, and a breast cancer scare. I was suddenly grateful for him and the money we had to keep someone like him on call. As much as I'd spent the past months feeling like an overprivileged ass, that privilege was nice when it could save your life. "He'll make sure they have all your old records and charts." Karl was often at his best when making a plan or managing a project. I once watched him organize an entire funeral for his great-aunt Betsy while stuck in traffic on the Long Island Expressway. But I didn't want to be managed. I wanted to be loved. I couldn't bring myself to puncture our polite discussion with my messy emotions. For the next five minutes I acquiesced to giving him the names of the doctors I'd seen in Darwin. We scheduled a time for me to talk to the girls the following day. "Don't worry about them," Karl said. "I told them you were going to be just fine."

"Karl—" I began again.

"Not now, Kate," he said softly. "Just get better. We'll be here when you're well."

I should have had a difficult time falling asleep after the call, but the pain medication wouldn't accommodate panicked insomnia. I fell asleep with the phone still at my ear and didn't wake up again until almost noon the next day. If I dreamed, I didn't remember it.

Derek had been right; the Darwin Private Hospital was indeed quite proper, with its teams of specialists, its slick technology, and its pomegranate and kale salads for lunch. The doctors had told me they could discharge me the next day. Derek had already gone ahead to his farm. Mia was flying in and would take me there. She promised it coincided with a leave she'd already planned. She was required to take four weeks off at least once a year. Mia explained that it was designed to make sure the directors of refugee camps didn't go stir-crazy, or fully native.

"Our farm is the perfect place to recuperate and rest. Stress will make a head injury worse. I promise you," she said. "Derek will be there and my dad will probably just ignore you the entire time. You'll go home better than when you left. Wasn't that always the plan?"

I did want to be in better shape than I was in now, especially when I saw the girls. I could hardly even lift my own phone. I napped like a baby every couple of hours and got dizzy if I stood up for too long. This was hardly an ideal time to reunite with my husband and children and figure out what our future looked like. Once again, I needed more time.

The next morning I was still groggy as the nurse wheeled me to the hospital's exit. "We're driving to your ranch in this?" I raised a hand to shield my eyes from the sun as Mia waited for me, leaning languidly against a dusty yellow taxi. My heart lifted seeing my friend standing outside the hospital. It seemed impossible that we'd known one another for only a few months. I felt like I'd known her my entire life.

She crossed the space between us, gave me a strong hug that was careful to avoid my ribs, and threw my duffel bag into the trunk before returning to help me out of the wheelchair. I hadn't been in a wheelchair since I was released from the hospital after the last time I gave birth. Karl had thought it was hilarious that Lenox Hill forced me to be in a wheelchair until the second we left their property and jogged in front of Tilly and me, videotaping our slow journey down the hospital corridors and onto Seventy-Seventh Street. I still had that video somewhere on my phone. My purple-faced newborn screamed the entire way. I could hear Isabel laugh at her little sister from her perch on her father's shoulders.

Mia fussed over me and insisted I lean on her while getting into the taxi.

"I'm so happy they're releasing you. I talked to your doctors. You're going to be fine. You just need some rest. How do you feel?"

The truth was I still felt shattered and weak.

"Much better," I said, and conjured a smile. "It's so good to see you."

"We're going to the bush airport," Mia said as the driver started the ignition. My friend wore a baggy white tank top. A red bandanna flopped lazily around her ponytail.

"I thought we were an hour's ride away?"

"We are. In a prop plane. This is the Northern Territory. Nothing is drivable."

I moved my hand up to my head.

"We don't fly that high, so no need to worry about the pressure. Does it hurt much?" Mia asked, shifting seamlessly from friend to medical professional.

"I need to take another pill in about fifteen minutes."

"We'll have you in bed in just over an hour."

I slumped down in the seat and let my head fall onto the ledge of her shoulder.

Darwin was a small city, and it felt like we were on the outskirts of it in no time at all. It was lush and more tropical than I expected. Soon enough we were on a single lane of asphalt. I wanted to ask if I would see a kangaroo hopping alongside the road, but I worried that would sound ridiculous. Then again, I never thought I'd be in the middle of an elephant traffic jam in a Thai jungle.

"They sure put the airport far outside the city."

"We aren't going to the airport." We turned down a red dirt path, dust billowing up to the windows.

The taxi stopped at a long metal hangar. A few dirty planes were parked in front.

"Get as close to that yellow one as you can. I don't want my friend to have to walk far," Mia instructed the driver. He continued driving the extra ten yards through the dirt.

Mia pulled out our bags and paid the driver. She let me hold on to her as I pulled myself to stand, and then Mia slung an arm around my hip to keep me steady.

"Your chariot, madam." She pointed to the two-passenger plane.

"Where's the pilot?"

Mia grinned. "You're looking at her."

I shouldn't have been surprised that Mia was a licensed bush pilot, and a damn good one at that. She expertly maneuvered her yellow Piper Cub off the ground in less than thirty seconds. I closed my eyes on takeoff and must have dozed because thirty minutes later I looked down to see nothing but deep red earth.

"Wow." I breathed in. "I've never seen anything like this."

I realized Mia couldn't hear me from the pilot's seat so I leaned back and let myself enjoy the view.

I saw Mia make a commotion in front of me. I realized she was gesturing for me to look down below the plane. I shifted my weight slowly to avoid any twinges of pain and craned my neck a little. We weren't too far off the ground. What I saw made me laugh out loud like a delighted child. Dozens of tawny kangaroos were moving directly under the plane, hopping around our small shadow. I saw Mia look back at me in her mirror. I gave her a wide smile and a thumbs-up.

As promised we landed less than an hour later on a narrow strip of cement surrounded by nothing but dirt and a blue pickup truck.

"Not much farther now." Mia helped me out of the plane. I leaned into her wiry frame for support the entire walk from the plane to the truck and realized for the tenth time that day that I never would have been able to travel back to New York by myself. It was the broken ribs that crippled me more than anything else. Most standing positions made me feel as though a hot knife were slicing me through my middle.

"It looks like *The Thorn Birds*," I murmured.

Mia threw her head back and laughed. "Book or movie?"

"Both."

"Richard Chamberlain didn't too it for me. Chamberlain seemed like a wet blanket . . . and you know . . . a pedophile."

"You're wrong. But then, I did love him when I was a little girl and way too young to be watching it."

"Grown women want someone who can throw them over their shoulder and carry them off to bed and spank them."

"Was your ex-husband like that?"

"Not in the least." Mia laughed again and pulled a Toblerone bar out of her backpack and handed it to me. "He was a Chamberlain."

I ripped open the candy bar and savored the sweet chocolate as I sighed long and low and took in the scenery. It reminded me a little of Zion National Park in Utah, with its grand red cliffs falling off into long swaths of desert. Karl and I went to a wedding close to Zion right after I came back to the States. We camped overnight in the park in a tiny two-person tent and hiked the entire Observation Point trail in a single afternoon. On the way back down, Karl pulled me into a crevice in the canyon just big enough for two bodies. He pressed my body against the hard rock wall and pushed himself into me right then and there. I hadn't thought about that day in ten years. I smiled at the memory.

"So Karl called," I said to Mia. I proceeded to tell her everything. By the time I'd finished, the sun had sunk closer to the horizon, turning the soft red earth a blazing orange.

She listened to me recount the entire phone call before saying anything in response. "What do you want to happen when you go back?" Mia asked.

It was a relevant and reasonable question, but it still made my pulse quicken. I *was* going home. The doctors had said it would be safe for me to fly in just a couple of weeks. I had officially run out of runway, it was time to end this interminable adventure. But it was very surreal—the day you knew was coming but still aren't prepared for. Yes, I was beyond excited to see my girls, but everything else—Karl, my friends, his mother—that was all more complicated. I still needed to figure out exactly what I did want to happen, and how much of it would be within my control. I ran away from my life in order to clarify what I wanted out of the next half of it, and I felt fueled by that clarity: I wanted more meaning. I wanted time to write. I wanted authentic friendships. I wanted to feel a real connection with my husband.

I had changed on this trip, fundamentally, for the better, but I had to remember that my life back home had stayed largely the same and that I was going to have to navigate a minefield of judgment and hurt feelings. Still, I was determined to keep this perspective when I went back and to live a life that I wasn't just proud of but that I enjoyed. I didn't give a damn that I was starting to think like an inspirational Pinterest meme.

"I want Karl to see how much this trip has changed me, how happy it's made me. I want to be with my family without losing myself again. I want to be happy."

Mia grinned at me and reached over to put her hand on my leg. "I'm happy that I'm a part of your journey. It makes me feel good that I could do anything to help. But what about the writing? What happened with that story you submitted to that literary magazine? Is it getting published?"

I hadn't written back to Ben Hirsch. Being published in *Zoetrope* seemed insignificant once I got the e-mail from Karl's lawyer and set out to help Htet. But now I had more time and I was determined to do as much writing as possible before I went home.

"They asked me to revise one of the stories. If they like the new version, they may publish it in the fall."

"Yahooooo!" Mia took both her hands off the steering wheel and threw them over her head in a V, her palms smacking the roof of the truck. I quickly grabbed the wheel to keep us on the road.

"That's incredible. That's something to be happy about," she said, grinning madly as she retook the wheel and gave it a hard slap for emphasis.

"I know." It was something to be happy about. I'd worked hard and I deserved it. I vowed then to respond to Hirsch as soon as I could get to a computer. I might not be able to do much for the next few weeks, but I could still write.

Five different times Mia stopped at rustic fences made of wood and barbed wire, stepped out to swing open a gate, drove the car through, and then stopped to close it. I offered to help, but she dismissed me. "You're a cripple," she said.

I finally spotted a faint light in the darkness about a half mile down the road. We passed beneath a wooden arch with a hanging shingle that announced the name of the property: BAHLOO STATION.

Mia paused for a moment and stared up at the sign. "My mom named this place. Bahloo. It's an old folktale. It might have started with the native folk. My mom's dad was part aboriginal. Bahloo was the name of the moon. He wasn't really a god, not the way my mom told it, at least. He was really more like the man in the moon." Mia's eyes began to tear up. I placed my fingers on top of hers on the steering wheel. "She always told us that Bahloo was looking out for us. Sometimes she told us he was checking up on us and he knew when we did something bad. We grew up convinced the moon was spying on us."

"I think I would have liked your mom," I said.

"Oh, everyone liked her. That was just one of a thousand stories she used to tell."

Mia put the car back into gear and drove below the arch to the house.

"Dad and Derek are probably still out with the herd. There's a cottage out back for you. It was Mom's studio. She did watercolors back there. There's a bathroom and the most comfortable bed in the world and a minifridge, and you never have to leave if you don't want to. You hungry?"

I nodded and let Mia carry my bag. I took in the lovely three-story Victorian farmhouse with a grand wraparound porch. The inside was neat and well loved. The walls of the entrance hallway were covered in photographs in mismatched frames of Derek and Mia and another boy with blond hair and Derek's eyes.

"That's Jack. He's in between Derek and me. He lives in Bondi, right on the beach, works at a bank. Makes a gazillion dollars and loves talking about it."

I searched for pictures of Mia's parents, but there only seemed to be photos of the children. I wondered if I would keep walls like these in our homes once my girls were grown and out of the house. Finally, I spied one wedding photo, but both the bride and groom were facing away from the camera, gazing off into the red desert, the sun setting in front of them. It was clear that Mia had inherited her perfect supermodel frame from her mother. The wedding dress was an ivory color, soiled by maroon dust along the train. It had a low sweetheart back. The groom's hand fit perfectly into the curve of her hip. I saw nothing of him except his sturdy build, wide shoulders, and thick dark hair that curled just below his ears.

"How old were your parents when they got married?" I asked Mia.

"Practically fetuses. Both eighteen. Straight out of high school. My mom was up the duff, but you can't tell in that picture. It's why she isn't facing the camera. If she turned around you'd see me in her belly." I did the math in my head. That made Mia's dad about fifty-six, much younger than I had expected.

Mia stared at the photo for a moment, and I could tell she was remembering her mother again by the quiet smile that lingered on her lips. I took her hand and gave it a squeeze to let her know I appreciated the picture as much as she did.

"Your mother is beautiful in that photo. Does Jack have kids?"

"Nope. My poor mum and pop—three grown kids and no grand-kids. Broke my mom's heart. Jack will at some point, though, once he stops dating teenagers. It's not too late for him. His ovaries haven't shriveled up and died."

"Stop it." I whacked her on the arm. "Your ovaries haven't shriveled up and died."

She gave me a nudge and pushed me farther down the hall to the kitchen. "Well, no, but they are on life support. I'm in half meno-pause, or early meno, according to my gyno. I'm lucky I haven't grown a mustache yet. The upside is I bleed only once every six months, which is handy in the jungle. So, what can I make you? I can bet you there are eggs and some cheese and some rib eye in the fridge and that's about it. So it's really an omelet or a steak. We don't worry too much about cholesterol here."

"A steak seems like a lot of trouble."

She shook her head and pulled a steak the size of my head out of the refrigerator along with an entire stick of butter. "You're on a cattle farm. I can fry you a steak in ten minutes."

Headlights beamed in through the short red-and-white-checked curtains covering the kitchen windows.

"Steak it is." It was easy to make myself at home. I began opening creaky old cabinets looking for a glass to fill with water to take my pain meds when I heard the front door open.

"Well look what the cat dragged in," I heard a man's deep voice call out to Mia as I found a tall pint glass. When I turned to meet her and Derek's dad the glass slipped from my hand and shattered on the kitchen tiles.

Standing in front of me, kicking mud from the sides of his boots, a lit cigarette still dangling from the edge of his lips, was one of the most handsome men I'd ever seen in my entire life.

Chapter Fourteen

If you'd asked me a year ago if an Australian version of the Marlboro Man with a two-day beard and dirt under his fingernails was my type, I would have laughed in your face.

But Dusty Williams is probably most women's type, even women, like me, who have long claimed they cared more about a man's intellect, sense of humor, and sensitive side than his muscles or his wide, strong hands.

Where had I gotten the idea that Mia and Derek's father was a little old man? I knew he was a rancher who still rode out with his herd every day. Yet when I heard the word *dad* spoken by someone my age, I pictured my own suburban father in the later years of his life, his gray hair mostly gone from his head and now growing out of his nose, snoring in a recliner when he wasn't complaining about his arthritis. My own dad was only a few years older than Dusty when he died, but the difference between the two of them was night and day.

I only looked away from the door when Mia plunked my steak on the table and flashed me a knowing smile that said, *He gets that a lot.*

I kneeled on the floor to hide my embarrassment, picking up the big shards of glass and placing them in my napkin. Mia stooped down with a handheld broom and dustbin to sweep up the tiny pieces. She gave my backside a smack to indicate I should get back in my chair and eat the steak before it got cold. She looked up at her father, who seemed amused to see us scrambling on the floor.

"I'm making steak. Want one? Where's Derek?"

"He's chasing Mikey. That *bogan* ran off again and got mixed in with the sheep when we lost the light. Throw one on for me."

"Mikey's the dog," Mia offered by way of explanation. "And this is my dad, Oliver. But everyone calls him Dusty. Even me . . . because he's never been a big fan of proper showers."

"Your friend made it." Dusty walked across the room and placed his massive palm on the top of my head and ruffled my hair like I was a five-year-old. "Derek and Mia have been bringing home strays since they were knee-high." Like a child I tried to wriggle from his grasp.

"I'm Kate." I stood with a wince and offered my hand instead.

He wiped his own palms off on his dirty Levi's, and gripped my hand. When he released it he ran his fingers through his thick salt-and-pepper hair. It was shorter, but still curled at the edges the way it had in his wedding photo from four decades earlier.

"Good to have you. It's nice to have the kids running around."

I'm a forty-year-old woman, I wanted to tell him. *I have two children of my own.* But I realized it would do no good. I was a friend to his children and therefore, to Dusty, I was a child myself.

"Did Mia show you the cottage? It ain't much, but you should be comfortable back there. Derek told me you got banged up. Two of you got attacked in Burma? I told him not to go pissing around up there. Adele and me went there when the junta was still on. I bought her a slab of jade the size of my foot, but we nearly got shot trying to get it out of the country."

I laughed too loud at his story. *Get ahold of yourself, Kate,* I thought. *He's just a guy, just Mia and Derek's dad.* I yawned and stretched my arms over my head, forgetting about my injured ribs. I let out a yawp like a cat whose tail has been trampled.

"Oh, honey." Mia moved to help me. "You've had a really long day." She looked at her dad. "It's been a lot of traveling. By the way, I think we need to check the engine on the Cub. It was making a noise I didn't love when we came in for the landing. And we need to clear the brush off the airstrip."

Dusty let out a long and low sigh. "There's a lot that needs to get done out here, but it won't be my job after this summer. We'll be fine until then. Why don't both you girls get some sleep. I can fix my own steak and something for Derek." He reached out to wrap his arms around Mia in a tight hug and gently kissed her on the top of her head the way I'd seen Karl do hundreds of times to our own girls. "I love you, monkey butt. I'm happy you're home."

I didn't wake up until close to noon the next day. My broken body craved sleep, and Mia had pulled down the shades for me to keep me from waking with the sun. The room was small but sweet, with white brick walls and a cozy daybed. Mia left me her old laptop and logged me onto the house Wi-Fi. After so long in my little Thai tree house, this felt like a five-star luxury hotel. It even had an en suite bathroom with hot water.

The first thing I did after getting out of bed was turn on that computer and e-mail Ben Hirsch from *Zoetrope*. I apologized for the delay and blamed an extended trip out of the country. That wasn't a lie, not entirely. His positive response was brief, but came quickly enough that I was able to convince myself he was still interested in my story. I wrote for four hours that first day and rested for the remaining twenty. Each day continued like that for an entire week. For dinner I joined Mia, Derek, and Dusty around the old wooden kitchen table and listened to them tell family stories I knew they'd told one another dozens of times before, including the time Mia brought home a baby dingo who'd lost his leg after it was caught in a barbed wire fence. They named him Tripod and he lived in the house for the next ten years.

I wrote and revised and revised and wrote and finally I had something I thought might just be worthy of publication. The pride that came over me when I hit send on that manuscript gave me an intense high, unlike anything I'd ever experienced. I knew it was good.

I couldn't wait to tell Karl. He'd been diligent about checking in on my recovery, mostly over text message, but I hadn't kept him updated on my writing. Now, I was ready to tell him.

I wanted to start my e-mail to him with something a little less personal. I knew that one of his top authors, Ellen Bloom, had a book coming out this month. Her novels always came out just in time for summer. They were endless tomes about recently divorced women finding love when they least expect it with someone adorably working-class — a plumber, carpenter, or policeman in a small beach town. If I remembered correctly this year it was the pizza guy in Montauk.

I googled Paradigm to check for a review, thinking it could be a nice thing to start my e-mail with.

But the most recent story about Paradigm had nothing to do with books.

Publishing Honcho Hooks Up with Heiress

I slammed the laptop so hard I worried I shattered the screen. It was the last thing I expected to see, and yet it also explained why Karl hadn't objected to my coming to Australia, to me staying away even longer, why he actually seemed happy when I spoke to him on the phone. Karl had moved on.

I slowly opened the screen again and began to read. My heart thumped harder and harder until I finally placed my hand over my breast, as if to keep it inside my body.

The newly single head of Paradigm Publishing, Karl Carmichael, stepped out on the red carpet for the movie version of last year's number one bestselling thriller, The Woman Under the Stairs, *with the beautiful and brilliant heiress to the international Hoxton hotel chain. Daphne Sarraf, twenty-seven, is an Oxford-educated PhD in evidence-based health care currently working for the World Health Organization. Her family's net worth is estimated to be just over one billion. Carmichael is a mature departure for Sarraf, who split last summer from Jake Wellsley, the lead singer for the indie rock band The Drags.*

A close friend of Sarraf revealed to Page Six that she and the publishing magnate have been canoodling for several months. Carmichael is currently estranged from his wife, Katharine, the mother of his two children.

Too many questions filled my brain. Did Karl know this story was being published, or worse, was it planted in the newspaper by the Paradigm public relations department in an effort to drive sales for *The Woman Under the Stairs*? Karl would never do that on his own, but I wouldn't put it past Donna, their Machiavellian head of marketing. And then there was this girl. And that's what I would call her from then on, the girl. I couldn't bear to say her name. Daphne was too pretty, too sweet, too perfect. And why couldn't she be less perfect? Why couldn't my husband's rebound be a cocktail waitress with a lisp and an unfortunate back tattoo? Why did she have to be beautiful, brilliant, and worst of all—a good person? I suppressed the urge to call Karl. What would that accomplish? And besides, it was the middle of the night and there might just be a gorgeous naked body lying next to him, her elegant toes touching his the way mine used to in the middle of the night. I gasped out loud then. Had she met my daughters? Did she sleep in my bed?

I wanted to crawl into my own bed and never get back out, but I could hear Mia rustling around in the main house, and I'd promised her I'd come for a drive with her today to check the perimeter of the property for broken fences.

I pulled a discarded pair of pants off the floor and looked at myself in the mirror. I liked this new woman staring back at me, the woman who'd finally started to pursue her passions again, who woke her brain back up, who was beginning to understand what she wanted out of the rest of her life. She was stronger, more confident, more sure of herself—*happier*.

But could this new version of Kate Carmichael compete with Daphne Sarraf?

Chapter Fifteen

Just as I felt myself at my very lowest, an e-mail arrived that changed everything.

I read it over and over. I read it quietly to myself. I read it out loud to Mia and Derek so many times I knew they were sick of hearing it, but they smiled through each subsequent recitation.

It wasn't an e-mail from Karl. It was from Ben Hirsch. The editor of *Zoetrope* wrote me back and told me that my revisions were perfect. He planned to run the story a few months from now. I was going to be a published writer. They'd pay me $300 for it. But that wasn't the part I kept reading. I recited his praise over and over:

> You have a rare talent for capturing a playful irony that is incredibly difficult for many writers to articulate. Your interplay with time and memory manages to stir emotions in the reader in surprising and exciting ways. Reading this piece has been a pleasure and I hope to hear more from you.

He wanted to hear more from me. I was a real talent. Screw Daphne.

After getting Ben's e-mail and learning about Daphne I was that much more motivated to make the most of my remaining time here.

Each morning I sat down at an antique writing desk pushed up against a window that overlooked the vast plain for as far as the eye could see. Mia told me the wooden desk belonged to her mother's mother, an outback poet whose work was still taught in Australian high schools. I was in such a zone of creative flow; within a week I had polished the first hundred pages of my novel I never thought I would write.

Mia read through the burgeoning novel during her final days at the ranch. She leaned back in her chair in the kitchen and kicked her dusty bare feet up on the table, pages in one hand, a heaping glass of wine in the other. I took a mental snapshot of her there. It was how I'd always remember her. We promised to see one another again soon. She'd come to New York. I'd try to bring the girls to Thailand. I hoped we'd keep those promises, but I knew better than anyone how life could get in the way. I was just grateful to have had this time with her. I'd been starved for meaningful friendships, and I'd gotten more than I ever could have wished for.

"You're so fucking good, Kate. No matter what happens with this. No matter what happens with your marriage, please always remember that," she said when she'd finished.

"I will," I promised, and meant it.

"Don't worry. I'll remind you," she said. "You won't be getting rid of me."

I helped Mia pack all of the things from the house she wanted to keep. We dismantled the gallery wall of photos in the hallway and carefully wrapped each picture in newspaper. We sent some to Jack and put some in boxes for Derek and Dusty.

Throughout the entire process, Mia hadn't shed a tear until we began going through her mother's paintings in the back cottage. She ran her finger over the soft pastels on a small canvas, no bigger than a children's picture book. Mia's mother painted a solemn silver moon in the corner. It's quiet light illuminated a small girl with fiery red hair lying on a boulder in the middle of the darkness.

"It's Bahloo and me," she whispered. "I haven't seen this one in years. It used to hang over my bed. Bahloo was always watching over me."

I stroked her hair and let her tears fall into her lap. "She's still watching over you," I said. "Bahloo and your mom. A mother never stops watching out for her children, even when she's separated from them." I knew this was true.

Mia nodded and wiped her tears away. "I know." She paused and began to wrap the painting in tissue paper. "She'd be happy we were leaving. She never wanted to spend her entire life here. She always thought the two of them would sell it one day and start a whole new kind of life. There just wasn't enough time.

"Oh! That reminds me. I almost forgot!" She reached into her back pocket and pulled out a tiny envelope. "Are you ready to take them back?"

I opened the lip of the small beige package and shook it into my hand. My rings. They were heavier than I remembered. The light from the window caught on the diamond as I blinked back a tear. I stared at them for a long time before I handed them to her. "Can you sell them?" I asked.

Her eyes widened.

"For Htet. And her family. I want you to sell them and give the money to Htet. She needs it more than I need these."

"Are you sure?" Mia asked.

I nodded. "I'm not sure about a lot of things, but I'm sure about this."

Before I knew it Mia was back in Thailand and Derek was spending most nights with Zoe. I'd met the girl about a half dozen times. In the beginning, when we first returned to the farm, I could sense her skepticism, her need for distance, her fear that Derek would leave her again. But he quickly proved himself slavishly devoted to her, and I knew it was only a matter of time before he ended up proposing. I liked her a lot. She was in many ways the opposite of Derek, quiet, reflective, and serious. I could tell that she offered a healthy counterbalance to his sometimes heedless freewheeling spirit.

Dusty and I orbited one another politely, like he was a landlord and I was a tenant. My habits changed. My recovery had demanded so much rest that I switched from being a night owl to going to bed soon after the sun set. I was often asleep by the time Dusty got in from the fields. He was attempting to castrate more than a thousand bulls before the sale and was intent that every inch of the farm be in perfect working order before he left.

"My dad would never want anyone thinking he sold them a bad bill of goods," Derek said, half complaining about all the work they were investing in something that would soon belong to someone else.

Derek was also good about replenishing the groceries, since it was the kind of thing Dusty apparently never remembered to do. "He's the kind of man who needs a woman," Zoe explained about Dusty one day. "He went straight from living with his mother to living with Derek's mom. I've watched him since I was a little girl. He's a man who doesn't know how to take care of himself."

So I was surprised one night when I wandered into the main house to fix myself a quick sandwich to find Dusty at the stove stirring something in a Dutch oven that smelled like heaven.

"I was just about to come out to get you." He smiled at me as I stood in the door. He wore clean jeans, a wrinkled blue oxford, and no shoes. He'd shaved. It was the first time I saw his face without a layer of stubble. Without the beard I noticed a friendly dimple in the center of his chin.

"Barefoot in the kitchen?" I smiled back at him, suddenly self-conscious of my unwashed hair, sweatpants, and ratty tank top.

"But not pregnant." He chuckled at my joke. "I'm making a cassoulet. It's almost finished. The key is to soak the beans the night before and to use pork shoulder in addition to bacon, but you need to let it get so tender it slides right off the bone. The secret to a good cassoulet is patience. If you don't give it time you can ruin everything."

My mouth must have hung open in surprise.

"What? You didn't think I could cook? My kids think I can't, but I know my way around a kitchen. I loved cooking for Adele, baking too. I just used to do it after we fed the little bastards franks and beans and put them to bed." He pulled a chair out from the kitchen table. "Sit down. Want a glass of wine?"

I nodded, still slightly in shock.

"Red or white? I think Australian whites are shit, but our Shiraz is some of the best in the world."

"I'll never say no to a good Shiraz."

"My kind of woman."

I felt my neck grow hot at his compliment.

"So, Kate, tell me more about yourself. I know you're a writer. You sit and stare out that window most days. Mia tells me you're going to write the Great American Novel."

I took a sip of the wine. He was right. It was one of the better reds I'd ever tasted. "Even talking about the Great American Novel makes me nauseated," I said honestly. "I just want to finish a novel. If it gets published, that would be a dream."

Dusty put the dish back into the oven, set the timer, and poured himself a generous glass of wine.

"It's funny how we lower our expectations as we get older, huh? I once thought I'd own the biggest, most profitable ranch in the Northern Territory. Now I'd be happy if I didn't have to sell out to the man just to keep it alive." He lifted his glass and clinked it against hers. "Cheers to us."

"Cheers to us," I agreed.

"What will you do after the sale is finished? Where will you go?" I asked him.

"That's a good question. The kids want me to travel, a regular old walkabout around the world. There will be enough money to live on when I turn over the land, probably for the rest of my life and some to leave behind. Jack asked me if I want to come live in Sydney, but he didn't mean it. He doesn't want an old man cramping his style, and besides, I don't know what I'd do, being around that many people all the time. I guess I could take up surfing."

The timer dinged on the oven. I rose to grab plates and begin setting the table while Dusty prepared the food. A comfortable silence settled between us, as if we'd been doing this, preparing dinner together, for years.

"This is the best cassoulet I've ever had," I said, and meant it. Cassoulet, I knew from experience, *was* an easy dish to ruin. I'd ruined plenty when I had tried to replicate a version I served when I was a waitress in Paris. These beans turned to butter in my mouth. The liquid was rich and hearty and warmed my entire body like a familiar hug. "I used to order this all the time when I lived in Paris."

"You lived in Paris?"

From there I filled Dusty in on my life before I took a break from my life. We talked about Paris and leaving Paris. How I met Karl and fell head over heels in a way I had never even thought was possible. He told me about Adele and how her unexpected pregnancy changed both their lives when they were still just babies themselves.

"We took a road trip as a honeymoon. She was five months along then. The second trimester was good for traveling. She had this sweet tummy, but none of the sickness of the early days. We took my dad's old camper van and drove from here to Ayers Rock. You could still climb it back then, and damned if Adele didn't beat me up to the top. It feels like you can see the whole world from the top of that rock. It makes you understand why it's so sacred. Then we went on down to Adelaide and over to Bells Beach and Melbourne and then up to Sydney and Brisbane. We snorkeled on the reef and then we drove home. A whole month, it took us. You know we hadn't been dating that long when she got pregnant. It was that trip where we really fell in love."

"That's incredible," I said. "Karl and I traveled before the girls and then a little when Izzy was born, but traveling with two seemed impossible."

Dusty nodded. "We didn't do much once Mia came." He paused, lost in thought. We both brought the final slurps of the soupy stew to our mouths. I closed my eyes to savor the last bite.

I was so lost in my thoughts, I was almost startled when Dusty spoke again. "Adele and I didn't have the perfect marriage. It's hard when you're that young. You're not fully formed humans yet. But then, I don't know if we would have done better if we'd been twenty-seven instead of eighteen. I know her eye wandered sometimes. I wasn't a damn saint. We fought like cats and dogs. If I had a dollar for every plate she threw at my damn head I wouldn't be selling this place now. But in the end I think we did OK. We did that trip again just a few months before she passed."

"The same road trip?" I asked.

"The same one. Different van. This one was all-modern. It had all her medical equipment in it. I did all of the driving this time. Instead of climbing the rock we slept in its shadow. But otherwise we took the exact same path. We camped in the same sites. We told all our old stories and we fell in love again, right before the end."

I didn't realize I was crying until Dusty passed me a napkin.

"It's not a sad story," he said, though I could see the tears start to pool in his own eyes. "We had a happy ending."

"She sounds like an amazing woman. You must miss her."

He finished his glass of wine in one long sip. "Every day. But we got to say our good-byes. She wanted me to live a good life when she was gone. Now I need to figure out what that life looks like. It ain't easy starting all over again."

"No." I shook my head. "No, it isn't."

Dusty stood and stretched his hand out to me. "I want to show you something. How are those ribs feeling?"

"Better. Much better, actually. I hardly notice them." When I took his hand to stand I felt a tingle of electricity run up my spine.

"Let's go for a ride. Grab yourself a sweater."

"I don't have anything that warm."

"No sweat, I'll get you one of mine."

He disappeared upstairs and returned with a man's heavy cardigan and another bottle of wine. He grabbed our wineglasses and held them by their stems in one hand.

I pulled the sweater around me. It smelled like old wool, tobacco, and something sweet, sweat mixed with dirt.

"Let's go."

Mikey, their spry old sheepdog, tried to jump in the back of the truck, but Dusty shooed him back into the house. The mutt barked at the windows as Dusty climbed behind the wheel and poured me a glass of wine for the drive.

"Where are we going?"

"You'll see. Patience is a virtue, Kate. In cassoulet and life." He sipped on his own glass of wine as he drove and I wondered for a second what would happen if we were pulled over. I'd had enough of dealing with the police in foreign countries. Then I remembered we were driving on Dusty's land and following his rules. I relaxed and let myself enjoy the wine as I stared into the ink-stained night.

"It's a new moon," Dusty commented, and smiled at me out the side of his mouth. I realized only then that Dusty was flirting with me. I allowed myself to enjoy it.

After all, Karl had moved on. Remembering Karl's new relationship made my entire body tense. I finished my glass of wine and squeezed my eyes shut to force the memory away.

I took in all of Dusty then, his rugged profile, the taut muscles of his shoulders straining against his shirt. He hadn't bothered with a sweater or jacket and I imagined he didn't need one. I stared at his hands on the wheel and thought about, just for a second, what they would feel like on my body. I was glad the dark could hide the blush that took over my cheeks.

We stopped every mile for Dusty to get out and unlatch a gate and finally began to climb up a steep ridge I didn't know existed. He parked the car at the top and hurried around the back to open my door like a gentleman.

We walked another thirty yards up the remainder of the hill, side-stepping the low desert shrubs. At some point Dusty reached down and grabbed my hand, as if it were the most natural thing in the world. I gave his fingers a squeeze to let him know I was happy he did. I knew how to do this. It was like riding a bike. It all came back to you if you'd only let it.

Finally, we came upon a large boulder all on its own that rose out of the earth as if it had been placed there specifically by some super-natural force. I squinted at the shape of it and imagined what it would look like if there were a full moon in the sky. It was the boulder from Adele's painting, the one of Bahloo looking over a young Mia. I was touched and a little apprehensive that Dusty would bring me to such a special place.

Before I could think any more about it, Dusty placed his hands on my waist.

"Will this hurt?" he asked in a low voice. "If I lift you up?"

I shook my head. He gently placed me on the rock as though I weighed nothing at all. I marveled at the smooth, flat surface, polished by years of winds and sands whipping across the highest point for miles. Dusty placed the wine and the glasses beside me and leaped up in one fluid motion.

"Best seat in the whole territory," he whispered, and lay down on the rock.

I lay beside him.

"It sure is."

There were more stars than I'd ever seen. Dusty pointed out the constellations unique to the southern hemisphere. The Southern Cross I knew, but I'd never heard of Vela or Carina.

"Vela means 'sails of the ship' in Latin," Dusty explained. "It was part of a larger constellation of the ship that Jason and the Argonauts used to search for the golden fleece."

"I see where Derek got his love of astronomy," I said.

Dusty nestled his arm beneath my shoulder so that I could place my head on his chest. My skull fit perfectly into the space just below his collarbone.

"Maybe I'll go back to school," he said in a voice dreamy from wine. "Get my own PhD."

"It's a good idea."

"It's something."

I don't know how long we lay like that. I listened to his heart echo in his chest and let my breathing match his. I might have fallen asleep. Dusty gave me a nudge.

"Kate?"

I tipped my head to his, certain he would kiss me and equally certain I would let him.

"We need to move. We need to go fast. A storm's rolling in."

I swiveled my head behind us and saw a mass of gray thunderheads cloaking the stars.

"We don't want to be caught out here. We'll be safe in the car."

He helped me off the boulder and this time I felt too much pressure on my injured rib. I let out a low yowl, which Dusty couldn't hear over the whipping wind.

"The storms come fast out here. I should have checked the radar." He pulled me behind him toward the truck.

"We can outrun her. Come on!"

He sped us down the ridge and back toward the house. I felt the wind rock the cab of the truck. Lightning struck something on the horizon behind us and lit the sky a terrifying purple. The crack of thunder was deafening. I held on to the dash for dear life. We'd abandoned our wine in our haste to flee the storm. We reached the house in less than half the time it had taken us to get out to the rock. The rain came down in sharp sheets, cutting into my skin, and I was soaked in the short distance between the driveway and the front door.

I squatted, shivering, next to the fire still burning in the living room. Dusty crouched next to me and tossed a new log onto the flames. He swiveled on his heel to face me and began to peel the sweater away from my quivering shoulders.

"You'll warm up faster if you take this off."

His breath was warm and hot against my cheek. I didn't say anything as I shrugged the sweater to the ground. He placed his palms against each of my cheeks and drew my face to his. I let myself melt into his kiss. My lips parted. His tongue found mine. We fell back onto the floor in front of the fire.

His body was broader and more solid than Karl's, his hands rougher, his lips chapped in a way Karl's never were. I felt a quickening of my pulse and an urgency to keep going. The wine had gone to my head, making me slightly dizzy. I found myself trying to remember what was supposed to come next.

We fumbled, a tangle of limbs that didn't know where to go. Dusty bit down on my lip too hard and I winced. I tried to throw my leg over his hip and kneed him straight in the groin. He recoiled, grunted, and fell away from me.

"Let's try this again." We both leaned in for another kiss and knocked noses. My ribs began to ache. I suddenly felt nauseated from the car ride and the wine and the smoke from the fire.

When I opened my eyes I realized that Dusty has collapsed against the base of the sofa with his hands covering his face.

"Are you OK?"

He swiped at his eyes, embarrassed that I'd noticed his tears. The light from the flames glinted off his wedding ring. He still hadn't taken it off. "You must think I'm an incredible pussy."

I shouldn't have laughed, but I did. And it turned out that was the right thing to do, because then Dusty laughed with me, and soon we couldn't stop laughing. Just like that the moment passed and it's like we both knew how ill-advised a tryst was; our hearts weren't in it. We opened another bottle of wine and continued to dry off by the fire.

"It used to be so easy with Adele." He shook his head. "I knew what to do. Not in the beginning, of course. In the beginning, we were kids. But after we got it all working it really worked."

I noticed my wineglass was empty and took a swig out of the bottle instead of pouring more. I rarely let myself get drunk, but this felt like the right occasion to have too much to drink. "I know what you mean. How quickly could you make her come?"

If he was taken aback by my question he didn't show it.

"Five minutes," he said with pride.

"Yeah. Karl could do it for me in less than two. I used to listen to other women talk about how they missed the kind of sex that went on for hours and hours and sometimes that's nice, don't get me wrong. But there's something to be said for efficiency too, for knowing how to get a job done."

"Cheers to that, my girl." A cloud passed over Dusty's face as he finished off the rest of the bottle. "Maybe I just won't find anyone new. Maybe I've passed my expiry date."

I wanted to invite him to come to New York, where I knew about a dozen single, beautiful, and brilliant women just past their fortieth birthday who were convinced they'd passed their expiry date who would gladly help him get back in the saddle, or climb into his saddle.

"You're not going to have any problem once you're ready."

He lay down on his side and propped himself up on his elbow. His cheeks were rusty and his expression loose from the wine. "What about you, Kate?"

"What about me?" I said, even though I knew what he was asking.

"Are you going to move on?"

I didn't tell him that the entire time we were fumbling around, lips touching, tongues touching, all I could think about was Karl. I thought about how Karl kissed, slow at first, like a butterfly landing on your lips, and then hard and fast, like a starving man desperate to be satiated. I thought about how Karl knew exactly where to touch me to make me aroused, the unusual places like the inside of my thigh and the skin just above my nipple. I didn't want to move on. I wanted my husband.

I thought then too about Dusty and Adele retracing the path where they fell in love. They'd put in such effort to make it happen before the end came. They had refused to let fate decide the path of their final days. They made plans. They took action. Maybe that was the answer. I needed to take action, to take control of my life and my marriage. I needed to make a plan.

If Karl and I could retrace our own path to falling in love, maybe we could start all over again.

In the moment, I knew just what I was going to do.

Dear Karl,

I dreamed about you last night. I dreamed about what you did the first night I didn't come home from Thailand. I saw you wake up and touch my side of the bed and stare at the ceiling with such an intense sadness in your eyes that when I woke up my own eyes were damp.

I have no way to know if this is what happened. We never talked about it.

I know you've moved on. I discovered it in the worst way possible. I saw a gossip item about your new relationship and a picture of you with Daphne. Seeing you with someone else was like a dagger to my heart. I have no right to be upset, but the truth is . . . I want you, I want to fight for you.

When I first left the States I blamed you for holding me back. I blamed our marriage for stalling my career. I blamed becoming a mother for putting me in a kind of purgatory for the past ten years.

I know now that I have no one to blame but myself. I let inertia get the best of me. I deserted my writing and I lost faith in myself. For too long, I let things happen to me. It was easier, even though it was making me miserable. I became my own worst enemy.

This time away has shown me that it's up to me to build my own fulfilling and meaningful life. I will work harder to be the woman who you married, the brave, curious writer who seized life by the balls and made our days a brand-new adventure. Before I came here I beat myself up for becoming a boring stay-at-home mom. Part of me blamed you for allowing that to happen. I know now that I am the one who let those parts of me slip away.

Please know that I wasn't running away from us. I was running to find a new version of myself. I know who I am again. It's hard to put into words exactly how good that feels.

For too many years you and I have been two vines, both searching for sunlight in different directions. But there is a part of us still twisted together at the roots. We can still find the sunlight together. We can make our future together. We can begin again.

Love,
Kate

Chapter Sixteen

The flight attendant stopped by my seat and asked if I would like a glass of champagne. I said yes, just a little. I pulled down the hard plastic tray from the seat in front of me and put the notebook I was writing in off to the side to make room for the drink.

"What are you working on?" she asked. European flight staff were so much kinder than their American counterparts, who mostly behaved as if you were lucky they hadn't smacked you in the face. I wondered if the European carriers paid better, or if their staff were simply less beaten down by demanding American travelers.

It still struck me as odd to think of myself working again after all these years. But that's what I was doing. I would have enough of a novel to give to an agent, about twenty thousand words, when I got home. I was a writer.

"I'm writing a book," I said.

I looked up at her as she filled my narrow glass all the way to the top. She wasn't American, but I couldn't pinpoint her nationality. She had sharp cheekbones that looked as though they were cut from glass, and bright red lipstick. Her dirty-blond hair was pulled into a high bun with a few perfect wisps that escaped to frame her pretty face.

"That's so impressive. I wish I had the patience to sit down and write a book. You should be proud of yourself."

"It took me a long time to get here." I turned back to my notebook. I did feel a surge of pride.

The plane hit an air pocket and my champagne wobbled. I finished the entire glass in one gulp, worried we would drop again and the contents would spill out and destroy everything.

I opened my photo app. In the first few years of the girls' lives I took pictures of every half smile, each twitch toward crawling, every step, every spoonful of peas. I meticulously organized all of them into files labeled by month—Isabel 0–3m, 6m–18m. But, like most mothers, as the years went on I got lazy and stopped taking so many pictures. I rarely uploaded them from my phone, and when that phone fell in the toilet an entire year of photos was lost forever. One thing was so obvious now, staring back at the past few years of our lives. There wasn't a single photo of Karl and me together. When we'd become parents, at least in these pictures, we'd ceased to be a couple.

That was about to change.

I was on my way to Paris. I had e-mailed Karl the morning after Dusty and I failed to rip one another's clothes off.

> I want to show you the woman I've become. I want you to have the chance to get to know her before we make any big decisions. We have a lot of talking to do when I get home, but first . . .
>
> Let's meet in Paris, Karl. I bought you a plane ticket. I'm sending the confirmation in an e-mail. I'll be at Le Select, in the same booth where we had our first date, next Friday.

In just twenty-four hours we would be blessedly alone. I'd booked the same suite at the George V where we stayed that first time Karl came to visit me when I lived in Paris. I'd have an entire day before he landed to get everything ready, including myself. I'd take a long bath, get a pedicure, maybe a blowout, I'd buy underwear!

I knew our reunion might be painful at first. I almost hoped for rage, screaming, tears. We needed to release some of that pressure. I thought of Dusty telling me Adele had broken every plate in their kitchen at some point. I entertained a brief fantasy of Karl and I decimating a room service cart, shattering crystal goblets and china saucers, and then falling into crisp linen sheets and fucking

for hours. I spent the next hour of the flight imagining all of the
various scenarios for our reunion until I nodded off with a smile
on my face.

The room at the George V was more beautiful than I remembered
and I nearly gasped as the bellhop opened the door into the grand
suite. I'd lived the past year in tiny rooms with dirty floors. My own feet
were still coated in red Northern Territory dust. Suddenly, I couldn't
get into the claw-foot bathtub fast enough. I shooed the young man
out the door and let my grimy clothes fall to a puddle at my feet. I ran
myself the hottest bath I'd ever taken and allowed the water to scorch
my skin. In all my fantasizing about what I would do here once I saw
Karl, I'd never imagined what I would wear. I cast a glance at the
beaten-down duffel bag and realized I had nothing that would wow
my husband.

I ordered a double espresso to the room, sat naked on the floor
of the balcony, staring at the Eiffel Tower and trying to shrug off my
exhaustion. I could step out the door of the hotel and be at Gucci,
Dior, or Lanvin within minutes, but I could no more imagine walking
into those soulless high-end boutiques than I could making small talk
with the salesgirl who would take one look at me and treat me like
Julia Roberts in *Pretty Woman* before Richard Gere showed up with
his gold card.

I'd walk to the Marais and find one of those adorable vintage shops
and buy something beautiful that would give me the confidence to
see my husband for the first time in nearly a year.

I was so excited that I was ready more than two hours before I was
supposed to meet Karl. I decided to walk to Le Select to burn off
some of the nervous energy. I took the long way, bypassing the Pont
de la Concorde in favor of the Pont Royal, which would allow me a

leisurely stroll through the Tuileries. I felt the hair on my neck stand at attention as I approached the old wooden bench where Karl had kissed me that first time. The memory of it made my thighs quiver. I wanted to sit there and close my eyes and relive that perfect first night, but there was another young couple kissing on the bench. I watched them for a moment, so engrossed in one another they had no idea I was there. I remembered what that felt like. It had been such a long time, but I knew it well. When the woman turned her face slightly I saw that she wasn't young at all. Upon closer inspection the two of them were even older than Karl and I. This, this more than anything, made me feel hopeful. Love, the kind of love that had you madly making out on a public park bench in Paris, was ageless.

I stopped on the bridge to gaze out at the Seine. I brushed my fingers across the rusty metal locks that lovestruck tourists kept fastening to all the Parisian bridges. The city authorities considered them an eyesore and came weekly with bolt cutters to remove them. But new ones appeared hours later. I laughed at how hopeless it was to try to put a stop to the follies of young love.

There was still time to spare when I squeezed into the tight quarters in front of the hostess stand at Le Select. I smoothed my sweaty palms over the thin blue crepe skirt I had bought. It hugged my thighs in a way that no longer made me self-conscious. I paired it with a man's pinstriped oxford, unbuttoned one button more than I usually would have dared; it was an homage to the outfit I was wearing the first night I met Karl. I felt confident, like that woman Karl had bumped into in that bookstore so many years ago—the woman who talked back and had opinions and dreams and wasn't afraid of showing a sliver of a black lace bra—the most expensive thing I'd purchased the previous afternoon.

A beautiful French girl with short bangs and a shorter skirt looked up at me with what I guessed was a perpetually irritated sneer on her face.

"Is the rest of your party here?" she demanded with a click of her tongue, hardly looking up from her clipboard.

"No. But he'll be here soon."

She released a heavy sigh. "I should not seat you then." She didn't say that she couldn't, merely that she shouldn't. I wasn't above begging to make sure this evening went perfectly.

"Please," I pleaded. "I'm meeting someone very important. I need to sit."

She waved her hand, as if to say my needs were inconsequential, but grabbed two menus anyway and led me back to the table in the corner that I'd meticulously requested last week. I gave a pat to the tabby cat asleep on the bar and smiled at the gray-haired bartender. Once I sat down I ordered a gimlet, neat. A double would have soothed my nerves, but I also wanted my wits about me. I'd practiced what I wanted to say since I'd booked Karl's plane ticket, but now, with my heart pounding in my head, I couldn't recall a thing.

I heard the door to the restaurant open. A musty summer breeze drifted through the door along with a young mother struggling to keep her phone at her ear as she dragged a stroller in behind her. Paris in August is hot and muggy, and most Parisians flee the city for southern beaches. There's a reason there are songs about springtime in Paris and not the summer.

The days were long and it would be light for another hour. I checked the time on my phone. I'd told Karl to meet me at six thirty and it was only a few minutes past the hour. My drink was empty, but I ordered a platter of oysters and an espresso to keep the waiter from hating me.

Six thirty came and went. Then, seven. Surely, he would come. I knew, since I booked his itinerary, that he would be coming straight from the airport. Perhaps there was traffic.

The waiter came again, this time with a concerned look in his eyes. He raised an eyebrow at the empty seat.

"I'm sorry. He must have been held up," I said. "I can order for both of us." I looked over the menu to try to decide what Karl would want. This wasn't how I imagined it. I didn't want us to dive right into plates of food. I'd wanted to draw things out, to let the evening unfold. But I felt obliged to order and selected a roast chicken for me and a filet mignon for Karl.

All around me other happy couples sat close to one another, whispering jokes and stories as they enjoyed their evening.

There was still no sign of my husband by the time the food arrived. I could tell the waiter felt sorry for me. "I can take it back to the kitchen to keep it warm," he said. I shook my head and averted my eyes.

"I'll eat it. I can pick at both of them. Just leave them."

I felt a growing awareness that I had miscalculated this evening. I'd planned this all so quickly that I was sure this romantic gesture would be enough to persuade Karl to come, but there had always been a part of me that knew he might not get on that plane.

By eight o'clock the steak was cold. I apologized to the waiter and offered a halfhearted explanation in English for why my companion had yet to appear. I gripped the side of the table as I said it, my knuckles turning white, unable to admit what I knew was true.

Karl was not coming.

I quietly paid my bill and left without making eye contact with the waiter or hostess. As I slipped out the door, a soft mist had begun to fall. I bowed my head against the drizzle.

I retraced my steps back to the hotel, feeling first a sense of terrible despair. And then, as I crossed the Seine, my phone buzzed in my pocket. A message from Karl:

Tilly's got a stomach bug. I'm sorry. I'll see you in New York.
Come home, Kate.

So, I wasn't just stood up, there was a reason he didn't show. I felt a flush of relief—even though I hated the thought that Tilly was sick.

I read his message over and over, parsing each word. I chose to see it as an open door. *I'll see you in New York.*

My relief morphed into another feeling. Something unexpected. A sense of conviction that despite everything, anything was still possible.

Epilogue

It was so hard to read the emotions on Karl's face—fear, confusion, anger—as he opened the envelope I thrust into his hands. He sifted through the pages. I knew they were in the right order. I'd made sure of that in the cab ride on the way over.

On top of the pile was every letter I'd written to my husband in the past year. I should have mailed them after I wrote them, but I never did. I'd been too afraid for him to read them.

I wasn't scared anymore.

Beneath the letters there were fifty pages of my novel. Only in hindsight did I realize I wrote the story of us. I couldn't finish without him.

Karl gripped the pages with both hands.

"I'm sorry about Paris," he said, looking at the papers, trying to make sense of what I had handed him. "I wanted to come." His eyes were apologetic. He meant it.

"Paris isn't going anywhere." I stood straighter. "And neither am I." I enjoyed the certainty in my voice.

Karl turned and placed the papers on the table we kept next to the door for mail and catalogs and keys and other detritus of our family's life. I took the opportunity to step closer to my own front door, and when he turned back we were so close I could smell him. I could have leaned over and kissed him, but I didn't.

In that moment our relationship flashed before me in vivid snapshots. I could also see snapshots from the future, a future in which there was a possibility we could find our way back to each other, stronger than ever, as the best versions of ourselves.

"I'm not the same woman who walked out on you a year ago," I said. "Can we start there?" What I regretted the most was not trusting him enough to show him who I really was. I had to put on a facade to survive. "I don't pretend to house a pearl. I am grit and soft tissue. I am flawed, but I am yours, if you'll have me."

I reached my hand to him. It lingered in the air for a moment before my husband brought his to meet it.

One year later . . .

The thick humid air covered my body like a warm cocoon. Tropical birds swooped above and around us, their incessant babble a cacophony of cheerful sounds. It reminded me of Thailand, but let's be honest, the Ritz Carlton Maui couldn't be further from the zen center . . . in more ways than one. It was Karl's idea, this escape to Hawaii. He planned it, booked it, and surprised us all with it, no help from Sara at all.

The four of us sat down to dinner on the beach, barefoot, toes in the sand. The girls and I wore matching colorful sarongs, made by Buppha and mailed over to us just a few weeks before. A scrum of hula dancers in grass skirts and coconut bras swished by. Tilly leaped up from the table to imitate their manic hip swiveling. I stood and grabbed Izzy's hand to start my own shimmy, a move I wouldn't have dared in public a year ago. My husband laughed and, to my surprise, joined us.

We collapsed back into our chairs, exhausted and giddy from the impromptu performance. Karl had never looked more handsome. He gave me a sly smile with a nod toward the hammock strung between two palm trees just past the pool. I felt a shy blush creep from my breasts to my cheeks. We'd snuck out of our room and into that hammock shortly before dawn, while the girls were asleep, with the intention of chastely watching the sunrise. But then Karl kissed the front of my neck, softly at first, then with an increasing hunger, a hunger I'd missed for so long. He lifted my tank top over my head in one fell swoop and then slid his mouth down to my breasts, going back and forth between each one, caressing, stroking, nibbling, and licking with a frenzy that made me weak. When he finally pulled off his linen pants and thrust inside me, I was beyond ready. I came quickly and urgently, biting Karl on the shoulder as I did, hard enough to leave a mark.

I blushed looking at his shoulder now, knowing that that memento was right there under his white button-down shirt. He grinned back as if he could read my mind.

"Tonight . . . again?" he mouthed silently, his hand creeping up my bare thigh, a look of delight crossing his features as he realized there was nothing beneath my sarong.

"Tonight," I said out loud. The girls had no idea what I was talking about.

A beautiful waitress, who reminded me of a younger Mia with her long red hair and porcelain skin, delivered our food. I watched her check out my husband and felt a slight thrill, a second shot of electricity between my thighs.

The girls chattered excitedly about the giant sea turtle they had seen earlier that day. I leaned over to cut a piece of Tilly's fish for her and the quotidian delight of this mundane task actually delighted me.

I'm happy. I'm fucking happy. The thought was a marvel considering how hard it was to get here. Standing on my doorstep a year ago, I didn't know if my husband would take me back.

Karl didn't sweep me into his arms and plant a long, passionate kiss on my lips right there on our stairs. My life isn't a Lifetime movie, after all. But he did tentatively keep the metaphorical door open for the next few months. I didn't move back in right away. As luck would have it, one of Karl's authors was vacating his studio apartment in the West Village, right on Jane Street, a few doors down from the first apartment we had lived in together. The writer, one of those confirmed bachelor types from another era, was delighted to have me house and cat sit while he went off on book tour. Aside from the fickle felines who insisted on drinking from the toilet bowl and shitting in my shoe, the cozy room was a little slice of paradise. That's where Karl and I finally tumbled back in bed, one stormy evening after a long dinner at Barbuto, our first real step back to each other. That night Karl whispered to me, "I love you, Kate. But more importantly, I want you and I need you. Sometimes you don't realize what you have or want until it's gone. Don't leave me again, promise?" The desperation in his eyes filled me with guilt—how could I have left this man? And how could he have forgiven me for doing so? I chose to see both scenarios as a testament to the strength of our connection. I moved back into our house and our bed the following weekend.

Not that it was instantly perfect—there were plenty of tears, mine and his. There was screaming and door slamming and vows to end it once and for all. We needed that, though. We'd been too civil for too goddamn long. Now our emotions were real and raw and honest and often messy. We spent late nights talking about what kind of life we wanted to have, how we were going to recommit to our dreams—and to each other. Karl promised to work less and to challenge me to write more. I vowed to be more open and honest. I promised never to run away again. We both agreed it was important that we remembered what it was like to screw like twenty-year-olds whenever we could, like, say, in a hammock under the stars.

I understood, more than ever, that I was an incredibly lucky woman. Sometimes I woke up and wondered whether I deserved this second chance at happiness, but I tried hard to keep those kinds of thoughts at bay. If I learned anything from my year away it's that we all have to fight for our happiness. And that we all deserve a second chance, no matter what it takes to get there.

Now, here on our last night in paradise after a truly magical week, it all felt worth it. It was one of those moments where everything was exactly how it should be.

The waitress returned with a sly smile on her face. She looked at Karl like they were exchanging some kind of inside joke and plunked a whole coconut in front of me.

"Thank you?" I said it like a question. "Appetizer?"

"You can turn it into a bra," Tilly said, and both girls giggled.

I knocked on the outside and realized it was split in two.

"Open it," Karl said.

My head fell to the side in confusion. "OK." I picked up the half coconut and just as quickly dropped it on the ground with a gasp.

I gazed down at the plain gold band, catching the light from the tiki torches around us. I hadn't worn a ring since I asked Mia to pawn them in Thailand.

I looked up at Karl. For a second I was the girl in the Paris book-shop again, heart racing, flush with one thought: *It's you.*

It had always been Karl. And we had always been destined for a happy ending. Right then, that night at the dinner table, in front of the kids, he took my hand. And, for the second time in our relation-ship, he proposed.

Acknowledgments

I always wanted to write a novel, but for a long time I didn't believe that I could. It took a village of people to make me believe that this was actually possible.

Thank you to Liza, my fearless and exacting editor. You never let me give up. You pushed me to be a better writer. I was so blessed to get to work with you, but I am even more grateful to count you as a friend.

I thought about my daughters every day as I wrote this book. I love the two of you more than you will ever know. I want you both to be proud of me as you grow up into brilliant and interesting women.

Ten years ago I met a man in a bookshop in Paris and my life changed forever. He believed in me, so I believed in me too. Charles, you are my rock, my inspiration, and the love of my life.